CARI Z

WHERE THERE'S

A WILL

PANOPULIS

Riptide Publishing
PO Box 1537
Burnsville, NC 28714
www.riptidepublishing.com

Where There's a Will
Copyright © 2016 by Cari Z

Cover art: L.C. Chase, lcchase.com/design.htm
Editor: Carole-ann Galloway
Layout: L.C. Chase, lcchase.com/design.htm

ISBN: 978-1-62649-406-0

First edition
May, 2016

Also available in ebook:
ISBN: 978-1-62649-405-3

CARI Z

WHERE THERE'S A WILL

PANOPOLIS

RIPTIDE
PUBLISHING

Even Villains need Heroes (to fight), and I liked the one I came up with so much I gave him a story of his own. I hope you enjoy it.

Heroes are made by the paths they choose, not the powers they're graced with.
—Brodi Ashton, *Everneath*

TABLE OF CONTENTS

CHAPTER ONE

SuperTruther here, folks, your source for everything that's happening behind the curtain here in Panopolis. And let me tell you, the further I look, the more I realize that the curtain is waaay bigger than you'd ever expect. Because the battle in Panopolis, despite what we've been told, isn't as simple as Heroes versus Villains. There's no clear-cut line between the people doing good and the people doing evil, and what distinction there is gets blurrier by the day.

Can we call Mastermind a Villain, when he's made Z Street and its surrounding neighborhoods safer in the past few months than the established do-gooders have done in years? Edward Dinges has better reason to despise Panopolis than most, after being experimented on in the Abattoir, broken out by the Bombardier, and fighting to survive as Mastermind. Now he's got a power strong enough to sideline some of our most powerful Heroes. So where are his conquests? Where are his crimes? Why do he and the Villains who follow him—and there are plenty, despite what the mainstream media would have you believe—leave their calling cards in brick and mortar instead of wrack and ruin? Can a Villain make you feel safer than a Hero?

And what do you do when you can't tell the difference anymore?

People say I'm a Hero.

That's pretty much *all* that people ever say about me, actually. It was all that ever needed to be said in Panopolis. Heroes were bigger than life, but little more than names on a television or shouted from a street corner for the majority of folks. Hell, most people probably didn't even know my real name. Craig Haney wasn't an exciting guy. I'd been a fairly average kid, raised by my grandmother after my parents were killed during a battle between Earthquake and Sky King. I'd grown into a fairly average man who wasn't smart enough to make it through college, so I'd gone into the police academy instead. I'd been a decent cop, but that was all I'd been. Then came the accident, and shortly after that, Freight Train was born.

I missed being Craig sometimes. Don't get me wrong, I got into the police to protect and serve, and I was doing more of that than ever as a bona fide Hero. I liked taking care of people, and I liked being a power for good. I especially liked the fact that I could go toe-to-toe with some of the baddest Villains to set foot in Panopolis, and come out on top. That was what I did now—it was my reason for being. I had to be the best Hero the city had ever seen, because I couldn't be anything else. Not with my force field keeping everyone and everything at a distance.

There were times when being completely untouchable was depressing. And then there were times like today, when I was so damn grateful for my power I could almost cry.

"Fucking *hell*," Mr. Fabulous snapped as he tried to scrape the remnants of a bright-pink bubble off his costume. He wasn't having much luck; it was incredibly sticky.

"At least it wasn't an acid one," I said as I scanned ahead for our quarry. The acid bubbles were bright green, and would have eaten through Mr. Fabulous's suit and into his skin in seconds. There were steaming pockmarks in the brick sidewalk where those ones had touched down. The blue bubbles froze things, which was a little better but not much if they hit you. All in all, the pink ones were fairly tame.

"Oh yeah, wonderful," Mr. Fabulous said as he swiped fruitlessly at his shoulder. I pulled him aside before he stepped into an acid crater, but he shrugged away my hand. "Unless you know a quick way to get this shit off, don't bother me."

Mr. Fabulous and I shared a manager and were both heavily sponsored by GenCorp, so we were often called in for the same jobs. He had super speed and super strength, and was one of the few Heroes I knew of who didn't also have pretty unsuper side effects to go along with his powers. Mr. Fabulous wore what I guess I'd call a tactical tuxedo, good against bullets and knives, and close-fitting enough that there were whole blogs devoted to his ass in those pants. I might have bookmarked one of them. Or two.

Hey, I might not be able to touch anyone but myself, but I could appreciate a nice ass, okay? In fact, his ass was the nicest thing about Mr. Fabulous. His personality sure wasn't anything to write home about.

Another bubble floated back toward us: blue, nasty. I popped it with the trash can lid I'd picked up a block back, and a sheen of ice spread across the front of the metal. I could see it, but I barely felt the temperature difference. Distantly, I heard the familiar strains of Bubbles the Clown's theme song, sung at a shrill and desperate pitch. We were getting close.

Mr. Fabulous was still trying to scrape pink off his shoulder. "Zane, what the hell does it matter?" I muttered as I snagged another blue bubble out of the air before it could hit the door of an apartment building. This wasn't the nicest corner of Panopolis—nothing really was nice so close to Spartan Park—but there were plenty of residences around, and plenty of people who could be hurt by these bubbles if we didn't move fast. "Just leave it alone and focus!"

"It matters because pink isn't a good color on me, and don't call me 'Zane' in public." His bow-shaped mouth tightened. "I don't want to be filmed wearing pink!"

I shook my head. "This problem isn't big enough for any of the news crews to be here yet." *And it won't be if we do our damn jobs.*

Mr. Fabulous stopped in his tracks. "Wait. Haven't you talked to Ianthe?"

"Ianthe?" I only knew one Ianthe, and she was my lawyer. Well, *our* lawyer. The lawyer for most Heroes in Panopolis, actually. "Why would I need to talk to her? Are we being sued?" It wouldn't be the first time.

"No, to sign the waiver!"

"What waiver are you talking about?"

Mr. Fabulous stared at me in utter horror, like I'd said, *What do you mean, we can't eat kittens for breakfast?* He spluttered, but I didn't have time to waste waiting for his mouth to work again. I moved on, and the strains of the song became clearer as I reached the edge of the park.

"Say hello to Bubbles the Clown! Bubbles is playful, Bubbles is great!" There was a muted *sploosh*ing noise, and a moment later a bright-green bubble wafted over the little hill ahead and up to the fountain next to me, bursting as soon as it touched the statue of Panopolis's original Hero, the Spartan, which was set at the very top. I winced as the acid began to eat off his nose.

"Say good-bye to that nasty frown; Bubbles puts kids in a happy state!" This time the song was interrupted by an enormous sob.

I ran over the hill ahead of me, and there he was. Bubbles the Clown, one of Panopolis's longtime minor celebrities, in his trademark polka-dot onesie. His head was covered with his usual perfectly coiffed, canary-yellow wig, sproingy locks spiraling out in all directions like a cluster of question marks. His white face paint was a mess though, and the red he used on his lips and cheeks was smeared across his face like open wounds. Bubbles was carrying three carefully contained buckets on a belt around his waist, and held in each hand several metal wands with circular hoops at their ends.

And the people in the park were just standing there, watching him release new bubbles into the air. Either they hadn't realized what the bubbles did, or they were in shock. I yelled ahead to the picnickers, "Clear out! Get away from the clown!"

"It's Freight Train!" a woman exclaimed.

"Grab your phone," someone else called. I wanted to smack him, but I had a lot of experience at working crowds at this point. Repetition was key.

"Get away from the park!" As I got within a few dozen meters, Bubbles seemed to snap out of his funk and turned to me. It was hard to tell his expression behind the oversized red nose, but I thought he was angry. He certainly sounded angry.

"Bubbles will sing you the A-B-Cs," he hissed, dunking one of his wands into the blue bucket. He made a big bubble this time, so big he could—and did—spin a full circle and connect the ends together again, like a bubble donut. It settled onto the ground around him and burst, turning the grass to solid ice.

He plunged the wand into the green bucket next, a furious, frothy dunking. When he withdrew it this time, he'd made a lattice of bubbles in the hoop, and blew them straight at me, tiny and impossible to dodge completely. "Bubbles will teach you the 1-2-3s!"

"Shit," was all I had time to say before the bubbles reached me. I held my makeshift shield out, but the first few ate right through it, and the rest glommed onto me and burst over my force field like huge drops of acid rain. Someone screamed.

They did nothing except eat into my uniform, of course. The acid melted away, its residue pooling at my feet like my own personal toxic-waste dump. Bits of blue fabric drifted in the goo for a moment before they vanished. I stepped to the side to save my boots from completely disintegrating.

At least the bubbles had missed my crotch. I didn't want to be photographed naked in the middle of a fight. Again.

"Ooh, thanks for taking the brunt of that," Mr. Fabulous said as he sauntered up next to me, finally un-pinked. "I think it's time to get rid of this clown, don't you?" He smiled and waved at the growing crowd. "Shall I take this Villain down a peg or two?" he called out.

"You should be getting them away from here, not encouraging them to stay and watch," I muttered, but Mr. Fabulous ignored me.

"Get him, Fabulous!"

"Oh my god, you look amazing!"

"Can I touch you? Please?"

He winked at the person who'd asked the last question. "Maybe later," he said, before turning and zipping toward Bubbles the Clown at ten times the speed of a normal person.

Unfortunately for him, it turned out that the ice Bubbles had laid down was *extremely* slippery, especially when he was going so fast. As soon as Mr. Fabulous hit the frozen grass, his graceful runner's form turned into an awkward lunge as he tried to stay on his feet. He slid right past Bubbles the Clown, and tripped as soon as his feet hit regular ground again, rolling head over feet across the lawn.

That got some shaky laughs from the observers. More to the point, their laughter got Bubbles's attention. He turned toward them, malice written in every line of his body. "Bubbles the Clown brings chuckles and joy," he sang, refilling his left wand with acid green. I gave up on yelling at the crowd to disperse and started for the madman myself, slowly and carefully. Unfortunately, my cautious pace gave him the chance to lay down another wide layer of bubbles around himself with his right hand, this time in pink.

My force field kept things from touching me directly, but that didn't mean they didn't affect me at all. If the ground was sticky, then I was going to have to fight to get across it in my boots. And Bubbles seemed to realize that, because he ignored me and blew another round of acid death at the gawkers filming this. The crowd finally began to look up from their filming and back away as the bubbles wobbled in their direction.

"Fuck, just *shoot* the guy already," someone yelled shakily.

I would've, except that Heroes didn't use guns. Cops could carry them, but we couldn't. We were supposed to be above that sort of thing, supposed to use Truth and Justice and whatever power we had at our disposal to apprehend Villains, not kill them. At times like this, that rule really sucked. I churned through the pink muck at my feet, struggling to reach Bubbles before one of his shots got someone in the crowd. Mr. Fabulous was on his feet again and fighting his own way in. *Just a bit farther* . . .

"Bubbles sings lessons to all girls and boys!" Bubbles the Clown shrieked. "You wanna pay attention to me *now*, you sorry little shits? After my show got the ax thanks to a lack of viewers? Screw you!" He raised the wand to his face, inhaled deeply, and then—

Something whipped toward Bubbles from out of the shadows, wrapping twice around his neck before I could do more than blink in surprise. Bubbles dropped both wands and clutched at the thin black cord and its glowing red ends—ends that glowed brighter and brighter . . .

"Everybody get down!" I shouted.

A second later, the ends exploded.

It was a pretty small explosion, all things considered. Just enough to turn Bubbles's neck to red and white slurry, not enough to destroy his head completely. His body crumpled to the ground, buckets spilling out across the grass like the world's worst Impressionist painting. His head hit a second later, facedown in a green pool. It started to hiss.

"Oh my *god*, really?" Mr. Fabulous exclaimed. I glanced over and saw him coated with a fine spray of gore, the same that had hit me. Of course, it had sloughed off of me. "*Really*? This is my day today?" He glared angrily out at the crowd. "Stop filming!"

"Uhm . . ." One of the guys with a camera phone lowered it and looked at us uncertainly. "Which of you guys did that?"

"They didn't!" The girl who'd wanted to touch Mr. Fabulous was staring raptly at the nearby alley. "It must have been the Mad Bombardier!" There was no one there now, but she was likely right. Bombs of any kind usually meant Raul.

"Bubbles the Clown may have had a point," Mr. Fabulous grumbled to me as he rubbed a hand over his dripping face. "People have no concept of loyalty."

I shrugged. "Hey, nobody got hurt." Except for Bubbles. I'd have to thank Raul, if I ever got out of this pink shit. Sirens were closing in on us now. Hopefully the police had a hazmat team on standby, 'cause we were gonna need one.

"I'm *glad* you didn't sign the waiver now, actually; that's probably the reason the camera crew isn't working today. It wouldn't do to have professionals getting this on record."

"What are you talking about?" I demanded before turning to a bystander, who was creeping awfully close to the rainbow ruin on the ground. "Sir, please step away from the goo."

"Talk to Ianthe," was all Mr. Fabulous said as he freed himself from the sticky ground. "She'll explain it. And you look like you've got things well in hand here!" He stretched out cautiously and clapped me on the shoulder. I was decidedly pleased to not be able to feel it. "See you tonight, Freight Train."

And with that, Mr. Fabulous, that jerk face, walked back the way we'd come, leaving me to handle the crowd and fill in the cops.

At least I had a nice view of his best feature as he abandoned me to the hard part of Heroing.

That's the honest truth, right there. Fighting? It wasn't so hard. I mean, I got that it can be for some people, but it wasn't for me. I was untouchable, literally. Nobody could physically hurt me. Keeping other people from being hurt, though? That was tough work. People were curious: they wanted to watch; they wanted to see what was going on. Wrangling them could be a full-time job, and it was one I hadn't taken seriously enough for a long time. A lot of Heroes still didn't give much of a damn, but with public opinion the way it was now, that was slowly changing. You had to attempt to shield the crowd these days, or your sponsors would pitch a fit.

The cops pulled up, sirens blaring and lights flashing, and the gawkers gradually started to disperse. I finally shook myself free of the goop and waited at the edge of the mess, staring at what remained of Bubbles the Clown. At the rate the acid was eating him away, he'd be gone before they could figure out how to contain his chemicals.

"Aw no, Bubbles," one of the cops said sadly as she walked over. "Poor guy! What happened to him?"

Well, no point in beating around the bush. "He went crazy and started trying to kill a whole bunch of people with acid and—" What was that other stuff? "Maybe some sort of liquid nitrogen compound? Freeze goo, whatever."

"Freeze. Goo." The cop looked at me like I was talking a different language. "Bubbles the Clown tried to *kill* people?"

"Yep."

"I always knew that clown was bad business," another cop—Pete Grier, I think we used to work together—said as he came up beside us. "All that singing and cheer and shit? That's not normal."

"It was an act; it was part of his show," the first officer retorted. Her name tag read *R. Flanders*. "Oh wow, I can hardly believe it. I watched him all the time when I was a kid." She hummed the melody of his song, and I couldn't quite keep down my shudder. I'd never hear that song the same way again. "You're saying he went crazy?"

"I don't know what happened to him"—although he'd mentioned his show being canceled—"but he was definitely trying to hurt people out here."

"And he . . . what, tripped and fell in his own goop?"

"The Mad Bombardier blew his head off!" one of the more enthusiastic observers added. "He saved us all!"

Pete's eyebrows crawled so high they almost disappeared into his hat. "The Bombardier? You serious?"

"Yes! Who else lurks in the shadows dispensing justice against the worst of his own kind?" The girl goggled at us. "Jeez, don't any of you read SuperTruther? That's, like, the Mad Bombardier's calling card."

"That and the fact that Bubbles's neck exploded," I said, not wanting to admit right then that I *did* follow SuperTruther's blog. It was a controversial subject. "Someone blew it up, and it wasn't me."

"Damn," Pete said. Both cops had disappointed expressions on their faces. "You let the Bombardier get the drop on you?" Pete shook his head. "What are you Heroes doing, getting beaten to the punch by Villains these days?"

"Was Mastermind with him?" R. Flanders seemed sympathetic. "Did he mind-control you?"

God fucking damn it. That rumor was one of the stupidest things I'd ever told a reporter. "I didn't see Mastermind," I said flatly. "And I didn't see the Mad Bombardier either, but whoever it was killed Bubbles the Clown, and probably saved lives in the process. You guys got a handle on this?"

"Oh, sure." A hazmat van was pulling up now, spilling people in full-body suits across the pavement as soon as it stopped.

"Great. Then I'm going to head out."

"New call?"

I shook my head. "I've got an appointment."

I didn't quite run back to my car, but I wanted to. I was already sick of dealing with people, and it wasn't even noon yet. I started up my Humvee, which was liberally plastered in GenCorp logos and product ads, and headed for the clinic. I might have business waiting with Ianthe, but first I had to check in with my doctors. It was standard procedure after a run-in with Villains.

GenCorp was my major sponsor. In fact, GenCorp was the major sponsor of close to seventy-five percent of Heroes. They put a lot of time and money into us, including providing apartments, free medical care, a living stipend, and a share of the profits from our merchandise. Not a *huge* share; I mean, I wasn't gonna make a mint off the few percent I got from sales of Freight Train dolls and T-shirts, but my bank never yelled at me when I made payments on Memaw's apartment on top of everything else, so there was that. And the medical care was, unfortunately, not something I'd ever be able to go without at this point. Not until Mastermind and his crew figured out what was going on with my force field.

See, the thing was— The thing was, GenCorp was lying to me. They had been lying to me for years, lying about my force field, about how tough it was to work with, about how they were trying to come up with a cure but nothing yet, so sorry, maybe next month! For years I thought the best they could do, the absolute most they could give me, was the bare minimum to keep me alive. A way to eat, a way to get rid of the evidence afterward, and a way to clean off the worst of my body's sweat and oil. They made specialized straws to feed me through, imbued with a force field that could penetrate my own. Those things were doled out like they were more precious than diamonds, and for years I swallowed that down. I believed it. I let myself get used to isolation as much as I could, which—

Look, I was a shit, okay? I was so eager for somebody, for anybody, that I acted like a bastard. Before Mastermind was Mastermind, he was just Edward Dinges: nice guy, worked in a bank; I saved his life once. He was grateful, and I was desperate, and I didn't listen when he said he wasn't interested in dating me. Even *worse*, I got my grandmother involved.

Turned out, Edward's boyfriend was the Mad Bombardier, a notorious Villain who specialized in explosives. When Edward had kicked me to the curb, my memaw, who'd been his neighbor, had handed over the recordings she'd made of him and Raul—yeah, I know, so fuckin' illegal, but no one cared—to the cops. They'd arrested Edward, and I . . . I hadn't done anything about it. Didn't try to stop it, just watched him get found guilty of "aiding and abetting a Villain" and sent to the Abattoir. He got out, but no thanks to me.

Edward had been willing to give me a second chance, though. In exchange for helping him break out of GenCorp's research facility three months back, Edward had promised to help me discover why GenCorp was giving me the runaround. He'd stolen information off a computer there, said he was going to decrypt it and get back to me.

It was slow going, but I trusted him to keep me in the loop. After all, he'd been the one who discovered GenCorp had so many of the straws that could penetrate my force field, they kept 'em in packs of twenty. They used them to keep me in line, keep me obedient. Keep me desperate for anything they would give me. It had worked for years, and as long as I didn't know how to make 'em on my own, I was a captive audience. I couldn't trust GenCorp to have my best interests in mind.

Just because I didn't trust them, didn't mean I could ignore them, though. GenCorp had a standard procedure after any Villain interaction, major or minor: you got checked out by medical. I drove over to GenCorp's newly rebuilt research center, now with reinforced walls and plenty of internal surveillance, something that hadn't existed before Mastermind's break-in. As little as they wanted their actions being recorded, they wanted Villains making off with their data even less.

The clinic had a private entrance in the back of the building, with biometric locks designed to let in only GenCorp health workers, registered Heroes, and their next of kin. Too many reporters had tried to con their way in here, and after Mastermind's break-in, the board had become paranoid.

I walked into the waiting room and up to the front desk. Phyllis stared at me over half-moon spectacles. She'd worked at GenCorp longer than anyone else I knew of, and had long ago stopped being impressed with Heroes, if she ever had been. She was close to my memaw's age, and filled me with a similar sense of nervousness.

"Hi, Phyllis."

"Mr. Haney." Did I mention she knew our real names? And actually used them? No one else on the staff here used mine, despite me asking them to. I'd stopped trying after six months. "I assume you're here thanks to Bubbles the Clown."

I winced. "You heard about that, huh?"

"Mr. Richards the younger has already stopped by."

Zane. Of course he'd been here and gone, he'd booked it from the scene so fast. "Yeah, that's why I'm here."

She handed over a clipboard with a single piece of paper on it, and a pen. "You know the drill, Mr. Haney."

"Yes, ma'am." It was a reflex, calling scary old ladies "ma'am." Phyllis just rolled her eyes and shooed me away from her desk.

I sat down and started filling out the Villain Interaction Incident Report form. *Time, date, place, name of Villain/s involved, cause of interaction, estimated civilian casualties—* At least there were none of those. I did have to think about how to phrase "saved from one Villain by another" without sounding like a complete wuss, though.

"Spartan Park, huh?"

"What?" I started and glanced over at the girl sitting next to me. It took me a second to place her; I hardly ever saw her out of her suit. "Hey, Firebolt."

"So, Spartan Park got some action today, yeah?" Her tone was casual, but I could practically hear her bones creak from how hard she was twisting her fingers together. "Sounds like it was a rough one." She eyed my tattered suit with interest. "Was it an isolated incident, you think?"

"Probably." I mean, as far as I knew, Bubbles had just lost it. "I'm pretty sure it was."

"Fuck." She separated her fingers long enough to run one quivering hand through her hair. Firebolt had been a circus performer who did fire-breathing tricks before a bad fuel mix led to her getting an asbestos-coated GI tract. Now she was a Hero, wearing a special flameproof suit and breathing flames out of specially made masks, and going after Villains like an avenging angel. A bright-orange, marshmallow-shaped angel.

She didn't seem so hot at the moment, though. Her skin was almost gray, and her eyes were bloodshot. She looked like she'd been skipping meals too.

"Why is that bad?" I asked. "Because I've gotta say, you don't seem ready for a fight right now."

Firebolt's thin lips twisted unhappily. "I got dropped by TidyWood Stoves."

"Oh, that sucks." Getting dropped by a sponsor was bad news. It meant that they thought you'd screwed up so badly that they were better off without you. It meant your brand was going south. And an irretrievably bad brand meant only one thing: termination of employment by the city. If a Hero couldn't get work in Panopolis, where there was so much Villainy to combat, well . . . the odds of a smaller city hiring them on was next to nil, and the special medical treatment most of us needed to survive was too expensive to pay for out of pocket.

Firebolt had fucked up bad during Mastermind's bank robbery three months ago, almost roasting the place's manager alive in the vault. He'd been outspoken against her ever since then, and the networks had been listening, especially in light of Mastermind's comparatively good press. She sniffed, clearly about two seconds from breaking down.

"Shit. I'm sorry." It was lame, but I didn't know what else to say.

"Yeah, me too." She swallowed hard. "I mean, I get it. I screwed up before, but I need another chance, you know? I need to show my sponsors I can do this, really do it, or— So, look. If you ever need backup on a job, could you give me a call?" Her hand twitched toward mine, not quite close enough to touch, not that it mattered. Her nails were bitten down to the quick. "Because I've got to redeem myself soon, or I'm toast."

"Sure, let me have your number." I pulled out my phone, then realized that it had fallen victim to an acid bubble. No matter how durable they made the cases, I managed to go through these things like candy. "Damn."

"Holy crap." Firebolt stared at the partially disintegrated phone with wide eyes. "Um . . . how about I just write it down for you?" She jotted it on the edge of her paperwork and handed the scrap over to me.

"Great. Do you want mine too?" She nodded, and I rattled the number off for her, which she dutifully wrote down. Weird, I'd expected her to put it straight into her phone. "I'll see what I can do for you." Maybe I could put a good word in with my manager. Ray was a corporate hard-ass, but he usually made an effort to accommodate me. "Let me talk to some people."

"Thanks, Freight Train." She made an obvious effort to smile. "I appreciate it."

"No problem."

"Mr. Haney." Phyllis interrupted our weird moment, adding a grabby hand gesture. "Your paperwork, please."

"Right." I got up to hand it to her just as one of the bright-eyed interns—I didn't know where GenCorp found them, but they were too cheerful sometimes—led a man in a blue button-down shirt, dark gray slacks, and a gray jacket into the waiting room. He was wearing a visitor's badge, but the way the intern kept glancing at him like she expected him to bite suggested he wasn't just here for the tour.

"This is our Hero Health and Wellness Clinic." She somehow managed to make her quiet murmur carry like she was shouting. "GenCorp is committed to maintaining every aspect of its Heroes' well-being, with treatments ranging from minor checkups to psychiatric counseling to major surgery. Your department hasn't historically had a lot of direct contact with the clinic, but personally I find it reassuring that our Heroes are close at hand, especially with madmen like Mastermind running around the city."

"I'm sure you do." The guy didn't bother to lower his own voice, or keep the edge of irritation out of it that was almost everyone's reaction to prolonged intern exposure. He had a bit of an accent—nothing I could place from just four words—and was tall and lean, maybe three or four inches taller than me. He was also completely bald, with pale-blue eyes slightly magnified by thick, dark-framed glasses. Probably an egghead of some kind; GenCorp had cleaned house after Mastermind's break-in, so there were a lot of new staff around. There was no way a lanky, bald science geek should be so hot, but just looking at him made me want to bite my lower lip.

"Mr. Haney."

I reluctantly glanced over at Phyllis before the visitor and I could make eye contact. "Yeah?"

She snapped her fingers. "*Paperwork.*"

"Right." I handed it over, and she waved me toward the back.

"You're in five today. The nurse decided to combine this with your usual appointment."

Five. Great. Time for my weekly colon cleanse. It was a gross necessity of my life, one mitigated since I'd gone exclusively on a specialized Nutrigro smoothie diet. Now I got all the protein, carbs, and fat I needed in two drinks a day, and the formula was designed to produce very little waste.

The only person who'd ever tasted one of my custom smoothies other than me was Edward, when he'd had me over for dinner once. I'd thought he was going to spit it out on the floor. I couldn't blame him. The taste definitely took some getting used to. Did I miss cheeseburgers and fries? Shit, did I miss *beer*? Absolutely. But the smoothie diet was worth it to keep other people out of my ass in the not-fun way.

Not that I'd had the fun way in years. Fuck if I was going to dwell on that now, though.

I headed back to exam room number five, where a nurse was waiting patiently for me. There was a doctor in charge of the clinic, but he was just that: "the doctor." No name, not that that was unusual with GenCorp's bigwigs: most of the directors were strictly anonymous, and so was the doctor who supposedly read our reports and supervised GenCorp's Heroes' health.

I'd never met the doctor, and I didn't care to. My post-Villain incident checkups were rote by this point, and the weekly maintenance didn't take much time. Just a few injections to inhibit the stuff that made me messy—hair growth, sweating, and bad breath, that I knew of—and the *other* thing, and then I was good to go.

The process was silent and detached, and over in about an hour.

"Everything appears to be normal," the nurse said, as I stood up and refastened my pants. My uniform used to be one shiny piece, but let's be honest: nobody looks all that good in a Lycra bodysuit. I much preferred the simple blue pants and long-sleeved shirt that I wore now. Or I would have if they were less in pieces. I needed to remember to stow a change of clothes in the Humvee. "Do you have anything you'd like me to bring to the doctor's attention, Freight Train?"

"Nope. I'm doing good."

"I'm glad to hear that. We'll see you next week, unless you run into another Villain before then."

Run into. Yeah, like I'd bump shoulders with one while I was out grocery shopping or something. "Sure."

Firebolt was gone by the time I got back to the waiting room, and so was the newcomer. Too bad; I would have liked to have seen Mister Hot Scientist again. Not talk to him, though; the last thing I needed to do was embarrass myself by opening my dumb mouth. The science staff did so much work to keep us Heroes alive: made medical breakthroughs and came up with shit that probably would have won Nobel Prizes if it weren't proprietary. Yeah, some of 'em were also lying bastards, but I thought—I hoped—that most of them genuinely cared about their work, and the good stuff it did. Such as keeping a plebe like me alive.

I didn't deserve to be a Hero, not really. I knew that down to my bones. But I couldn't help what I'd become, so the least I could do was be a Hero in a decent set of clothes. I'd drop by my apartment and change before I went to see Ianthe.

There were definite perks to being a popular Hero in Panopolis, and one of them was the apartment that GenCorp had fitted me with. I got the whole bottom floor of a building four blocks from GenCorp's headquarters, which was way more space than I needed. I didn't have a vintage car collection or a bunch of pre-Raphaelite artwork to house (and if I had to hear about Zane's goddamn Rossetti again I was going to punch him in the face). So most of my apartment was empty space, a vast cement-floored expanse that I'd bought a Roomba to go wild in. All I required was a bedroom, a fridge for my shakes, a space for my couch and TV, and my home gym. I didn't work out in public gyms anymore—too many gawkers. People were often surprised that I needed to work to stay in shape. Like having a force field was supposed to bulk up my muscles or something. Ha. Nope. I had a full set of weights and an elliptical machine in my spare room; for some reason, I kept breaking treadmills.

I fastened my three locks, reset the alarm, and checked that the window blinds were down before I let myself relax. There was a lot of money in selling "candid shots" of Heroes to the tabloids, and I'd been in them too often to be casual about it. The last time had been, huh, almost a year ago. It had been a picture of me and Edward in a bookstore, him handing me a novel with a little smile on his face. At first I'd liked that picture, until I'd figured out that his smile was too strained to be genuine. He'd been tolerating me, not liking me. That had been a rough lesson to learn, but I'd gotten it through my thick head eventually.

I stripped out of my holey uniform and dropped it, and my ruined phone, in the trash can, then ambled back to my bedroom and flopped down on my enormous bed, bouncing my ancient stuffed tiger onto the floor. I couldn't feel the softness of the comforter beneath me, or smell the detergent that I used to enjoy, but I liked the way the bed caught me, a gentle jostle that was the friendliest touch I got most days. I reached over to the bed stand for my backup phone—I went through too many of the things to not keep a backup at home. Plenty of new messages lit up the phone's display. Shoot. I closed my eyes and lifted it to my ear.

"Hey there, how's my favorite Hero doing?" Ray's voice burst through the phone like a firework, bright and loud and always a little shocking. "I saw some amateur video of your tussle this morning—bad luck, huh? I'll see if I can get it taken down. We don't need people to see you and Mr. Fabulous being beaten to the punch, am I right? What am I saying, I'm always right."

His tone went from blithe to serious. "Hey, I set up an appointment for you with Ianthe at four, okay? She's got paperwork for you to sign. Nothing major, just something that will do *wonders* for your career if it takes off like I know it will! So make sure you sign it ASAP, FT. Fabulous may be the first from the mark in this new wave, but as soon as people get to know you better, I'm sure there'll be as much demand for you."

What the hell is he talking about? I frowned as he finished up.

"Gotta go, contracts to negotiate, people to schmooze! And speaking of schmoozing, you're expected at GenCorp's Future Stars of Industry gala tonight, remember? Don't forget, and don't try to call in sick; we all know you don't get sick, buddy. Wear your tux, okay? It's black tie. Bye for now, FT!"

I'd been working with Ray for close to five years, and he still called me "FT." Like he couldn't remember Craig or something. And what the hell was I supposed to be signing, anyway?

The next message was from Ianthe's office. Excellent, maybe I'd get some answers.

"Craig, this is Viv for Ianthe Delavigne. I'm sorry, but we're going to have to reschedule your appointment at four today. Ms. Delavigne is unfortunately indisposed." Damn. That happened a lot with her; hopefully she was okay. "We'll see you tomorrow at two, if that's acceptable. Thank you for your understanding."

Well, Ray would be pissed, and so would Zane, but fuck them. I waited for the next message to start.

"Craig, it's your memaw." So it was. "I just saw you on the television. What on earth was that? I thought you took care of the bomb-y guy months ago! You're not falling back into your bad habits, are you? Remember"—I said the next part with her—"laziness is a recipe for failure."

She heaved a sigh over the phone. "Don't be like your father, Craig—my *god*, the laziness of that man. Your mother wasn't that bright, but she was so pretty, she could have had almost anyone, you know, and she chose, what, a handyman? She could have had a lawyer! A *lawyer*, and you know how much money they make—you're paying yours enough. You know the company will pay for your lawyer if you use one of theirs, don't you? You could be—"

I deleted the message. I'd heard it all before anyway. *Don't be lazy like your dad, don't be stupid like your mom, not that you can help it, honey.* Yeah, I'd skip that refrain this time around.

The next message was Memaw again. "And I forgot to mention, you're coming over tomorrow for Sunday dinner. You can tell me about your week. Only the good parts, though."

I deleted that one too. Like I ever forgot a Sunday dinner.

Two messages from people requesting interviews, both of which were trashed. If people wanted publicity from me, they could get in touch through Ray. That was what he was there for, after all. If this kept up I'd have to change my number again. The last message began to play.

"Hi, Craig, it's your friend from down the road." My breath caught in my throat, and I had to actively stop myself from gripping the phone so hard I crushed it. "I was just calling to let you know your cat's gotten out again. Maybe you could come pick it up later tonight? Tomorrow night's okay too, if that works better. I'm in Apartment Three. Thanks, see you soon!" Edward's message ended, and I exhaled slowly.

I hadn't had a pet in years. The cat was a code. He had news for me, hopefully about the information he'd stolen from GenCorp that he'd been trying to decrypt ever since. "Apartment Three" meant he'd be in the third safe house I was acquainted with, a place well outside of Z Street territory but nowhere near the Hero-heavy downtown. I glanced at the time. Shit, was it only one in the afternoon? I didn't want to wait another ten hours for—

Wait, no. I had the gala to go to. And Ray wasn't gonna let me off easy, either; if I showed up, then I was going to have to stay the whole time. Which meant I wasn't going to get out of it in time to meet with Edward tonight. I groaned and slapped a hand over my eyes.

I was over Edward, I *was*. So what if he was one of the only people who ever used my name or was nice to me without fawning over me? He was incredibly, completely, and absolutely off-limits. Raul had made that clear to me, not that he'd needed to. I might be kind of slow, but I learned from my mistakes. The elaborate and detailed threat from the Mad Bombardier on how he would destroy me, force field or not, had been unnecessary. And a little frightening.

I glanced at the clock again. No meeting with Ianthe, no meeting with Edward . . . and I wasn't about to go over to Memaw's until tomorrow. Looked like I had time for a workout, and a few episodes of *The Blue Planet* before I'd need to start getting ready for the party. Nothing like David Attenborough to chill out to after such a frustrating morning.

CHAPTER TWO

Ah, the glitterati of Panopolis. It's a combination of minor celebrities shoring up their support from the dark-suited movers and shakers, corporate businesspeople, and Heroes. Throw a bunch of plus ones looking to climb the social ladder in there, and I can safely say that I've never seen so many bloodless battles play out in a single room.

I wish I could compare the process to chess, or even checkers, but it's more like a game of shuffleboard. Everybody's slinging their weight around, trying to knock themselves into a better position by taking out someone else. Whoever hosts the event gets to do the mental math of winners versus losers at the end of the night, and the prize is increased invitations, increased access, increased influence.

Oh, to be a fly on the wall during one of these affairs . . .

You know those dreams where you're doing something and everyone is staring at you, and you have no idea what's wrong? And nobody will tell you, and there's no door that'll let you leave—they just all lead back to the same place? That was what my social obligations for GenCorp felt like to me: an inescapable maze of people I didn't know giving me attention I didn't want. Some of them I could beg off of, but tonight? Tonight it was all hands on deck.

Here was the thing about public events: I actually liked them. No, honest—I liked getting to be Freight Train for events like ribbon cuttings or dedications or, y'know, Hero Day at the local zoo. People know what to expect from me when I'm in uniform, and I know how to give it to them. It's not all kissing babies and shaking hands, but getting to sign autographs for kids who come over dressed up like me is always pretty cool.

Private events, on the other hand . . . *ugh*. They meant playing by a bunch of rules I wasn't comfortable with. I hadn't grown up going to fancy parties; the fanciest thing I'd been to before I became Freight Train was my high school senior prom, where my date and I had gotten super drunk and ended up vomiting side by side behind the auditorium before we ever got around to kissing, much less actually fooling around. He was so embarrassed he never spoke to me again after that. I think he ended up working as a plumber in Spokane.

The point was that it took years before I stopped making a fool out of myself at these parties. All the rules about when to speak, what to say, how to greet people with the appropriate level of politeness, how to excuse myself from the banquet part of the evening without being rude . . . they drove me nuts. Mostly, going to society events had been a crash course in learning to keep my mouth shut. I was there to provide some politician or celebrity or, in this case, corporation with Hero cachet, nothing more.

The Future Stars of Industry gala was GenCorp's annual party for its investors. GenCorp trotted out their top brass, big brains, and super brawn for the edification of the shareholders, while surrounding their guests with expensive booze and tiny, never-ending appetizers. People flew in from all over the world for this party, to see and be seen, to discuss deals and futures and important stuff, while getting happily soused under the watchful eye of GenCorp.

I wore my only tuxedo, its bow tie tighter than a noose around my neck. It was a few years old by now, but I wasn't going to waste money on another one. If I was lucky, I'd get called out tonight by a Villain who'd do me a favor and dispose of this damn suit before I had to wear it again. My shiny shoes squeaked slightly as I made my third circuit around the ballroom, exchanging pleasantries with people who had to read my name tag to figure out who I was.

"Ooh, Freight Train, how exciting!" one older man exclaimed. "I saw you on CBS the other day, that thing with the squid? Very impressive!"

"Thank you, sir." I'd never been happier that I couldn't be squeezed to death than when that giant squid had reached out of its tank with its tentacles to wrap me up as enthusiastically as a toddler who'd just been introduced to tape.

"It seems like they need to get better security at the zoo," the woman with him commented. "This is the third time someone's broken in to experiment on the animals, isn't it? It's so sad."

"Panopolis should designate a Hero for the zoo." The man stared at me expectantly. "Sound like something you'd be interested in, Freight Train?"

"I . . ." What? What could I say to that? If I said no, then it would come off like I hated animals. If I went with yes, then I was shirking my larger responsibilities. I had no clue who these people were, but I'd been misquoted often enough that I was wary of saying anything that could be taken the wrong way.

"Freight Train, there you are!" Salvation came in the form of a familiar blonde woman with big hair and a gleaming dress. She smiled brightly at the couple beside me, who were clearly as suckered by her razzle-dazzle as everyone was at first. "Do you two mind terribly if I steal him away? I wanted to talk to you about the interview." She didn't wait for them to agree, just took me by the arm and pulled me toward the wall.

Jean Parks was one of the few people who never hesitated when it came to touching me, even though she didn't like the buzz of the force field. It helped that we were old friends, but her tenacity helped even more. She might have been a friend, but she was a reporter first and foremost, and ruthless when it came to sniffing out a story. I didn't trust her any further than I could throw her, but Jean went easier on me than she could have where I was concerned. Case in point: right now.

"You could have broken that story," I said as she steered me toward a bunting on the wall. The folds of fabric were thick enough that you could almost disappear back into them if you pushed a little. "'Freight Train: zoo savior.' Or maybe 'Freight Train: animal abandoner.' Whatever you think makes for a better headline."

"Oh please." Jean rolled her eyes and snagged a flute of champagne from a passing waitress. The bubbly gold liquid was the same shade as her dress, and almost as sparkly. "People don't want to hear about you being a jackass, Craig; you're Panopolis's poster child for Heroes. And everybody knows we can't waste you on securing the zoo.

Anyway, a freaking X-ray scanner would catch nine-tenths of what Villains smuggle in there, but the city council says it's not in the budget."

"Huh." That figured. X-ray scanners were practical, and therefore forbidden.

"Yeah, huh." She took a drink, then sidled closer to me. "While we're on the subject of Villains, though, I have to ask . . . do you have any idea how I could get in contact with Mastermind?"

I almost choked on air. "What— Why would I know that?"

"You're his nemesis, aren't you?" she demanded. "You get called in whenever he's making trouble! Or, more recently, saving people, cleaning up Z Street—I hear he's opening a clinic!"

"You follow SuperTruther, don't you?" SuperTruther was a blogger who made it his—or her, nobody knew—business to dig up the worst of Panopolis's dirt and spread it around. SuperTruther was on Panopolis PD's Most Wanted list for espionage, thanks to his almost magical ability to infiltrate places and make contact with people that just shouldn't be possible. Hell, I was half expecting him to do an exposé on me someday, revealing my unholy alliance with some of our city's biggest Villains. It was just the kind of sensational story that Jean would probably love to get her hands on, friend or not. "You're allowed to use SuperTruther as a source?"

She shrugged. "What my boss doesn't know won't hurt him. Have you been down there, though? Is it true?"

"I haven't delved deep enough into Z Street to know." Plus, I didn't exactly get weekly updates from Edward. Cleaning up Zosimos Street, the epicenter of Villainous activity in Panopolis, was a process that would take years, and he didn't seem to have time to send a memo every step of the way. "He has been pretty active down there, though."

"So he has. One of our most notorious Villains, trying to better his neighborhood." Jean's eyes narrowed thoughtfully as she swirled her champagne. "Or maybe setting up the infrastructure to take it over completely and turn it and all its residents into his slaves."

"Those are your only options?"

She shrugged. "Those are the only ones that will sell, and that's the only thing my boss cares about lately. I'd rather peddle the truth, but I can't do that if I can't interview the guy."

"You can't interview a Villain."

"Why not?" she demanded. "Mastermind has gone out of his way to ensure the safety of civilians in his conflicts with the establishment. He isn't going to hurt me, and he's got such a story to tell! Why wouldn't he want to do an interview with me? Especially if you were there to facilitate it?" She smiled winsomely at me. "Come on, I know you've got a soft spot for the guy. If you could be there to guarantee our safety, to promise a cease-fire for, oh, just a couple of hours? I could have the story of the century!"

If I stared at her any harder, my eyes would fall out. "You're crazy if you think Edward would trust me for something like that."

Jean honest-to-God batted her eyelashes at me. "Aw, you still call him 'Edward'? You're so cute! See, *this* is why he would go along with it! Because he probably knows that, deep down inside, you're a big squishy marshmallow of a man. Do you still keep Tiggles the Tiger next to your pillow?"

"Please shut up," I moaned. "You promised not to use anything you learned about me when we were *kids* against me, remember?" Jean had been my neighbor before my folks died. Playdates had happened. Secrets had been learned.

"The sooner you agree to help facilitate an interview, the sooner I'll stop bringing up your— *Oof.*" Jean stumbled into my arms, her champagne splashing over the front of my tuxedo. She turned with a snarl to confront the guy who'd just walked into her.

She was beaten to the punch.

"I'm so sorry!" Zane smiled apologetically at her. "I'm afraid I was going too fast. Did any of that get on your dress?"

Jean lost her scowl. I might be her favorite Hero, but Mr. Fabulous wasn't someone she could afford to snap at. He had just as much influence in the Hero community as I did. More in some ways, since his dad was a member of the city council and had been for decades. "I'm fine. Fortunately Freight Train was here to break my fall and take the brunt of my drink."

Zane turned his smile on me, and it was way less apologetic now, kind of a smirk. "Good thing you've got a force field, then, right?"

"His tuxedo *doesn't* have one," Jean pointed out.

"He hates dressing up anyway, don't you Freight Train?" He leaned in close to me and whispered, "For fuck's sake, *sign the fucking paperwork* already. I'm sick of delaying the shooting schedule!" Then he backed off and turned his charm on Jean again. "Let's go find you another glass, shall we? And we can talk about mediating that interview you want."

Jean bit her lip, apparently torn, which was dumb. She didn't need to worry about me. "Go ahead," I said. "I'm about to turn into a pumpkin anyway."

Ten minutes to midnight, and once it was here I was gone—Ray could just suck it. I hadn't seen him for more than a minute since I first arrived; he was a schmooze machine. Zane got his way and took Jean off on his arm, and I stared down at my sodden tuxedo with a frown.

"It probably won't stain," a voice offered from my left. I almost did a double take. I hadn't even noticed the man standing there, and I definitely had reason to. It was the scientist from earlier, the one who'd been getting the tour. Now he was in a—I think it was a dark-gray suit? I wasn't quite able to tell until he stepped away from the bunting. Before that it was almost like his head was floating in space above a vaguely man-shaped piece of velvet decor. Weird.

But away from the dark-red decoration, his suit had reasserted itself, as had the gray shirt he wore, and a tie that just barely kept him from being completely monochrome thanks to a faint white pinstripe running through the fabric. His blue eyes seemed bigger when I stood a few feet from him, accentuated by those thick black frames. I couldn't make myself look away.

I could, however, make myself speak, if only to end the awkward silence that we had going on now. "Yeah, but I kinda wish it would." I tugged at the shirt a bit. "I'm not a real fan of formal wear."

"Only politicians and professional sycophants are fans of this sort of formal wear."

I chuckled. "Yeah?"

I could have smacked myself—"Yeah," like that was a really intelligent answer, but what the hell. No one came to me expecting rocket science, and I got an answer out of him anyway.

"Indeed. Those people who cling hardest to society's ideas of formality and decorum are usually those who would rather be judged on their appearance than their actions. There's nothing wrong with looking nice, of course, but I daresay you get more done on a daily basis in your uniform than you ever would in a tuxedo."

"Well." I shrugged. "A tuxedo's not exactly fighting gear."

"If I recall correctly, Mr. Fabulous fights in a tuxedo." The man smiled, just barely. "Which do you think that makes him? Politician or sycophant?"

"Ah . . ." I wanted to say "both," but I wasn't going to badmouth a fellow Hero to a guy I didn't even know. "Sorry, what's your name?"

"No, I apologize for not introducing myself sooner." He held out a hand. "Ari Mansourian. I'm the new head of GenCorp's R&D department."

"Wow, that explains the chameleon suit!" Suave, so suave. I wanted to pull a Wicked Witch and melt into the floor, but Ari seemed pleased.

"Something like that, yes. I saved my newest prototype for social situations I'd rather avoid. It's amazing how many people will look right past you if you make an effort to blend in."

"I wish I could wear one of those outfits," I said wistfully. "But I'm supposed to be seen. I'm Craig Haney. Or, well, Freight Train." I finally shook his hand, lightly, so the touch wouldn't shock him too much. "But I guess you already knew that."

"I did. I'm interested in knowing other things, however." Instead of letting go of my hand, he brought it closer to his face. "Fascinating. So it doesn't extend to affect the cloth?"

"Nope." I let him keep my hand, even though my heart sank a little. Naturally he was more interested in my force field than he was me. He was a scientist.

"But there must be a kinetic element to it, correct? An aspect of the field that shifts within it to make impact easier for you."

"Um." Heat bloomed at the base of my neck. "I'm not sure what you mean."

"The force field doesn't only shield you from touch; it facilitates your destructive impact, doesn't it?" One dark eyebrow rose expectantly. "Otherwise you could bang away at walls all day but never smash through them. Hence, a kinetic component."

"I have no idea."

His eyebrows shot up. "You mean you don't know how your own force field works?"

The heat had completely covered my face by now. "It never came up? I mean, they totally did research when the accident happened, enough to figure out how to keep me alive, but they weren't wild about answering my questions back then."

"That's ridiculous." He took a deep breath and let it out slowly. "But then, I don't know why I'm surprised."

"Yeah." I rubbed my free hand over the back of my burning neck. "Why would they tell a grunt like me, huh?"

Unexpectedly, Dr. Mansourian shook his head. "That's not what I meant, not at all. You're the *first* person who should be informed of the full import of your abilities. They're yours. How else will you make informed decisions about your treatment?"

"What treatment?"

He blinked at me. "Everything. Medical, psychological, rehabilitative if you wish it . . . your *treatment*. I saw you in the clinic earlier today. Weren't you there for treatment of some kind?"

"Uh . . . yeah? I mean, I go in after a tussle with a Villain, but mostly I just show up there for maintenance."

"Main-ten-ance." He cut the word to bits as he spoke it, his tongue sharper than a knife. "What does that mean?"

"You know." I gestured at myself. "Keeping it clean, mostly."

Dr. Mansourian frowned. "That sounds rather dissociative."

What was he talking about? "I go in once a week unless I've been in a fight. The rest of the time, I take care of things on my own. I can't get sick, and they give me stuff to eat that covers all my vitamins and minerals and stuff." I tried on a smile, just to see if he'd buy it. "It's fine, really. Sort of ideal, in a way." I mean, who wanted to get sick? I couldn't even remember what having the sniffles felt like.

I wanted to remember that.

Dr. Mansourian looked at me for a long time before finally releasing my hand. I hadn't even realized he was still holding it. Not that I could feel it either way, but it was nice not to have been dropped like a radioactive potato.

"You know, one of my newer areas of research is improvement and streamlining of Hero-adaptive technologies. Giving you better tools to get your job done, that kind of thing," he clarified when I gave him a blank stare. "I believe the CEO of GenCorp would very much like me to create a fabric that is better able to withstand the destruction you face so often, among other things."

"Yeah, they're probably sick of seeing my bare ass make national news." My blush, which had been receding, flooded back full force. "I mean—"

Dr. Mansourian didn't seem bothered. "You're exactly correct. Would you be willing to help me test out some options?"

I knew my mouth was open, but I couldn't quite force it to shut. "You want *me* to help *you* with something science-y? Really?"

"As long as your schedule permits it, of course." He tilted his head a little as he looked at me, the light playing off his bare scalp. "What do you think?"

"I'd . . ." *be cool, be cool,* "like that." I internally wiped my own forehead with relief at not blurting *freaking love that, holy shit, are you serious?* "Whenever's good for you."

"Let's try for this next week, then, as long as you're not called away. Say, Monday at noon? I'll meet you in GenCorp's lobby."

"Great." I could barely believe it. I was going on a science date. Well, not a *date*, and I wouldn't be the one doing the science, but still. My inner eight-year-old, the one who wanted to be a marine biologist when he grew up, was doing a happy dance. "Thanks."

"No, no." When Dr. Mansourian smiled this time it was wide, his teeth on full display. "Thank *you*."

CHAPTER THREE

I get messages all the time from people trying to shame me out of staying undercover, never mind that I'm on the police's Most Wanted list. Is it a matter of mystique? Do I hate the limelight? Is it because I'm afraid? Every Hero or Villain's real identity is known these days; even the Mad Bombardier's real face has been exposed at this point. Isn't my message about making the process more transparent? How can I advocate for that when I keep my own identity hidden? I understand those criticisms, I do. I also know that the last time I told someone who I was, I barely escaped with my life. It's one thing to hide your machinations behind a company's firewall, another to expose yourself when every official is looking for a scapegoat.

The truth is, we don't know how much we don't know about what really goes on here in Panopolis. The media shows us the Heroes and the mayor and everyone else associated with the beautiful people, but those guys aren't the real movers and shakers. Demetri Granger might be the CEO of GenCorp, but he's not making the decisions. All of that goes through a board of directors, and that board is never named in any of GenCorp's documentation. This is common practice with big business in Panopolis: they explain it by saying that anonymity is crucial to preserving their health and well-being, since Panopolis is full of evildoers who might come after them if they learn their true identities. But without knowing who they are, we can't make them take responsibility for what they do.

How effective can we hope our laws, for everything from environmental regulation to antitrust investigations, are when we can't even see the people we're supposed to apply them to?

I liked visiting Ianthe.

Not because I was sweet on her or anything. I was never interested in girls that way, and even if I had been, Ianthe had always been way out of my league. I hadn't even met her until after my accident. Ianthe was a few years older than me, and she'd gone to Panopolis Preparation Academy, the fanciest school in the city. Her brother Julian and I had both been football players, though, and our teams had partied together a few times after games. Ianthe had always been at the parties too, taller than the other girls, and most of the boys, in her five-inch stilettos. She'd never seemed like a peer to me, more like the sort of person you admired from a safe, silent distance.

One time, Julian had hosted the party at his house. I'd never seen so much booze before in my entire life. And they'd had a *butler* back then, and he'd fetched new kegs when Julian had asked. Back then, that had been unutterably cool to me. Once I became a cop the memory palled a bit, since the guy had basically been facilitating a shit-ton of underage drinking, but I'd chalked it up to a youthful shenanigan not to be repeated. At the time, I'd never thought I'd party in a big old house like that again.

It was more like a mansion, actually. Scratch that: it totally was a mansion, one of the few that were left from the first few generations of Heroes. Back in the forties and fifties, Heroes had been an even bigger deal than they were now, in part because they had still been very rare. People who could survive the changes that medical experiments and industrial accidents wrought without modern medicine to support them had been one in a million, and they'd been treated like royalty. Ianthe's mother, Phaedra Delavigne, had been a child when she first got her power in the fifties, the result of a drug trial for treating multiple sclerosis that made her body extremely mutable. Ten other children had been melted into piles of flesh putty, but the doctors in charge of the trial hadn't been punished thanks to bringing about Morpho Girl, the teenage Hero prodigy. Morpho Girl got a mansion, a huge stipend from the city, and a fan following of horny teenage boys.

She'd battled evil, got married, had two kids, got divorced, and eventually lost her mind in the early eighties thanks to severe drug and alcohol abuse. As soon as they turned eighteen, her kids, under pressure from the city to carry on their mother's legacy and make the massive public investment in her worthwhile, had accepted doses of the same treatment that had changed their mother. They'd been trying to make the Morpho Girl powers into a dynasty.

Their gamble had backfired. Julian had died, probably melted into one of those flesh putty people, and Ianthe had become partially paralyzed and stuck in a wheelchair. She'd given up on being a Hero and set her sights on law school instead.

Ianthe had gotten to keep the mansion, though, and would as long as her mother was alive and shut up in part of it, with full-time caregivers keeping Phaedra going. Ianthe ran her law practice out of a sitting room on the bottom floor. It was pretty there, airy and bright, and made people feel welcome if they had to wait to see her. Which I didn't, since Vivian liked me enough not to hold me up too much.

Vivian was Ianthe's personal assistant, and had been with her ever since she'd opened her practice. She was a head shorter than me, had a wicked sense of humor, and would cut anyone who glanced at Ianthe wrong. Zane had always hated her, but I was just glad that Ianthe had someone around to help her get stuff done. She couldn't run all of her own errands anymore; on days that Vivian was busy elsewhere, Ianthe didn't take appointments. They were a well-oiled machine, and today Vivian waved me through into the office without even pausing in her argument with someone on the phone.

Ianthe looked up with a smile as I shut her office door behind me. "Hi, Craig. Thanks for being flexible about our meeting."

I sat down in the chair across from her. "It didn't bother me at all, although I think Zane's about to kill me for putting things off."

Ianthe abandoned her stack of papers with a sigh. "He told you about the show, then?"

Show? "No, he just said something about a waiver I needed to sign."

"That little *shit*."

I stared at Ianthe for a second. She practically never swore, and especially not about her clients. Ianthe was classy, from the top of her dark, curly-haired head down to the points of her designer shoes—flats now, but fancy. "Not good, I guess?"

"If you're asking about the details of the deal, I can't say," Ianthe replied coolly, brushing a curl off her forehead. "I don't know anything now that Mr. Fabulous is no longer my client."

Wait, that couldn't— What? "But he's been your client forever."

"Even forever comes to an end, apparently. Zane accepted corporate representation last week."

I might not be the sharpest knife or anything, but even I knew that was dumb. "Isn't that a conflict of interest? Since he's already—" what was the term? "—fiscally involved with them? I mean, he works for them. What's gonna make them give him a fair deal in legal stuff?"

"That's an excellent question," Ianthe agreed. "And the answer is: nothing beyond Zane's own sharp eyes, which are admittedly quite good at striking deals that financially benefit him. For example, his new reality show."

His *what*? I waited for Ianthe to laugh or say she was joking, but her lips stayed firm and flat. "Oh." Now I understood the references Zane had been making to filming.

"GenCorp actually came to him with the idea months ago. I advised him against going along with it, since the work you both do can be sensitive, not to mention graphically violent at times," Ianthe said somberly. "It's not the sort of thing that people need to see splashed even further over their media. And the possibility for lawsuits from bystanders peripherally involved in the episodes is staggering. I told him no." She shrugged her slender shoulders. "So he went and found a new lawyer who enthusiastically told him *yes*."

"He's making bank, huh?"

"He will be, yes. And then GenCorp will take his inevitably huge legal fees out of his entertainment salary, and he'll end up even more of an indentured servant to them than you all are already." Ianthe's voice shook a little as she spoke, and when I looked closer I could see that her hands were trembling.

"Hey, whoa." I got up and came around the desk to stand beside her. Her power wheelchair was on, so I helped her back it out to give her some distance, and pulled my own chair around so I could sit next to her. I wished I could pat her on the shoulder or something. "You're clearly not feeling good. What am I even doing here today? You should be in bed. We could have rescheduled again."

Ianthe smiled, but she didn't seem happy. "Unfortunately, we're on a tight schedule. A response by Monday isn't only encouraged, it's compulsory. Failure to deliver the waiver by then or to present a brief on why you refuse to sign it means we'll be found in contempt."

"How can they find us in contempt? It's not a criminal case."

"No, it's not," Ianthe said with a sigh. "But the court in question is granting Zane, and through him GenCorp, special status with this project."

Aha. "Special status" meant lots of money. It wasn't the first time the legal system in Panopolis was proving to be less than airtight when it came to following the law, and it wouldn't be the last. "Well, shit."

That got a genuine laugh from her. "Exactly."

"I probably can't refuse to sign it, huh?"

"You can," she said fiercely. "Yes, you can. It'll mean a fight, and GenCorp might get involved since they own a lot of your subsidiary and merchandising rights, but you can certainly refuse. It's not like you need the extra income, after all."

Yeah, sure. "Eh, sounds like more trouble than it's worth." I didn't want to pick a fight with GenCorp. I might feel like Goliath in the Heroing world, but compared to GenCorp I wasn't any bigger than David's left nut. "Just lay it out for me. And can I at least get you a glass of water or a couple Tylenol or something?" Anything to help stop the tremors.

She shook her head and waved me back to my seat. "I'll be fine. You're my only appointment today, and I'll make this as painless for both of us as possible."

Basically they wanted me to agree to let the production company use any footage of me where I was in a shot with Zane, with no expectation of compensation.

"They offered to pay for your appearances, but that would technically embroil you in the same messy net Zane's in, only without the status that he's been given," Ianthe told me. "I got rid of the clauses that would have let them use individual footage of you taken during an incident where Mr. Fabulous is also present, and that would let them make you the focus of the episodes in any way. They have no excuse for following you or staking out your home, unless Mr. Fabulous is visiting, and I don't think you invite him over that often."

"Try never."

"Good." She turned to the next page of the document.

Even going fast, it still took a couple of hours to go over all of the waiver's provisions and clauses. Legalese gave me a headache like nothing else, and I was grateful to finally be ushered out of the place at a little after four by Vivian, who seemed to know my schedule better than I did. I had just enough time to make it to Memaw's without her kicking up a fuss about me being late.

Dinner was strained. Things hadn't been good between me and Memaw ever since Edward's arrest. Some of that was guilt on my part. I hadn't stood up for the guy; I'd let Memaw tell me something had to be wrong with Edward for him not to want me: it had been for the best, he was no good, he was a liar, he was everything wrong with society today. I hadn't believed it, not really, but I hadn't spoken out either.

I'd never be able to make up for what happened to Edward. He hadn't explicitly told me what had happened to him during his brief stay in the Abattoir, but I'd gleaned enough to know it hadn't been good. His ability—a kind of empathy control—had been a hard one for everybody to get a handle on, including Edward, and honestly I still wasn't sure exactly how he'd done away with Maggot three months ago. Maggot had been the Villain who forced Edward to break into GenCorp in the first place, in fact. I guess I had him to thank for the deal Edward and I had now, in a roundabout way. It was simple: Edward and I stayed out of each other's way, and helped where we could. It was a friendlier working relationship than I had with most other Heroes.

I couldn't expect Memaw to understand that. When she made up her mind about something or someone, there was no convincing her otherwise. Edward was bad, I should try harder, and my dad was a lazy bum. Three concrete tenets in her Church of Obstinacy, three of many that she brought up every. Damn. Sunday dinner.

"Oh, honey," she sighed as she inspected the bouquet I'd brought along. "Half of these are on the verge of wilting already; didn't you check them in the store? Why didn't you check them in the store?"

"They're not wilting, Memaw."

"They are. Look at this!" She yanked out a yellow gerbera daisy and brandished it under my nose. "This is falling apart! Those poor petals are going to be gone by tomorrow."

She put the bouquet in the water-filled vase on the sideboard, and didn't glance their way again.

"Gifts are only nice to receive when it's clear that the giver has put *thought* into them, Craig," she told me as she took her usual dinner out of the oven: chicken and potato casserole, my favorite. It made my mouth water every time. That was one of the best and worst things about Sunday dinners with Memaw: seeing my favorite food, but knowing that I couldn't eat it.

"I'll check the next bouquet better." I pulled out the shake I'd brought along. Mmm, salty, chewy meat-ish sludge. Maybe someday I'd ask for another flavor.

"Don't bother if it's going to be too much work for you, honey."

I held my snort back as Memaw filled her plate with chicken and potatoes, poured a huge glass of Moscato, and joined me at the table. Like I'd bother coming if I didn't bring her flowers. Memaw was a stickler for protocol, and bouquets were part of it.

"So," she began, "tell me the latest good news."

"Well, I made three arrests earlier this week. No casualties at all." They hadn't even been proper Villains, just a team of robbers who hit up a drive-thru bank on the edge of downtown. They'd actually tried to shoot me. It had been kind of funny.

"That's nice. Why didn't that one make the papers?"

"I guess because it wasn't very exciting."

"Craig, honey." Memaw took a big sip of her wine. "Shouldn't they leave small-time criminals to lesser Heroes? I don't like how GenCorp is scheduling you."

"I was the closest Hero on hand; it made sense for me to take care of it."

"You're going to get slow if they keep this up, though. Maybe that's why things went so badly with that clown fellow."

I sighed. "That one went okay, Memaw. No one was injured except for Bubbles the Clown." Bubbles had been injured enough for everybody, frankly.

"But it wasn't *you* who did the injuring! At least it wasn't that Fabulous boy either; I can't stand him." She frowned down at her plate. "I'm not sure having the Mad Bombardier handle the problem for you is any better. I can't believe he hasn't been captured yet and sent to the Abattoir. It's where people like him belong—him and that awful Edward Dinges. *Mastermind*," she said with a sneer. "Whatever *that* means. When are you finally going to go after them, Craig?"

"They're not a high priority. Not while they're taking out other Villains for the city."

"But they're getting too much publicity! Some people are actually *happy* that they're interfering like this, did you know that? I don't think you should be so complacent, honey. I mean, what if they did something so popular that no one cared about you anymore? What would you do if you couldn't be a Hero?"

I examined the faded rose pattern on the tablecloth. It had been my mom's tablecloth, one of the few things that Memaw had kept after I came to live with her. Most of it had been thrown away because Memaw had said it didn't match the décor. "I don't know."

I'd thought about it, from time to time. What would I be doing if I wasn't a Hero? If I'd never become a Hero? Probably I'd still be a cop, maybe a casualty of some big battle at this point; the Panopolis police force had a bad record with keeping officers safe. Would I go back, if a miracle took away my force field? I didn't have training in anything else, and I was really too old for college now anyway. If I could even get into college—my grades had never been the best. I'd tried, I'd tried so hard, but learning from books had always been tough for me.

Maybe I'd be a carpenter like my dad. A professional handyman. I was good with my hands. Of course, then Memaw would disown me, but what did that matter? It was just a fantasy anyway. "I don't know," I said again.

Memaw patted the tablecloth a few inches from my hand. She didn't like to touch me; she said my force field was too uncomfortable. "You'd better pick up the pace, then, honey. You make a good Hero, when you're trying. What else happened this week?"

"I met a guy." The words slipped out of my mouth before I had a chance to reel them back, and I groaned internally as Memaw's eyes lit up. She was always trying to set me up with someone lately, and I was always telling her to stop. I didn't want to go on any more blind dates with the kids of her friends, people who were so excited to meet me at first, and so disappointed by the end of the night.

"A guy! What kind of guy? Is he another Hero? Please tell me you're not dating Mr. Fabulous, honey. He seems so high maintenance."

We could definitely agree on that. "No, he's a new scientist at GenCorp. His name's Ari Mansourian."

"Ari. *Aaaah*-ri, huh. And his last name is Mansourian? Where's that come from?"

"I'm not sure."

"It doesn't sound like a local name." She pursed her wrinkled lips for a moment. "Ah well, that's okay. A scientist! My gosh, honey, what did you two find to talk about?"

We talked about how tuxedos are a sign of being a tool. "Um, my force field."

"Oh, that's good." She smiled broadly at me. "It's nice he's interested in that—that way you won't have to make much conversation to keep his attention. Are you going on another date? What does he look like? When are you going to bring him by?"

"Slow down, Memaw." I definitely didn't want her sticking her nose into the situation. Besides . . . "We haven't gone on an actual date yet. We met at GenCorp yesterday and got to talking."

"Is he handsome?"

"Um . . . I think so."

I swear Memaw almost rolled her eyes at me. "I mean is he *objectively* handsome, honey? You've picked some weird ones in the past. Honestly, that Edward Dinges didn't know how to use a comb."

"Well, that won't be a problem for this guy. He doesn't have any hair."

It was the wrong thing to say. For someone who'd grown up in a lower-middle-class neighborhood and had never been a beauty queen herself, my memaw could be really judgmental about a person's appearance. "He's bald? Craig, honestly, how old is this man? Is he a cradle robber, going after you?"

"Memaw—"

"Don't you 'Memaw' me in that tone. Answer the question!"

I was saved from embarrassed obedience by the sudden buzz of my phone. I pulled it out of the special holster on the small of my back and checked the new message. It was from downtown's central police precinct, the one quartered beside the courthouse. *Unidentified package in central square.*

Goddamn it, if this was a bomb, I was going to kick Raul's ass.

Big. Assistance needed. Big . . . that was a weird descriptor to add in there. How big was it?

Guess I'd find out soon enough. It was only a five-minute drive from here. *En route 5 min*, I texted back, and then put the phone away. "Sorry, Memaw, I've got to go."

She looked disappointed. "You didn't even stay long enough for dessert."

Yeah, the chocolate-chunk brownies that I never got to eat, just got to watch *her* eat. I was more than happy to skip that experience this time around. "Duty calls."

She sighed. "I suppose." She turned her cheek to face me, and I kissed the air next to it. "Fight hard, honey. Don't be afraid to jump right in there."

"I will, Memaw." I got up and left her to her half-eaten dinner and wilted flowers with a sigh of relief. Sometimes Sunday dinners could be a real pain in the ass.

CHAPTER FOUR

Progress is a decidedly relative concept. I'm just putting that out there as something the Absolutists and True Believers in our minisociety should maybe take some time to consider. Statistics are all well and good, but you can lie with math as easily as you can with words, folks. It's all in how you ask the questions.

For example, official Villain attacks are down by almost sixty percent in the past six months. Pretty impressive reduction in crime, right? Fewer people getting blown to kingdom come by vengeful bombardiers, that's lovely. But you know what's gone up a corresponding amount in that same time frame? Normal crime levels: the everyday robberies and murders and assaults that aren't historically the responsibility of Heroes; those crimes taken care of by the police. So can we really call it a reduction, when it seems more like a reallocation?

The fewer the big-name Villains, the more the small-time criminals, perhaps? One wonders if our police force remembers how to deal with people like that anymore.

I had a special siren on the top of my car, and whirling lights made people get out of my way real fast on the roads. I parked in front of the courthouse four minutes after leaving Memaw's, and was pleased to see that cops were already working to keep the crowd back from the package.

It was an actual fucking *package*, with wrapping paper and a bow on top and everything. Like a birthday present, only a hundred times bigger than normal. You could have fit a car in this. Two cars, stacked on top of each other. There were noises coming from the thing, banging and chittering, occasionally hitting the inside of the box hard enough to rattle it.

"Huh." Weird. I turned to the nearest cop, who looked intensely relieved to see me. "How did this even get here?"

"A tow truck dropped it off."

Okay, that made sense but wasn't exactly what I was asking. "You let a tow truck with an enormous present on the back of it pull up in front of the courthouse, dump the present on the ground, and drive off without asking any questions?"

The cop shrugged. "It wouldn't be the first time in the last few months something like this has happened. I mean, did you see the stuff that was dropped off for Mayor Wright's birthday celebration last month? The flock of pink plastic flamingos was the least of it, Freight Train."

That might be true, but I didn't care. "You're trying to tell me that you thought the mayor might have an enormous box filled with, what, strippers or flamingos abandoned in a public thoroughfare in the middle of the evening? I assume you've checked in with him."

"I'm . . . almost positive that we have."

"Where's Chief Burnside?" She should have been all over this.

"They moved her to the north side of Z Street at the end of last month, sir. We've got Chief Studer now. He doesn't work on weekends."

The fuck he doesn't. "So you call him and tell him it's an emergency!"

The cop rubbed his hands together so hard I worried he'd give himself blisters. I could see the whites around his eyes. "I did! And he said he was busy and to call one station over, but they're out in force helping Petra deal with a hostage situation! So I contacted you!"

"And that was good," I said as soothingly as I could manage. "That was the right thing to do. I'll handle this." Whatever *this* was. I needed to take a closer look, but first . . . I owed someone a chance. I pulled out my phone and made a call.

Five rings in, Firebolt picked up. "Yes, hi, I'm here, yes, hello? Freight Train?"

"Yeah. Where are you?"

"Seventeenth and Mapleton." That was on the seedy side of downtown, close to Z Street. "Where do I need to be?"

"The courthouse. Just for backup, Firebolt. I don't think this is gonna be a messy one." I hoped it wouldn't be, at least.

"Sure!" The prospect of not getting to breathe flames at her enemies didn't seem to faze her. "I'll be there in five."

"See you then." I hung up and moved nearer to the box. The pattern was shiny and blue, and when I peered closer, faint holographic Vs jumped out at me. *Damn* it. I had an idea of what was going on now, and I was gonna wring some necks tonight. Fucking showboating Villains.

Well, hopefully the thing wasn't going to blow up. "There's a tag," I noted as I walked around the thing. Cameras and phones were flashing from fifty feet back, but the perimeter was holding nicely. "*For Your Halls Of Justice.*"

"It sounds like there's something alive in there," the cop in charge said uneasily. I checked his name tag: Vin Morrison. Aw, one letter away from greatness.

Once I concentrated, I could detect what sounded like *lots* of movement, on tiny feet. "I think you're right."

"What do you want me to do?"

"We need to move the box to a more secure location before we try anything else. We should—"

"Freight Train!"

Oh, shit. It was Mr. Fabulous, bursting through the wall of police like they weren't there. That wasn't exactly abnormal, but the half-dozen civilians that followed behind him sure were. Half a dozen civilians carrying video equipment and microphones on sticks and a bunch of other stuff that didn't need to be this close to an unidentified but probably dangerous object. There was even one girl there with a makeup kit, fluttering closer to Mr. Fabulous with a sponge before he shooed her away.

"Mr. Fabulous," I said as calmly as I could while he was a little ways out. Once he was at my side I dropped my voice and hissed, "What the hell is this?"

"Oh, come on, I got a call from the mayor that something was going down in front of the courthouse. What could I do, not respond?" He smirked at me. "What, are you getting shy about sharing the limelight?"

"No, but I'm kinda pissed that you're bringing civilians in this close to a potential conflict zone."

"It's a *present*." He drew the word out like it was made of taffy. "A literal *gift*; how dangerous could it be? It's a great job to break my crew in with. Thanks for signing that waiver, by the way." He turned to one of his cameramen. "Are you guys in position?"

"Looks good, we're rolling."

"Perfect." Mr. Fabulous threw his shoulders back and clapped his hands together. "So! Let's just open this gift, shall we?"

"Not here," I cut in. "We need to move it someplace more secure."

Mr. Fabulous scoffed. "Are you kidding me? It's so scenic here, like something straight out of a movie. No, we're opening it now."

"We can't—"

But he'd already darted off on feet that moved too fast for me to track. He grabbed a handful of paper and sprinted around the box in a series of rapid circles, tearing the wrapping away in thin strips. The crowd shrieked as the package's contents were revealed.

It was actually two glass boxes, pressed in tight side by side. Each was completely clear, with air holes drilled in the sides to allow for the passage of air. In the right-hand box was a person—maybe a woman? It was hard to say, her clothes were so tattered and filthy, and her hair was so matted. She crouched on her hands and knees, cooing at the contents of the other box, clucking and seeming to do her best to distract them from us. And *they* were . . .

Rats. Massive brown-and-gray rats. So many that they were piled on top of each other, the box too narrow to allow all of them space at the bottom of it. They were like a roiling, furry maelstrom, snapping and squeaking and biting constantly. And when they bit, these rats bit *hard*. I saw one sever another's toe and had had enough. "We're moving these. Now."

"But where did they even come from?" Mr. Fabulous asked dramatically.

"You'd know if you'd bothered to talk to the cops," I snapped. "Anonymous delivery via tow truck. Why they were put here, I've got no idea." I turned to the woman and raised my voice. "Who are you?"

"Don't hurt them." Her voice was low and rough, her hands were wringing together so fiercely I thought she might take her own skin off. "They didn't know what they were doing. They were hungry; it was an accident! Don't hurt my friends."

"What did they do?" Mr. Fabulous demanded.

"Nothing!"

"We can't interrogate her here," I murmured.

"You started it," he shot back before returning to the captive woman. "Come on, then! What did they do?"

"Nothing too bad, nothing, I promise! They were clean-up only, making Z Street a cleaner place, like we're supposed to!"

Mr. Fabulous leaned closer to the glass box. "Cleaner how?"

"Eating the bodies! Dead bodies only, just the dead ones, how were they to know a few of them were a little bit alive?" She spread her hands helplessly. "Just an accident, I swear!"

My meat shake roiled in my stomach. "They ate people alive?"

"It was a merciful death," the woman whispered. "More merciful than leaving them to die slow and terrible and alone! When I told my friends to stop, they listened to me; they always listen to me. If I had known, I would never have told them to. Free them, they'll be good, we'll be good!"

"Who captured them?"

The woman's expression went sullen. "Nobody."

Mr. Fabulous scoffed. One of the microphones drifted closer to us. "So they climbed inside this box on their own?"

"No!"

"Then *what*?"

"They came because I called them!" She pounded a filthy hand on the glass. "Because I didn't want to be alone! Caught in glass with nothing to touch, no heartbeats to soothe me, nothing! They came to be with me! They only came to be with me; be kind to them, be kind!"

Mr. Fabulous shook his head. "Lady, you are one kiwi short of a fruit basket."

Someone laughed, and Mr. Fabulous turned a gleaming smile in their direction before looking back. "We'll take care of you in a minute. For now . . ."

He picked up the box of rats, hefting it easily into the air despite its size. The rodents squealed, and the woman shrieked in mirrored fear. "I'll run this down to the lake and drown these guys lickety-split."

"No!" The woman howled out the denial. "No, don't hurt them! Don't hurt my friends, don't hurt them, don't don't don't!"

"You lost the right to have a say in their fate when you chose to—"

A puffy orange figure shouldered its way through the cops and ran toward us, stopping a few feet back. "Am I too late? What did I miss?" Firebolt panted. Her hands were covered with simple gauntlets today, but her mask had its usual fire-spray feature on, like a flat, wide duck's bill. Attached to the corners of her mouth were metal tubes that led to a secured pack of special lighter fluid in the back of her fireproof suit.

Mr. Fabulous frowned at her. "Who the hell are you?"

"I called her," I told him, then turned to Firebolt. "And you didn't miss much. We're just figuring out what to do with the rat queen and her subjects here."

"Don't hurt them!" the woman shrieked again.

"Why the hell would you call for backup that wasn't me?" Mr. Fabulous demanded.

I blinked at him in disbelief. "I thought you always said you were no one's backup."

"Well, that's *true*, but I should still be the first person you call when something is going on. Freight Train and I make a pretty good team," he said with a wink to one of his camera people. "When he lets me do the planning, that is."

I was making a plan to hand Mr. Fabulous his ass on a platter. "The point is—"

The woman in the box made a high-pitched squeak, and suddenly the rats inside of it ran straight toward her, piling heavily on one side. The box tilted quickly and precariously, and Mr. Fabulous didn't have time to recover his balance before it tumbled to the ground. The glass shattered, and a moment later the rats were free.

"Run, friends!" she yelled. "Run run run! Bite your way to freedom!"

"Don't let them reach the civilians," I shouted, grabbing for rats as fast as I could. Panic broke out as the rats flooded the area. A member of the camera crew cursed and dropped his gear as a rat began to climb his leg.

They couldn't bite me, but I wasn't good at catching them either. Mr. Fabulous ran some of them down and herded them toward their shattered box, but there were too many for him to handle them all. We needed a better way to corral them.

"Stand back!" Firebolt took a deep breath, and then a gout of bright yellow flame poured out of the mouthpiece of her mask. The pulsing mass of rats caught fire, and . . .

It turned into one of those times that Heroing really sucked. I was okay with putting bad people into a certain amount of pain; most of them had knowingly brought it on themselves. But the rats? What had they done, other than listen to a crazy lady who'd turned them into the world's grossest murder squad? And burning to death? All it had going for it was it was pretty fast, I guess. Not that some of them didn't try to run away. They did. They just didn't get too far.

The woman in the box was completely freaking out now, a couple of people had been bitten and were bleeding profusely, and Firebolt's shoulders were hunched as she glanced between me and Mr. Fabulous. She had probably done the only thing that she could think of in the moment, but it wasn't a comfortable or a pretty one. And Mr. Fabulous . . . he was mad. More like furious, actually.

He stalked over to Firebolt and poked her in the middle of her chest. "What the fuck was that?"

"Um . . ."

"Who asked you to come in and save the day, huh? I had this under control!"

"Freight Train kind of asked me, and—"

"Anything that happens downtown is a job for Class One Heroes only, you upstart piece of shit. You think you belong in here with us? And *you*," he rounded on me, "have been worse than useless here!"

I was in no mood to take that from him tonight. "I said we should move the box to a secure location before opening it. I didn't say we should pick it up and grandstand on a goddamn soapbox, and then *drop* the fucking thing so it breaks all over the concrete."

Mr. Fabulous's eyes narrowed. "We'll discuss this later." He went to help his camera crew, and I turned back to Firebolt.

"Ignore him," I said. "You did okay. It wasn't a nice solution, but at least it stopped them."

"What else could I have done?" she asked, her eyes wide beneath her mask.

Oh, there were so many things . . . "Waited for me to pour out a ring of gasoline around them and then set that on fire to contain them? Or done the same with your own fuel?"

Her metallic voice was downhearted. "Oh. I didn't even think of that."

"I know." I had to take a share of the responsibility for this; I had known she was undertrained when I phoned her for backup. "We'll work on it, okay?"

"Okay," she said. "Thanks for calling me."

"You're welcome. Head on to the clinic and get checked out." I'd be there soon enough myself, as soon as I dealt with the rat queen and the cops.

Some days never stopped sucking, it seemed.

Five hours later I walked through the door of Apartment Three ready to breathe fire of my own. Apartment Three was a derelict boathouse on the edge of Lake Juniper, across the water from the Abattoir, which you could just barely see on the far shore. The boathouse was the sort of place you'd never know existed if you hadn't been escorted there. The sky out here was pitch-black at midnight, only lit by stars made hazy from Panopolis's ever-present smog. There were no street lamps, and the moon was just a sliver tonight, barely slicing through the darkness over the horizon.

Apartment Three appeared the same on the outside as any number of the boathouses on this part of the shore, with dingy windows and peeling paint. In reality, the windows had been airbrushed to appear that way, and were completely opaque. If someone looked closely at the door, they'd notice that the simple knob and lock combination wasn't actually connected to anything. Turning over the rusting paint can a few feet away revealed a keypad, though, and after I punched in the code, there was a quiet hiss of the security system disarming and releasing the locks. I stepped inside and did my best not to slam the door shut behind me.

Three people were already inside, poring over a blueprint spread out on the table in the middle of the small but well-lit room. As soon as they saw me, they rolled it up and set it aside, and Edward came around the table with a faint smile. "Hi, Craig."

Oh, fuck him and his "hi" tonight.

"What the hell was that show outside the courthouse today?" I demanded, ignoring his outstretched hand. Edward frowned, and Raul flanked him silently.

"What show?" Edward's dark hair was sticking up in a hundred different directions. I'd spent nights wondering about the texture of that hair, once upon a time. Now all I wanted to do was slap its owner upside the head.

"Dressing that maniac and her rats up like a present and sticking it in the middle of the street? Do you have any idea how many people could have been hurt?"

Edward shook his head. "What are you talking about?"

Raul, on the other hand, stared straight at the third person. He was down by one eye after a nasty confrontation with Maggot, but his remaining eye did the job of two pretty easily when it came to glaring. The black eye patch didn't hurt the intimidation factor either. "Oh, Daya. Really?"

"What?" she asked brightly. Clearly the glare had lost its power over her. Daya was the Villain I knew as Vibro, a dark-skinned woman with lavender hair and a wide smile. I'd only met her once before, but I knew better than to trust her. "I was making a statement!"

"What kind of statement was that, exactly?" I clenched my hands to my own biceps. Otherwise I might do something unwise. "That you think the courthouse deserves to be overrun with rats, or that we can't take care of the crazy psycho who eggs them on? We had to set her rats on fire. On *fire*. You know how far a rat can run when it's on fire before it dies?" I knew, down to the inch.

"You gave them Zena?" Edward sounded disappointed. "We had a plan for her!"

Daya put her hands on her hips. "And it was a bad plan. You can't save everybody, Edward, and you shouldn't try to. There are always going to be people who don't work into the grand scheme of things."

"I was getting there. I was starting to change her mind," Edward argued. "With a little more work, maybe I could have made a real difference in her."

That didn't seem right. "I thought you didn't do mind control."

"I don't," he insisted. "I've been working at creating a lasting emotional effect in a person, though. Connecting to their feelings and engendering action through them."

"Yeah, that still strikes me as mind control."

"It's not! It's— Think of it like an antianxiety pill, only without the side effects. I mean, yeah, I can make a few suggestions, try to keep a person calm or put a simple, beneficial impulse into their heads, but mind control? No way."

We'd have to agree to disagree. "So what, when your pill thing didn't work, Vibro set Rat Lady loose on the cops?"

Daya rolled her eyes. "No. I handed Zena, and her rats, over to the regular authorities to see what *they* would do with her. The rats were contained. It's not my fault some Hero stumbled and let the little beasts break free. You'd think the police would have recognized her anyway. A person with her reputation should have been treated as a more serious threat."

Okay, there was a lot I wasn't following here. "Why was she a threat? Who exactly is Zena?"

Raul finally broke his silence. "Dr. Zena Parsons, a zoologist at the university back in the early nineties. She did research into animal communication, and was convinced that with the proper understanding, humans and animals would be able to speak coherently to one another. Dr. Parsons applied for grants for advanced trials, and when denied, she experimented upon herself and her lab rats. She did indeed discover a means of communicating with them, with the help of a few minor surgeries and a couple of very dangerous chemical injections."

He shrugged. "It drove her mad. The university fired her, her insurance dropped her, and once she could no longer afford medical care, she fled to Z Street. She lived in the shadows for decades, before we began to thin out the bigger, badder Villains. We tried to work with her, but she—"

"She fed people to her rats," Edward finished, tilting his head up toward the light as he sighed. He looked a bit too pale to be healthy. "During a cold spell a while ago, when the homeless took shelter in abandoned buildings. She'd sneak her rat pack in and let them feed on whoever was too sick to run. We didn't find out until she'd killed almost an entire block. She said her rats deserved to eat too, that she was doing us a favor clearing out the old and weak."

"Aggressive little beasts. It took a lot of work to round them all up," Raul commented, glancing at his hand. It did look nibbled around the edges, with Band-Aids covering several of his fingers.

Wait, that didn't track. "She said she called them into the box so she wouldn't be alone."

"She lied," Raul said flatly. "She set them on us. She's quite the liar, our Zena, or hadn't you noticed?"

"And we hadn't *decided* what to do with the rats yet, but I was working on rehabilitating Zena, remember?" Edward said, glaring at Raul. It might have been petty of me—screw that, it was definitely petty of me—but I was glad to see them argue. They got along so well, it almost seemed like they were the perfect couple. Apparently not.

"We weren't about to feed and care for the rats ourselves. We had neither the time nor the means," Raul retorted. "And you have other, larger concerns to deal with than rehabilitating a woman whose very touch left you nauseous. So I delegated to Daya." He resumed glaring at Vibro. "But as a gift in front of the courthouse? Is there no room within you for subtlety?"

"Think of it as a test," she suggested. "A chance for them to prove they can do a better job handling Villains than us Villains can. A test that they failed, by the way." She pivoted to me with a mocking grin. "I saw footage of Mr. Fabulous dropping the box. Not very Heroic of him."

I wasn't Zane's biggest fan, but I felt the need to defend him a little. "He couldn't have known that she could order rats around. They unbalanced the thing."

"Hey, if *you* can see that it's a bad idea to go casually hoisting a box of rats into the air out in the open in front of a crowd of onlookers, then it should have been obvious to him."

That stung, despite being true. I opened my mouth to defend myself, but Edward beat me to it. "Daya, you should go now."

Her smirk softened into apology, but not at me. "Edward, come on, let me stay. I promise to play nice from here on out."

"We won't be long," Raul said. "And your brother will already be wondering what's keeping you. Go on, we'll be just another minute."

Daya stared at them both for a long moment before nodding. "Whatever you want, boss." She straightened up, brushed past me, and walked out the door.

"You're too easy on her," Raul commented.

Edward sighed. "I know, but that's what you're helping me with, right? Keeping people in line?"

"How *do* you keep a bunch of Villains in line?" I was genuinely curious; it didn't seem possible that so many people with big, often violent personalities would follow Edward's lead. He was too nice. I mean, I knew he had a rep that made him seem a hundred feet tall, but how could anyone be scared of him once they'd met him?

Raul turned a sharp grin on me. "He simply gives them their options: to work with us, or to fight against us. Those who refuse, he takes by the hand."

Oh. "He mind whammies them."

"It isn't a mind whammy," Edward sighed. "Jesus Christ, you know that."

"Heart whammy, then. Hit 'em in the emotions, or whatever." I'd never felt Edward's empathic power, you had to touch skin to skin for that, but apparently he packed a real wallop. "You force them to agree with you?"

"No!"

"Most are willing to join us once they understand our goals," Raul interjected. "Some are too vicious to let live when they fight against us. Others, well . . . others are insane, and cannot be controlled by our limited means, but perhaps don't deserve to die. Like Zena. So we gave her to you to take care of."

And a fine job we'd done there. "She got sent to the Abattoir tonight."

Edward flinched. "Oh, no."

I felt bad about that, but . . . "You had to know she would." There was no other place for captured Villains in Panopolis.

"I was going to keep working with her! I was sure I could—"

"You were making yourself sick." Raul took Edward's hands in his own and lifted them to his chest. "Too sick to even get out of bed yesterday morning. You can't save anyone else if you aren't saving yourself first, love. And when you cannot save yourself, or you forget to, then I do so for you."

"Raul . . ."

They were about to get mushy. It hurt to watch them touch like this, doing what I never could with so much ease. If only they'd get to the point so I could get out of here. "Why did you call me? Is it about the data?"

"Oh, right!" Edward freed one hand and reached into his pocket. "Our hacker finally figured out a way to unscramble part of the information on the drive. Ze thinks it's probably a chemical formula of some kind, and also wanted me to tell you that if ze had known this was going to be so heavily guarded, ze would have advised Maggot against going after it at all. Apparently each file is encoded differently, and beyond the most basic information they're almost impossible to crack. Even unscrambled, ze couldn't really understand the data, and we don't have any biochemists on our team." He handed me a small silver thumb drive. "It's better than nothing, though. We'll keep working on it."

I put the drive in my pocket with a sigh. It sure as hell wasn't gonna do me any good, but I'd rather have something I couldn't understand than nothing at all. "Thanks."

"And I'm sorry about Zena and the rats."

I gave him the ghost of a smile. "It's not your fault, apparently. Besides, we should have handled them better."

"True," Raul said.

My smile evaporated as I looked at him, but he held up a hand. "But at least you tried. To try and fail is better than to never try at all."

That was probably a compliment. "Thanks."

"We'll let you know when we have more data for you."

Sounded like "good-bye" to me.

"Okay." I turned to leave, and then glanced back at Raul. "By the way, it would be nice if next time you decide to personally lend a hand, you don't blow our target's head off."

Raul smirked insincerely. "I'll try."

I bet you will. "Great."

CHAPTER FIVE

I've made no bones about my feelings when it comes to power and privilege here in Panopolis. Hero or Villain, regular Joe or big-name CEO, no one should be immune to the magnifying glass of oversight. Sometimes, though, we take it a little too far.

From where I sit, I can see three different tabloids. Every single one of them has a Super on the cover, and every single one of them is screaming about that person's personal life. I know, I know: live your life in a bubble, you're going to be scrutinized whether you want it or not. But after reading and researching, I've come to the conclusion that ninety-five percent of everything printed about both Heroes and Villains is bullshit. We want to know all about them, but we don't seem to care whether any of our information is correct. It's taxation of the soul without representation of the truth, and we the consumers are the tax men in this poor metaphor of mine.

On Monday at noon, I showed up at GenCorp for my meeting with Dr. Mansourian, and tried to act innocuous. It shouldn't have been so hard: I was in jeans, a sweatshirt, and a ball cap, not my uniform, and the place was crowded enough that I could have been mistaken for a tourist. Or in the past I could have. These days, security was a little more conscious.

I'd gotten so used to entering the building through the back, I completely forgot that they'd made major changes since Edward broke in. Everyone who came through the front door had to go through a metal detector, then a physical frisk, while their stuff was opened up and checked out, just like at the airport. There was also a special wand they passed over the head, looking for what, I wasn't sure, but they let me in, so apparently I passed.

An intern met me almost as soon as I entered the lobby.

"Freight Train!" She seemed oddly familiar . . . Oh, yeah. It was the same girl who'd been showing around Ari last time. I hadn't caught her name then, but now she was wearing a name tag.

"Hi, um . . . Tuh-sering?"

"Oh, the T is silent, but don't worry about it," she assured me. "What an honor to meet you in person at last, sir." She held out a hand, and only jumped a little when we shook. "What can I do for you today?"

"Well, I've got a meeting in a few minutes, but—"

"With whom? Would you like me to page them and inform them you're here? Or I can send a memo! I'm allowed access to the company's internal memo system."

She sounded way happier about that than she probably should. "Nah, that's okay, I'll wait."

Tsering frowned. "But why wait when you don't need to?"

"Because he might be in the middle of something important and not have time to come and meet me yet."

"What's more important than meeting with a Hero?"

"I can think of about a million things," I said seriously. I was about to name a few of them when a sudden soft but urgent call of "Matty!" drew my attention. A woman standing in line for the tour was staring at me— No, wait, not quite at me. At my leg. Or . . .

I glanced down. There was a little kid, way little, crouched over my shoe. The leg of my pants had caught on the top of my sneaker, and he was poking a tiny finger at the triangle of bare skin that could be seen there. I didn't feel it, of course, but he seemed fascinated.

"Matty, get back here!"

I wiggled my foot, and the kid looked up at me and grinned. "Hi!" he said.

I grinned back. "Hi."

"That is *not* appropriate," Tsering said, more surprised than severe, but the boy's smile dropped away.

"Nah, it's fine," I told him. "Pretty cool, huh?"

"Yeah," he said, all shy now but still meeting my eyes. His mother had given up on subtlety and was headed over to us, blushing furiously.

"I think so too." And I did, even if I also thought it sucked. I mean, c'mon, I had a *force field*. If I'd been able to turn it off whenever I wanted, it would have been the best thing ever. "You like Heroes, Matty?"

"Yeah!"

His mother reached us and grabbed for his hand. "I'm so sorry; he saw you and ran off before I even recognized you!" Her blush deepened. "Not that I don't know who you are. I just—"

"It's fine," I said before turning my attention back to the kid. "I mean, not that you ran away from your mom, because that's not fine, but I like talking to new people. Who's your favorite Hero, Matty?"

"Um . . . I like Mr. Fabulous!"

That figured. "He's pretty cool," I agreed.

"And I like Keen."

"Keen is *way* cool." I didn't know her well, but apparently her enhanced reflexes made her an almost unbeatable hand-to-hand fighter.

Matty nodded along with me. "But you're my most favorite, Freight Train."

"Oh." I wasn't incredibly surprised—Ray did get my name plastered on a lot of stuff—but it was one thing to read about my "positive market saturation" and another to be told I was someone's favorite Hero in person. "It's so great to hear that, Matty."

"Taking the tour was his idea," his mother confessed. "His cousin came with a school group last week and got a signed picture of you. I told Matty he was too young to really appreciate it, but he insisted."

"Oh wow." I looked down at Matty, who was grinning again. "You wanted a picture, huh?"

"I can get a promotional one for him—" Tsering began, but I cut her off.

"Actually, how about you get one right now?" I asked his mom. "Does your phone do that?" She nodded. "Great." I crouched down next to him, and he threw his arms around my neck. So much of his bare skin against my force field made him jump, but he gamely held on until his mom had taken the photo. She turned the phone around to show me; the kid couldn't have been smiling any harder.

"Good one," I told him. "And you hung on even though I know it doesn't feel very nice, so I think that deserves something special." I took off my ball cap and gently tucked it onto his head.

If he tried to open his eyes wider, they'd pop out.

"What do you say, Matty?" his mom prompted.

"Thank you," he whispered, shy again.

"You're welcome, Matty."

Tsering gaped for a moment before turning to me. "Are casual photos like that allowed?" she whispered. "I thought footage of GenCorp property was proprietary if taken inside the company building."

I could see why she was confused—I'd had to have Ianthe explain this to me too. "That's only for things that GenCorp has exclusive intellectual and property rights to."

"Exactly! Like . . ." She made a wavy hand gesture that seemed to say *like you*, and something in my expression must have given away my displeasure, because she suddenly became very interested in the other side of the room. "Oh, the tour is ready to head out! Let me escort you folks over there."

She ushered Matty and his mom toward the tour group, with Matty glancing back every other step. I gave him a little wave, and then looked away.

Lucky for me, the next person I saw was Dr. Mansourian coming down the stairs. "Hey!"

"Good afternoon, Mr. Haney." He was dressed more like a regular scientist now, with a white lab coat over his regular clothes and an official badge stuck to his lapel. "I'm sorry I'm late; it's a bit of a process becoming accustomed to a new floor plan."

"No problem, I get it." I shook his hand, and *really* wished I could feel it. "I kept busy."

"I could see that." His smile was warm. "A fan, I take it?"

"Ah, yeah, but I think he's got a thing for Heroes in general. He's at that age." I remembered that age: young enough to be aware but too young to be nervous or afraid. For me it had lasted right up until I lost my folks in my last year of junior high. I guess I'd always been naïve.

"I can see I have a lot to learn about Hero and civilian interactions in Panopolis." Before I could ask what he meant, Dr. Mansourian gestured toward the staircase. "Please, come with me."

I followed him up the stairs and down a long hallway filled with offices. At first the walls were clear, and I could see people working away at desks inside. Farther down, though, all of the glass was replaced with solid walls. "Why no windows here?" I asked as we approached a large door.

"Because having windows to your research and development department is asking for trouble," Dr. Mansourian replied as he got us through the door. One set down, two more to go if I remembered correctly. At least we didn't have to suit up in hazmat gear. "A better application of a force field like yours would be the securing of an environment against catastrophic accidents, but apparently that research hasn't been done yet."

"Do catastrophic accidents happen often?"

"More often than they should, I've found." We took a left and walked through a steel door into a fairly large room. It had a metal table along one wall and a computer station, but apart from that it was mostly empty except for a tablet and a few other devices I didn't recognize sitting out on the tabletop. "Not in this facility, as far as I know, but consider your own situation," he continued. "I've read the police report; it's included in your file."

I winced. "Ah." Of course he'd read the police report. That meant he knew just how dumb I'd been. "That was my fault, though. I should have taken more care."

Dr. Mansourian raised one dark eyebrow. "That isn't what I got from the report."

"We were responding to a potential chemical hazard. I should have waited before going into Ward's place."

"But Leon Ward had a daughter, whose mother had reported her missing a day earlier. It was your concern for her that led you to breach the doors."

True, but he hadn't been there. He didn't know how it had actually happened. I'd smelled the chemicals; I'd known something in there was dangerous and that I wasn't equipped to handle it. I'd gone in anyway, and had collided with the container where Ward had been mixing his experimental force field elixir. I'd brought it on myself.

Now probably wasn't the time to argue the point, though, so I changed the subject. "What do you want me to do, Dr. Mansourian?"

"First off, please call me Ari. It's much faster to scream in case of an emergency." He smiled.

"Then you should call me Craig," I said. "It's about as easy to scream as Freight Train, but I like hearing it better." *In bed*, my traitorous mind added, and my cheeks started to get hot. Shit. Was I ever going to be able to relax around this guy?

"Craig, then." He picked up a tablet and swiped at it. "May I ask you some questions before we get started on the actual testing? I'd like to fill in a few blanks in your file, but if anything I ask makes you uncomfortable, you can certainly tell me so, and I'll back off."

That would be novel. "Yeah, sure. Shoot."

"Have you noticed any variation in the strength of your force field since you've had it?"

"Nope. Well, except for right at first," I amended. "It was really strong at the beginning: it reached out for, like, an inch from my skin. Then it went way down for a while; people could barely feel it." I didn't like to think about that time. I'd been so hopeful it would just go away. "But it evened out eventually."

"Evened out?" Ari's eyebrow went up again. "You mean it increased in intensity once more?"

"Yeah. Something about . . ." What had the scientist in charge here said then? "Hormonal fluctuations? How my body chemicals reacted with the elixir stuff?"

Ari made a note on his tablet. "Interesting. Were there any other times of imbalance?"

"Nope." I'd been solid as a damn rock ever since.

"Apart from air, have you noticed anything else that can penetrate the force field?"

"Nope again." I'd been lucky that air could get through, all things considered. Coming close to death by dehydration had been bad, but dying of asphyxiation wouldn't have been much nicer.

"But light can penetrate it."

"Oh." That was true. "I guess it can. I don't really think of light as a *thing* like that."

"That's understandable," Ari said. "And yet, light has physical properties that any quantum physicist would love to expound upon to you."

"I suppose I'm lucky I don't know any quantum physicists," I joked.

"Well, you do now."

"I thought you were a . . ." I actually didn't know, but I was pretty sure quantum physics wasn't what GenCorp scientists were being paid to research.

"I have two doctorates, and recently finished my MD overseas." Ari politely ignored my dropped jaw. "I couldn't find any better way to get the practical knowledge I wanted of the human body without pursuing medicine. I'm actually on-call at the clinic downstairs, in case of emergencies. My other degrees are in bioengineering and, as you now know, quantum physics."

"Oh."

He chuckled and shook his head. "I know, it's rather excessive."

Excessive wasn't what *I'd* been thinking. *How the hell am I going to get through an afternoon with this guy without making a complete idiot of myself?* Memaw was right—I had no idea what we could talk about that wasn't my force field.

Ari continued. "I've spent more time in labs and lectures than I have working in the actual industry. Internships don't count, I'm afraid. Which is apparently why, despite my vaunted title," he frowned down at his tablet, "I'm not yet cleared for access on *all* aspects of your file. But that's fine; we can work around the deficiencies for now."

"Yeah, whatever you want," I said quietly. The little line between his eyebrows didn't go away as he looked up at me, though.

"No, not whatever *I* want," he corrected me gently. "Rather, whatever is acceptable to you. I didn't ask you here to torture you or subject you to procedures that are going to make you uncomfortable. That's the last thing I want. You came here as a favor to me, and I appreciate that, but you're under no obligation to stay if you'd rather not. There are plenty of projects I can work on that don't require a Hero's active assistance."

Oh, no way was I going to chicken out and make him invite some other Hero into his lab! What if he asked Mr. Fabulous, and he came with a huge camera crew to tape it for his stupid show? What if he asked Firebolt, and she accidentally set something important on fire? No, I wasn't quitting before we'd even begun.

"I'm happy to help however I can," I told him. "I just hope you don't expect me to do much other than move where you tell me to."

Ari raised one eyebrow again. Damn, that was sexy. Why couldn't I do that? "Are you expecting me to ask you to assist in something that you'll find morally objectionable? Because I can assure you, that's not my intent."

"No, I just..." I rubbed my hand across the back of my neck. "It's just, I don't think I'll be able to keep up, talking-wise. I never even went to college."

"So, I can't expect to engage you in a discussion of the latest finding on pentaquarks and whether or not they're bound tightly together or as a looser meson-baryon molecule?" Ari tsked. "I'm trying to keep you here, Craig, not drive you away with esoteric scientific theories. You don't have to be a scientist to do experiments, just like I don't have to be a Hero to make positive changes in the world." He gave me a small smile. "Which is fortunate, because I don't think I'm cut out for that kind of excitement." Ari turned and picked something up off his table. "How about we start with this?"

Wait, I recognized that thing. It was... "A laser pointer?"

"Yes. I want to test the resiliency of your force field against light. I promise not to point it at your eyes or anywhere else that might cause you harm."

"Whatever you want."

"Well, laser pointers are a good start." He made a few more notes, then pressed a button at the top of his tablet. "I've set this to record everything we do, so we have a reference and so there's documentation to refer to if corporate wonders why I'm keeping so much of your time to myself." He pointed at the bare far wall. "If you would stand over there, please."

I went and stood there. I knew it wasn't going to hurt or anything, but I couldn't help squaring my shoulders off like I was going into a fight. It was a nervous reaction, but Ari was nice and didn't call me on it. He just said, "Test One," and turned on the laser pointer.

I glanced at my stomach, where he was aiming it. The little red light showed up clearly. "Seems like a nope to me."

"We'll see. If you would pick up your shirt, please."

He wanted my shirt off? I was glad I'd spent so much time on crunches. I lifted the cloth, and the red dot was still there. I glanced at Ari but found him staring down at himself bemusedly.

There was a matching red dot on his own shirt. Or rather, right below it, since he was taller than me. It was actually just under the line of his belt, which . . . I looked back up quickly.

"Interesting," he said.

"Yeah?"

"Oh yes. I'd expected it to absorb the light somehow, not to reflect it so directly." He turned the pointer off and stroked his chin with one finger. "Tell me, do you ever get sunburns?"

"Sunburns? Um, no."

"Which is also interesting, since you're so fair. Your force field clearly allows in UV light from the sun, which is the type of light that causes burns, but you don't get them." He smiled his big, toothy smile, which I'd pegged by this point as the one that meant he was really pleased. "I'll know more when I get the detailed chemical breakdown of your force field, but that indicates a very unexpected flexibility in its components. The man who designed it must have been a genius."

"Yeah, he was. Leon Ward was a scientist, but he taught himself most of it. Sold some of his patents to GenCorp, made a ton of money."

Ari leaned slightly toward me. "What happened to him?"

"Nothing happened, exactly; he was just insane." That was what I'd been told, at any rate. "He was so paranoid that the government was gonna get him and suck his secrets out of his skull that he set his house on fire, took his daughter, and ran. By the time he was found, both of them were dead. He drove his car into a river." I hadn't been at that scene; I'd already been taken to the hospital after getting doused in chemicals at Ward's house.

If Ari had noticed that my voice had gone hoarse, he didn't mention it. He just said, "Do you mind if we move on to the next type of light?"

"Nah, knock yourself out."

"Let's hope not."

For an hour we did short tests on a bunch of different types of the electromagnetic spectrum: visible light, ultraviolet, infrared, and even a little bit with microwaves and X-rays. Ari was focused, but it didn't stop him from talking to me, explaining everything he was doing, and asking my permission. I could actually follow some of it.

"It's fascinating, the things that are allowed through the force field and those that aren't," he told me as he measured the output from his portable X-ray machine. "Like this, for example. I'm getting absolutely nothing from the machine, even at very low radiation levels. So X-ray is completely out, but ultraviolet is variable. We don't exactly have the facilities ready to test for gamma, but I'm willing to bet that it won't penetrate either." He grinned at me again. "I can't wait to see how your field responds to different frequencies of sound."

Hey, if he was happy, I was happy. "Okay. When do we start that?"

Ari glanced at his watch. "Not today, I'm afraid. I've kept you long enough as it is. And I've got labs to organize and staff to get to know as well."

"Oh, of course." I stretched far enough that my back popped, then reached for my shirt. After a while, it had been easier to leave it off. I pulled it over my head and straightened it out, then waited for Ari to say something else. He was staring at my stomach, though. "Ari?"

"Hmm?" He glanced up, and then shook his head a little. "I'm sorry; I was sort of . . . drifting. What did you say?"

"Just, um . . ." What had I been saying? "When would you like me to come back?"

"When can you be spared from your Hero duties?" he countered. "Because I believe I'm the one with regular hours here. I'm ready to work around your schedule, Craig."

"Yeah, Villains don't really follow a schedule." I wiggled my phone. "I just head out when I'm called."

"That leaves you with a lot of uncertainty, and I don't want to diminish your already-ambiguous free time. How about next Monday again?"

Not until next Monday? That was longer than I wanted to wait to spend time with Ari again, but the guy was busy, and probably trying to be nice about it. "Sure, that would be good. But I've gotta tell you, I've got a lot more downtime than you think I do."

"Really?" He pulled out his own phone. "In that case, let's exchange numbers. Perhaps if you're free, you can show me some of your favorite places."

I hesitated. "Outside of GenCorp?"

Ari snorted. "I certainly hope that most of your favorite places are outside of this building, Craig. Otherwise I'll be seriously worried."

This—this sounded suspiciously like a date. An open-ended invitation on a date. Was he serious?

"I'm quite serious," Ari said.

It was my turn to snort. "Are you a mind reader or something?"

"I leave feats like that to the Mastermind. I'm perfectly happy with myself the way I am." He shrugged. "I'm rather accustomed to interpreting facial expressions and body language, though. Scientists aren't always the best verbal communicators, so it helps to be able to read between the lines, so to speak."

"Well, you're a pretty good communicator yourself."

"Thank you." He smiled again. "I've worked hard to become so." We exchanged numbers, and he looked me straight in the eyes. "I have few commitments in this city so far, apart from work, so remember, you'll be doing me a favor if you call me."

"I . . . Okay."

"Good." We stared at each other for a long moment. "Is there anything else I can do for you today?"

"I do need an escort back," I pointed out. "Unless you want me to bust through every door from here to the lobby."

Ari was too composed to blush like me, but his chin lifted slightly. "Yes, of course." He swiped his ID to open his door, then ushered me through with a graceful gesture. "After you, Craig."

Man, it felt good to hear someone say my name.

CHAPTER SIX

Panopolis is a city where miracles really do happen. I've never seen anything like it in any other place I've visited, and I've visited the major metropolises of three different continents. Nowhere else in the world has both private and public support for scientific discovery, medical innovation, and high-minded technical fuckery like Panopolis. Did you know that our university's engineering department hosts a contest every year where teams create Hero homunculi, juice them up with whatever power the creators are interested in, and then run them through a gauntlet of different physical trials? Whoever's is least damaged at the end of the race wins.

GenCorp and its cronies do the same thing, only with our actual Heroes. We hear a lot about how great those folks are, out there saving us from the problems our society has made for itself. One has to wonder, though . . . how close are some of our Heroes' calls in the field? How long can they go before the damage gets too bad?

We're a city of miracle cures. How often have we saved our Heroes from the brink of ruin, only to pat them on the head and shove them back out there?

I didn't plan on waiting to call Ari, not after he'd made it clear that he was okay with it. I didn't eat out, obviously, but there were a few restaurants I remembered liking that he might enjoy. Or I could get tickets to the opera or something. I wasn't all that fond of classy things like opera myself, but Ari seemed like the kind of guy who'd get behind people singing loudly in other languages. I'd put up with it if it meant spending some time with him outside of the lab.

I wasn't kidding myself that Ari was interested in being anything other than a friend. The guy was brand-new to town, new to his job, maybe new to America altogether; he was looking for company, and I was a convenient way to get it. But it was nice, being asked to hang out like I was a normal person, like I could go and do things with a guy without worrying about being interrupted by a bank robbery—although those were rarer and rarer these days—or a corporate break-in, which were becoming more and more common.

Nobody who was born in Panopolis would have asked me out like that, so casually. The natives of Panopolis had been raised to be fairly respectful of Heroes, and that meant keeping a respectful distance too. That was one of the things I'd liked best about Edward: he hadn't seen me as off-limits because I was a Hero. He hadn't become my friend with weird, homespun ideas about what a Hero's life was like based on the odd rumors that followed a person around in Panopolis. Stupid stuff, like that only my soul mate would be able to reach through my force field and touch me at last. I'd had people discreetly groping me for weeks while that one had circulated. Jeez, it was *science*, not freaking magic, that had made me the way I was.

I hadn't intended to make Ari wait, but I ended up doing so anyway. The first bump in the road was the meeting with Ray I got called to that evening.

Ray lived in a high-rise downtown, the biggest and swankiest building in all of Panopolis. It had the best security too, right down to fingerprinting the normal people who came to visit before letting them into the lobby. Since I couldn't be fingerprinted, I was left waiting for a call from Ray to the guards before I was let inside. Finally I made my way up to Ray's penthouse, expecting—I don't know, some talk about the papers I'd signed with Ianthe? Not what I was about to get.

"FT!" He greeted me with a wide grin and an expansive wave. His teeth were even whiter than mine, and that was saying something. Ray was about my height, with thick blond hair and bright-blue eyes. He looked kind of like I might, if I dyed everything and spent a lot more money on my clothes. "Get in here, buddy, get in here! How's my resident genius, huh?"

Well, that was a nickname I'd never heard applied to me before.

"What are you talking about?" I asked as I sat on the edge of his couch. He had these leather couches, perfectly cream-colored and pristine, and so deep that if I tried to sit all the way back on one my feet would practically be dangling off the floor. He poured himself a drink as he explained.

"I'm talking about your brilliant idea to bring Firebolt in on your last job!"

"Yeah?" That was nice to hear. "You met with her, then? Because she could use a leg up, and I thought that you could—"

"Right, about that: I called her *after* I saw the preliminary footage from your fight with the Rat Queen. There was some good stuff there, FT, really good stuff for Mr. Fabulous, but handing the big finish off to her . . . I've got to say, I wasn't sure about that at first."

"I didn't hand anything off, I—"

"Oh hey, no," he waved his beverage-less hand as he sat down across from me. "I'm not blaming you, big guy. It's at least as much Mr. Fabulous's fault as it is yours, there's no sense in crying over spilled blood and all that. What I was going to say, though," he added as if I'd been the one interrupting, and not him, "is that it was actually a great play! She's the sort of raw talent that could be molded into a helpmate for a big-name Hero, you know? Perfect Sidekick material."

"Uhm." I might not know much, but I knew that wasn't right. "Wasn't the Sidekick program canceled five years ago?" It'd had too many liability issues, too many contract issues, too many arguments between Heroes and their Sidekicks over who had responsibility for what and how to share the limelight. There hadn't been the upward mobility Sidekicks had wanted, and Heroes hadn't wanted Sidekicks who grasped for more. In the end, the program had been canceled, and there were only Heroes of varying capability and popularity. It had the same basic effect with fewer hurt feelings.

"Old news, big guy, old news." Ray shook his head while still grinning, which made me wonder what the hell he meant by any of his body language. I could never get a handle on it. "The sponsors are thinking that it's time to bring back the Sidekick program, and I totally agree with them. It opens up a lot of new and exciting merchandising potential."

Oh yeah. Merchandising potential. "But . . ."

"Of course the old issues are being taken into account," Ray said blithely. "The whos, the whats, the hows. They're starting with a pilot program, where the participants can be closely monitored and evaluated for compatibility."

I didn't like the sound of that. "So you want to turn Firebolt into a Sidekick."

"Not just *a* Sidekick. We want her to be Mr. Fabulous's Sidekick!" He set his drink down, gesticulating broadly. "It's the perfect opportunity! We can control most of the information that people get about her thanks to Mr. Fabulous's camera crews, so there won't be any need to fight for dominance—it's all going to be prescreened. She's got a power that's flashy but doesn't give viewers any chance to see her face, so the focus will stay on Mr. Fabulous, the way it should. Plus," and now he made a point of staring me straight in the eyes, "it will give her a chance to learn from one of Panopolis's best and bravest Heroes. Mr. Fabulous is looking forward to passing on his knowledge to the next generation."

Oh, I fucking bet he was. "Ray, I really don't think this is a good idea."

Ray shook his head. "I understand that you might be a little jealous, FT. You brought her in in the first place, after all. She's your find, but honestly, she jumped at the chance to work with Mr. Fabulous on a more permanent basis."

I could tell when I was on the losing side of an argument. "Are you managing her sponsors now too?" Because she'd better get some benefit out of this beyond the dubious honor of holding on to Zane's coattails.

"She's not a big enough fish for me to manage yet, big guy, but I know that GenCorp is increasing their sponsorship of her," Ray said with an easy grin. "She's been living on the street, can you believe that? On the fucking street!" He laughed, although I couldn't see the humor in that. "They're going to get her a place to live, make sure she's in good health: everything she could ever want. It's a good deal, a real good deal."

"Did you at least get her an appointment with Ianthe?"

"She's got a corporate lawyer, FT." He shook his finger in my direction. "And she's already signed on the dotted line, so no battling

WHERE THERE'S A WILL

about it now. Firebolt is happy, Mr. Fabulous is happy, and you should be happy! You did a good thing for her." He rubbed his hands together. "So, let's talk about possible Sidekicks for you."

Oh, hell no. "I'm not interested."

"FT, baby. If this goes over well with the network, then Sidekicks are going to become the standard when it comes to having your own reality show. If you want to move on to bigger and better things, then you're going to have to get with the program. That means picking a Sidekick."

"I don't want one."

"You're not going to pout about not getting Firebolt, are you?" He tilted his head. "I know that you and Mr. Fabulous have a healthy rivalry going, but really, it was her choice. If you'd offered first, I'm sure she would have taken you up on it, but you're behind the curve on the latest media applications of your superpower, big guy."

My hands were clenched so tight that I was starting to lose feeling in them. I forced my grip to relax. "I don't care about media applications," I said as calmly as I could. "I care about keeping people safe. I don't want my own reality show, Ray, and I don't think it's a good idea for Zane either. It puts people unnecessarily in harm's way."

"I told you, Firebolt already agreed—"

"I'm not talking about Firebolt"—although I was seriously bummed by that too—"I'm talking about his crew! One of them got bitten by enormous, man-eating rats yesterday. It could have been fatal."

"Well, that's why we have you guys!" Ray projected cheer, but his warmth was gone. "To keep those sorts of people safe. You can't control everybody, FT. You've got to do the best you can with whatever circumstances you find yourself in, and that means accounting for civilians. I thought you knew that."

"I'm accounting for them by pointing out that they shouldn't be so close to a Villain confrontation."

"And I'm telling you that the camera crew is nonnegotiable, so you're going to have to learn to deal with it." Ray picked his drink up and downed it. "Although, now that you mention it, maybe it's time for you and Mr. Fabulous to take on different jobs. Adapt to different roles, if you will."

I frowned. "What does that mean?"

"I'll let you know, big guy, I'll let you know." Ray stood up and showed me to the door. "Thanks for stopping by."

I left angrier and more confused than when I'd arrived. I tried to reach Firebolt, but the phone rang and rang. It had probably been a payphone if she'd been living on the streets. If we were going to connect, it would have to be her decision now. And it was too late to politely call Ari. Tomorrow. I'd phone him tomorrow.

Tomorrow turned into the first day of Ray's revenge; I got sent out on every minor, annoying job a Hero could possibly be needed for. I was sent to deal with a mugging half an hour after it had happened, which left the cops interviewing the victim scratching their heads about why I had bothered showing up. I got called in for a convenience-store robbery that was already being handled by Keen, who hadn't been pleased that I had stepped into her turf.

I even got called in for a cat that had gotten stuck up a tree. The owner had looked at me like she expected me to fly up there or something and get it, and had been disappointed when I'd suggested that we just wait for the fire department to get there. "Why did you come at all if you're not going to help?" she'd asked crossly.

"Good question," I'd muttered to myself.

In the meantime, Mr. Fabulous and Firebolt were called out to handle a jewel heist and a possible "contamination event" at First Presbyterian Hospital, which could have been anything from biological or chemical weapons to an outbreak of Ebola. That one hurt. I mean, I was literally immune to disease and biochemical attack. I should have been the first Hero contacted for a job like that, and instead I'd been sitting on my thumb waiting for the fire department to get a cranky old cat out of a willow tree.

After three days of this, I finally ran into Firebolt at GenCorp's clinic. She was fresh off an arson case—again, perfect for me to handle and completely wrong for her, but whatever—and I'd come in for my weekly maintenance after a day spent in the sewer, searching for a kid who'd gone down there on a dare to search for alligators. He'd found them, unfortunately—some asshole had seeded the sewers in a dozen major cities with a mutant species of alligator twenty years ago, and Panopolis, unlike New York, had never bothered to get rid of them.

I had changed my clothes but not my shoes, and from the looks I was getting, the funk still clung to me. At least there was no blood. The kid had been fine when I got to him, just scared stupid. The alligators were pretty placid critters, it turned out.

Firebolt jolted when she saw me walk in. "Freight Train!"

"Hey, Firebolt." I offered her a smile. "How's it going?"

"It's . . . ah . . ." She squirmed in her seat, her eyes never quite meeting mine. "Busy," she settled on at last.

"Good. Not too tough?"

"No!" She glanced around the waiting room, her teeth sunk so deep in her lower lip I was worried she'd bite through it. "No, not too tough at all. It's great, it's just great working with Mr. Fabulous."

"Yeah?" I peered more closely at her. She was sitting on the very edge of the seat, holding herself stiffly upright. Her expression wavered between smile and grimace.

"Oh yeah, I'm learning a lot." She looked down at the ground. "Of course, I still have a long way to go before I'm as good as I should be."

"How good is that, exactly?"

She laughed a little. "Well, I mean, you saw me with the rats. I need to learn other tactics, other . . . ways. Mr. Fabulous is a big help."

Sure he was. And Ray was an altruist, and GenCorp was a nonprofit. "Hey, I know we're not working together anymore"—not that we ever had been—"but if you've got questions, you know you can come to me with them too? Just in case you want another perspective."

Firebolt stared at me for a long moment before her shoulders finally relaxed, just slightly. "Thanks," she said. "I appreciate it."

I opened my mouth to reply, but Phyllis beat me to it. "Mr. Haney, come and get your paperwork. Miss Belz? The doctor will see you now."

Firebolt stood up slowly, straight like her whole spine had been fused.

"See you later," she said before heading into the back. I watched her go, until I couldn't ignore Phyllis's increasingly insistent gestures with the clipboard.

Oh boy, incident report. Where to begin? *Kid went into sewers to find alligators. Found them. I had to carry him out over my head while he screamed for his mommy. Lucky he has all his limbs.* That was the succinct version. I'd have to expand it if I didn't want the higher-ups to complain, though.

Half an hour later I escaped, maintenance done and a date set for my next session. It was dark when I got outside, and Firebolt was nowhere to be seen. Not that I'd expected her to wait around or anything, I just . . . It felt like it had been a while since I'd talked with anyone who wasn't asking me to be their savior, or demanding that I do something else to please them. It was a shame; we might not be friends, exactly, but it would have been nice if she'd wanted to hang out for a while. Like with Ari: he wanted to study my power, but he'd also asked to get together, just to see the sights. I wanted that. I was in the mood for that tonight.

Maybe if I'd smelled better, I would have, but as it was I wasn't fit for company. I got into my car and headed home instead, where I tossed my shoes in the trash, got a shake out of the fridge, and fell onto my bed. What a fucking *day*. The force field made my work easier sometimes, but it hadn't today.

I took my phone out of my pocket and turned it on, finally checking my messages. Memaw. Ray. No one I wanted to talk to, no one who would say anything to help me forget the ache in the small of my back, or the way my stomach groaned at me between meals.

I pulled up Ari's number. There was no photo next to his contact information yet, but I didn't need a picture to remember him perfectly. He was good-looking, he was so smart, he was fun . . . Still, it had been three days since we'd hung out in his lab. He'd probably made friends since then. He was probably out with them now. He didn't really expect me to call . . .

I hit Call before I could talk myself out of it.

Two rings later, we connected.

"Hello?" That one word was thicker with accent than anything else I'd heard from Ari's mouth. Maybe I'd called at a bad time? Woken him up? Shit.

"Hi, Ari?" I cleared my throat; I could barely hear myself, so there was no way he'd be able to. "It's Craig."

"Craig, yes, hello!" He immediately sounded more engaged. "Sorry, I didn't check to see who was calling before I picked up. I was wondering if I'd hear from you before Monday."

"Oh, well, it's been busy lately." *Stupid, but busy.* "But I didn't want you to think I'd forgotten you."

"I wasn't thinking that. I know your life is full of responsibility."

It was, and not full of much else lately. "It is, but . . . yeah. Anyway." I was losing at being articulate tonight.

"So, I haven't eaten yet," he said a moment later, breaking the silence. "Do you have time for a meal?"

I would *make* time for a meal. "Absolutely. Where do you want to go?"

"Hmm, I don't know many restaurants here. Is there anything you like that's close to this location?" He rattled off an address not too far from my apartment.

"There's a great Korean place close to there. It's a hole in the wall, but I remember it being good." My mouth watered just thinking about the last time I'd eaten at Korea Bowl. It had been my final meal before the force-field incident. Throwing out those leftovers had been painful.

Ari *hmmm*ed. "We should meet there."

"Yeah, that would be—" My phone beeped. "Gimme a sec, sorry." I checked the messages and groaned. "Ari, I've been called in. We'll have to meet another time."

"Oh, I understand." Was that disappointment I heard in his voice? It made me smile, just a bit. "Later, then. Thank you for the recommendation, I'll try them out."

"Do that." My phone beeped again, more insistently. "Sorry, I've really got to go."

"Go, then. Be safe."

That was another thing I didn't get a lot of: people worrying about my health. "I will be." I was Freight Train, after all. Nothing could touch me.

The directions on my phone sent me to a burned-out building on the north side of Z Street, on the very outskirts of Villain territory. It was a fresh burn, that much was clear: the three-story skeleton was still smoldering, and the air was hazy with smoke. The fire department was on the scene, but there were no working fire hydrants in the area, so they were making do with a tanker truck. The police were also there, cordoning off the street and dealing with the civilians, one of whom was crying and pleading from behind the yellow tape. A news crew pulled up at the same time I did, and I saw a familiar head of bright-blonde hair exit from their van. Jean was here, then. Great.

A cop came over as I exited my vehicle. "Oh, thank goodness."

"What's going on?" It seemed like the damage had already been done.

"We, ahm— We need help with a search-and-rescue operation here."

I shook my head. "It doesn't look like there's much chance of *rescue* at this point. What happened?"

"The fire was started during the pursuit of the Villain Vibro."

That didn't make any sense. "Vibro doesn't have a fire ability. She doesn't use explosives, either."

The cop seemed almost embarrassed. "No, it was started in *pursuit* of her. Actually, the building catching fire was an accident."

"An accident?" I stared at him. "Who the hell sets a building on fire by *accident*?" I had the sinking feeling that I knew, though. And now they wanted help with a search and rescue? "This place wasn't properly evacuated?"

"There was no time, Freight Train. The accelerant went up too fast. Several residents are missing, but there's a basement level that they might have fled to. They could still be alive, but it's too precarious for us to go in."

Well, that explained the screaming bystander. I sighed. This wasn't going to be good. "You want me to check the basement?"

"We can't afford to wait," the cop said, and he was right. Even if there was no hope of survival on scene, if we were on the news, we had to be seen doing everything in our power to save and safeguard the citizens on site. Not that I wouldn't have anyway, but this was a publicity lesson that had been drilled into me over and over once I had become a Hero, until I could recite it in my sleep. Heroes had to be active, not passive. We were a special class of people in Panopolis, a privileged class, but with that privilege came the expectation of going above and beyond for the public good. I'd been passive too much lately, with those dumb assignments Ray had been throwing my way. This might not be nice or fun, but there was something I could do here that might make a difference.

Speaking of assignments, though . . . "Why isn't the Hero responsible for this still here?"

"They— I mean, *he* had to continue pursuing the Villain in question."

Uh-huh. Yeah, I bet he had. *He* never stuck around to handle the dirty work, or the sometimes tragic consequences. "Right. I'm on it."

"Freight Train!" Jean shouted from behind the police tape. "Can you confirm that this fire was set by a Hero? Is this sort of reckless Hero behavior the new norm in Panopolis?" Her cameraman was giving her the cutting hand signal that usually meant *change it up*, but Jean resolutely ignored him.

As for the reckless behavior, I wished it wasn't, but . . . "No comment," I said, to Jean's apparent disappointment, and then turned back to the ruined building and stepped up to what used to be the front door.

The foundation here was cement, but it was patchy in places; this was a building that had been expanded from a smaller size, and definitely not to code. Smoldering rubble made the footprint hard to move through, and already I knew that I wasn't going to find anyone alive in here. The floor was so hot I could hear it crackling, and the air was hazy with radiated heat. I had to try, though.

There were a few doors set in the ground not yet covered by fallen beams and parts of wall, and I tried all of them. The first one was sealed shut, but the second I was able to pry open. It was dark down there, and cooler. There was even a wooden staircase. I took the steps carefully, leaving the door open.

"Hello?" I called out. No answer. I grabbed my phone and activated the flashlight app. "Hello?"

The room was long but thin, and with the haze I couldn't see that far inside, but maybe at the end . . . maybe down there was a . . . shape. A person? I headed toward it, light held out in front of me. "Is there anyone here? It's Freight Train, I'm here to rescue y—"

I barely had a moment to register the sudden shuddering of the ceiling above me before parts of it began to fall *onto* me. I could turn and run and probably make the stairs, but that shape in front of me— it could be a person. Or it might be an old pile of rags, but I had to know. I moved forward again, reaching out and down, getting close, almost there . . .

And the rest of the ceiling fell in on me.

Waking up was strange. I couldn't remember the last time I *hadn't* immediately known where I was when I opened my eyes. I might get tired, but I'd never been unable to drive myself home at the end of a job. I was Freight Train, and Freight Train didn't get knocked out. Or, I guess, not until tonight. Today. Whenever it was now. And wherever. The noises weren't the familiar sounds of my apartment: the quiet hum of the fridge or my ceiling fan. Here it was like I was surrounded, the sound pressing in more intimately: machines beeping, people talking, squeaky shoes on floors, and the quiet rustle of clothing as someone moved around me. There was a faint hiss beneath my nose, like a tiny, angry snake had made a house out of my face.

As soon as my eyelids fluttered open, a bright light shone directly into my eyes. I grunted and turned away from it. The movement didn't hurt, although I was oddly exhausted, and my chest ached like I'd been running too hard.

"There you are." The light vanished, and I turned my head to see the man standing next to me. My vision was partially obscured by something, some kind of mask that was removed even as I tried to focus. I blinked, and then blinked again.

"Ari?" I asked—wheezed, really, and what the hell had happened to me? "What . . ."

"It's 1 a.m. on Friday morning," he said, brisk tone offset by his gentle volume. "You're in GenCorp's clinic. You've been unconscious for approximately," he glanced at the clock on the wall, "two hours, fifteen minutes."

Unconscious. Weird. "How?"

"Do you remember what happened to you?" Ari countered. I stared at the ceiling and tried to concentrate. Ceiling . . . huh, I'd never bothered to look at the ceilings in the clinic before. I'd never had to look up at them: in and out, that was me. Not tonight, apparently. Ceilings, though . . .

"A ceiling collapsed on me."

"A *building* collapsed on you," Ari corrected. "That ceiling was another story's floor. Though the building was already mostly destroyed, there was still plenty of detritus to fall. When they found you, you were almost completely buried. They couldn't wake you up, so they brought you here. The nurse didn't feel comfortable treating you on her own, and I'm the closest clinic advisory staff on call." He smiled, but it wasn't his happy, toothy one. "It's a good thing, too. They were trying to give you pure oxygen, which won't penetrate your force field. I switched it out for a purified version of our air."

"Thanks." I tried a smile of my own. I don't think it was very convincing; my face was stiff. "Hey, I got to see you tonight after all."

"Not under the best circumstances."

"How'd I go unconscious?" I ran a swollen-feeling hand over my head, checking for bumps despite knowing they couldn't be there.

"From what I can tell, you asphyxiated. Lack of oxygen," he clarified, although I knew that word. "I had assumed that would be the weakness of your particular ability, but I didn't anticipate having my suspicions confirmed so dramatically."

"How . . ." My head hurt. "Can you tell me exactly what that means?"

Ari sighed. "You were buried alive," he began after a moment. "Surrounded so tightly by debris that no fresh air could reach you. Your force field extends only a small distance from your skin, and contains a minimal amount of air. Once that was gone, there was nothing left for you to breathe. Luckily you were dug out within a few minutes, according to the firemen. I could do little more than make you comfortable and wait for you to wake up." He took his thick-rimmed glasses off and rubbed his first two fingers over the bridge of his nose. "It was a disconcertingly long wait."

"Sorry."

"It's hardly your fault. You were doing what Heroes are made to do." His sharp consonants were even sharper than usual, spitting off his tongue like splinters. "You—" He bit back his words and took a deep breath. "How do you feel now?"

"Tired." That was it, mostly. "My chest hurts. But not as bad as it could."

"We administered painkillers and stimulants through one of your specialized syringes. I'm glad they're working."

Something he'd mentioned was still rattling around in my head. "You said you knew this would happen to me?"

"I considered the ways in which your ability might be confounded, and this was the method that seemed the most obvious."

"Being buried alive."

"From asphyxiation," Ari corrected again. "It could have happened if you were submerged in a liquid too. At any point where your air was taken away long enough that you exhausted the supply within your force field. I'm surprised it hasn't happened before, actually. You don't do Heroing underwater?"

"Not if I can help it. I can't swim, and Ray doesn't want me to be filmed wearing floaties. The closest I've been to underwater jobs is working in the sewers." I chuckled. I couldn't help it. "And thinking about how to kill me is a little creepy, I've gotta say."

Ari rolled his eyes. "I run the research and development lab here. Figuring out your weaknesses and how to compensate for them is *literally* my job description. I don't have to like it to want to do it well."

I understood that perspective. "Kind of like me and running into burning buildings."

"Only in an oblique way, my friend."

"Do you do that for everyone?" I got how it was a part of his job, but it couldn't be a fun one. Thinking about nothing but how to keep people from being killed all day . . . gruesome. "Or am I special?"

"You are special because you were the first Hero whose limitations I considered," Ari said, and that was actually comforting. "But no, you're not the only one. My research extends to all of GenCorp's Heroes. Focus on my finger."

He took me through some visual acuity tests, asked a few more questions to test my memory, and eventually concluded that I was probably going to be fine. "Which is very good news."

"Thanks." I was sitting up on the edge of the bed at this point, plucking at the thin fabric of the open-backed gown that someone had stuffed me into. I was glad I couldn't remember that part. I wasn't so glad I couldn't remember the rest of it. Not that I wanted to dwell on what I'd just gone through, but it was so strange to not remember. "Sorry for dragging you out in the middle of the night."

"You have nothing to apologize for."

"At least tell me you went for Korean food first."

"I did," Ari said. "It was delicious. You should come with me next time."

"I'd come and watch you eat," I offered.

Ari frowned. "It makes no sense to me that your diet is so tightly controlled. I'll be looking into that, I assure you."

It was strange to talk to someone who saw my smoothie diet as something to be considered, possibly even fixed, instead of a fact of my life. I didn't want to get into a discussion of bodily functions and the difficulties of cleanup tonight, so I just said, "Whatever makes you happy."

"As it seems you're incapable of pursuing things that are supposed to make *you* happy, I feel more comfortable taking on that task for you." He touched my hand, or rather, the force field right over it. "Do you feel well enough to stand?"

"Sure." I went ahead and stood up to prove it to him, and was genuinely surprised when my knees buckled. Ari reached for me but he couldn't get purchase, and I barely managed to catch myself on the edge of the bed. "Or not."

"Back in bed with you, then." He watched me roll onto the thin mattress with narrowed eyes. "You need a break. No Heroing for you for a while."

"I've got a job to do," I protested.

"And right now your job is to rest and recuperate. I will contact the people who need to know: your coworkers and your manager."

"Just my manager." The room was spinning. I shut my eyes. "I've been working solo lately."

"Why?"

"Punishment duty." I remembered to shut my mouth a little too late. That wasn't the sort of detail that should go beyond my own suspicions. I resisted the urge to slap my own forehead. "Wait . . . that's not true. It's not exactly a punishment; I've just been working easier cases lately. I don't need backup for that."

"Or common sense, apparently."

I sighed. "Cameras were there. You can't stand around and do nothing when people are watching."

"Who says that?"

"Everyone."

My eyes were closed, but I could tell when Ari turned the overhead light out. "Rest," he told me. "I'll handle things and wake you in the morning."

I shouldn't need anyone else to help me handle things. I was good at handling problems, I was the best. But I was tired, so tired, and my knees were still shaking despite lying down. I shouldn't feel fragile . . . but I did. "Okay."

"Good. Sleep well." He left, and I rolled over and groaned into my pillow.

Worst. Date night. Ever.

CHAPTER SEVEN

What would the world be like if there were no Heroes, no Villains? No superpowered people, just all of us on an even footing. Well, a more even footing. There's always going to be some metric for inequality and injustice, whether it's the color of your skin, the religion you practice, or the tax bracket you reside in. But consider this hypothetical anyway.

Or rather, consider this past reality. We didn't always have these people, folks. There was a time when we didn't have Heroes and Villains at our fingertips, wreaking havoc and playing God. They're a relatively recent invention, almost exclusively dating from WWII. Why then? Was it truly the great leaps forward in scientific technology, coupled with a new and vibrant disregard for safety, that led to the creation of so many bigger-than-human, larger-than-life personalities? Because we make most of them, people: check their origin stories. We make 'em, and then we break 'em.

Why can't we unmake them, then?

Apparently, I made the evening news. Or, rather, I *was* the evening news.

I figured this out not by seeing myself on television, but by seeing the crowd of reporters clustered outside the clinic when I walked into the waiting room Saturday morning, a full day after I'd been brought in. The staff had locked the doors, but that didn't keep the crowd from shouting questions as soon as they caught sight of me, their words muffled but still loud.

"Holy shit." I turned to Phyllis, who never seemed to leave her desk; I didn't know if she had another home, or if she'd commandeered the break room for herself. "What's all this?"

She didn't even glance over at me, just held out her phone. I took it and checked the screen: it was a video, paused on an image of Jean. I took a deep breath, and then hit Play.

"—no sign of Freight Train himself, although his manager Ray Givens assures us that the Hero has suffered no permanent damage." The shot cut to Ray, standing in front of a GenCorp banner and smiling affably.

"Freight Train is getting the best of care from GenCorp's top doctors," he said, somehow striking a balance between cheerful and concerned. "The incident has shaken us all, but nobody's tougher than Freight Train. One little collapsed building isn't going to keep him down for long."

"What do you say to allegations that Freight Train should never have gone into the wreckage in the first place?" someone called out.

"I say that second-guessing Heroes isn't in anyone's job description," Ray retorted.

"What about the fact that it appears the fire was set by another Hero or Heroes, who then fled the scene?"

"That's nothing but hearsay and speculation, and I think we're done here."

The video cut back to Jean. "We have reporters standing by outside GenCorp's clinic, waiting for confirmation of Freight Train's recovery. In the meantime, and for those of you just tuning in, let me set the stage. Last night, a conflagration erupted at the corner of—"

I stopped the video and looked over at Phyllis. "Can I use this to call my manager?" My phone had been nowhere to be seen when I'd gotten dressed, probably thoroughly crushed. Another one bit the dust. Phyllis waved me on, and I dialed Ray's number.

"If this is another reporter, I'm going to sue the ever-living—"

"It's me."

"FT! Buddy, where the hell have you been?"

I frowned. "In the clinic. I woke up ten minutes ago." He must have known this already; hadn't he called to check in on me? How else could he have said with such certainty that I was recovering?

"Really? Shit, I thought you just weren't answering your phone."

"Why would I do that?"

"Because of these goddamn reporters, that's why! Fucking vultures pouncing on every second word. *Do not* talk to them, FT, you hear me? Don't tell them a thing, that's what I'm here for."

Apparently he was going to talk about me one way or the other. "Well, tell them I'm fine now. I'm ready to go back to work." The skin between my shoulder blades prickled, and I glanced over my shoulder to find Ari glaring at me. I shrugged helplessly. Heroes didn't get breaks.

"Actually, I think you should take a break."

Wait, what? "What are you talking about?"

"This is the perfect opportunity for you to get some well-deserved R & R, big guy! Step back, take a breather, chill out for a while."

"More than I already have been?" I knew my annoyance had gotten through when Ray didn't respond instantly. "All my latest calls have been low-level jobs, Ray. I should be in on the difficult stuff; it's what I do."

"But look at what happened on one of these supposedly low-level calls!" Ray said, latching on to my words like he might a lifesaver in the middle of a hurricane. "You got knocked out, or something. They took you out of there on a stretcher, buddy; that's seriously disturbing! I think you need a longer break, a *real* one. Let things settle down. Let others carry the load. At least until Mr. Fabulous and Firebolt have finished getting footage for their first series run."

"*Ray.*" I squeezed my eyes shut. "I don't *care* about the television show, I don't care if they never mention me at all, but I should be helping protect Panopolis. It's my *job*. Don't take that away just because you want publicity for Zane."

"Are those sour grapes I detect?" Ray sounded almost mocking. "Anyone but you would be dying for a vacation after so long on the job, Freight Train. I suggest you take this one with good grace. I've got a plan for you, FT, and you'll be back to work in no time! But the more you argue with me now, the longer this hiatus could end up being."

I spun on my heel, ready to throw the phone into the wall regardless of what Phyllis would do to me afterward. But as I turned I caught Ari's eye. He was looking at me, with no judgment but *worry* on his face. I hated that I was worrying him.

"Fine," I ground out. "A break. But no more than one week."

"One week should do it!" Suddenly Ray was all sunshine again. "Enjoy your time off, FT. Stay home and catch up on Netflix. And remember, no talking to the press!" He hung up, and I wordlessly passed the phone back to Phyllis. Ari motioned me into the exam room I'd just come out of, and I went with him.

As soon as the door was closed, he asked, "What happened?"

"I'm benched for the next week."

The little line of disapproval popped up between Ari's thick eyebrows. "I informed your manager that you were recovering nicely last night. There's no reason for you to be benched for so long."

"I know!" My hands itched to punch something, but if I put a hole in one of the walls, I'd never live it down. "I told him that too. Ray's just using this as an excuse to keep me out of the public eye so he can get more fucking footage of Mr. Fabulous and Firebolt saving the fucking day, not that they did a very good job of that yesterday."

"What are you to do, then?"

"Nothing. Stay home." I knew better than to think his "suggestion" was anything less than an order. "I'm gonna go stir-crazy, though, I know it."

"And you have to obey this man?"

I swallowed down my immediate denial and tried to be honest without incriminating myself. "If I don't play nice with Ray, he could 'request' that I be benched even longer." Ray was my primary link to GenCorp and the one who okayed every call from the cops that came through, without ever consulting me.

Ari's brow furrow deepened. "He threatened you?"

"More like gave me a choice with only one good option." I scrubbed my hands over my face, then clasped my itchy fingers behind my neck and looked at the floor. "I hate it, but I've got to go along with it. At least I'll have an excuse not to do Sunday dinner with Memaw." I wasn't looking forward to fielding her innumerable questions.

"Very well, then." Ari's broad shoulders straightened. "We can work with your new limitations."

I stared at him for a moment. "We?"

"You and I have work of our own to do together. There are plenty of experiments that we can do outside of my formal lab, and I have a certain amount of leeway in my schedule. I can help stave off your boredom."

"You don't—" I shook my head. "You don't have to do that."

"I know." He took his keys from his pocket. "I'm parked underground, and my windows are tinted. We can get out of here now with no one the wiser."

"Sounds good." It sounded better than good; it sounded like a lifeline that I honestly hadn't been expecting to get. I wasn't about to question it, though. I could use one thing in my life going well right now.

I followed Ari down the hallway and waited for him to collect his belongings. That reminded me— "Shit, I've got to go get my car."

"We can take care of it later. I doubt anyone will steal a Hero's car."

"You'd be surprised, then," I said wryly as he led the way to the underground parking garage. "It's my third car in three years, and only one of those was totaled by Villains. The last time, a couple of kids found my keys in the wheel well and took it for a joyride while I battled Pinball. They crashed it into a bridge on the other side of town."

Ari beeped open a plain sedan that could have been either blue or black under the neon lights.

"No one was injured," I added when he didn't say anything. Did he think I was irresponsible? "I always get my cars specially reinforced, in case of attack. The kids busted it up, but they were okay."

"I wasn't actually that concerned with their well-being," Ari said as we got into his car.

He pulled his seat belt on, and then arched an eyebrow in my direction until I did the same. Seat belts. Hah.

"I was thinking," he continued as we headed for the ramp, "about why it is that Heroes are treated so casually here. Where I come from, I can guarantee you that no one would ever think of stealing a Hero's car for a joyride."

"Why not?"

His long fingers tapped the steering wheel. "Perhaps because of the obvious consequences that anyone with so much audacity would face at the hands of the state. Where I come from, Heroes are more than city employees: they're guardians of the central government, and employed by the same. To do anything that calls their authority into question is seen as an attack on the country's leaders. Where do you live?"

Oh, right. "Fifth and Bellaroque." Then I finally asked the question that had been preying on me for a while now. "Where are you from?"

"Eastern Europe," he replied. "Armenia, to be specific. Very much a former Soviet state, with all that that entails."

The only thing I knew for sure about the former Soviet Union was that it had fielded some of the most powerful Heroes in the business. Some of them had been so badass that they'd been labeled Villains by Western Europe and the US, and placed on terrorist watch lists. The mere sight of them close to a delicate border had been considered an act of aggression. "Is that where you learned about working with Supers?"

"It is where I began my work, yes."

"Did you ever work with any of the big guys? Like ..." I racked my brain for a moment. "Like the Russian Bear? Or Red Death?"

Ari smiled tightly. It was his unhappy smile. Damn it, I should have backed off. "I was rather young when the Soviet Union folded and the Super program there was disbanded. My working experience has been much more focused on research than immediate practical application."

"Sorry."

"You don't have to apologize. I was the one to bring it up. But the Soviet Super program ended on a very poor note, and I don't think any of us like to recall it."

"Right." Something had destroyed the research complex where the program had been located in Siberia, and taken out all life, human, animal, or otherwise, for fifty miles in every direction. Nothing had ever been definitively published as to *what* had happened, exactly, but as far as anyone not in Siberia knew, the site was abandoned. "I get why you don't want to talk about it. And I can take people telling me to mind my own business; you don't have to be nice to me." If I had a nickel for every time I'd been told to butt out—

"We're going to be research partners in the near future. We ought to be able to talk over our histories, if only so we can determine what we have in common. Our professional histories," he amended after a moment. "Work, education, and the like."

"About that." Time to disappoint him. "I have absolutely no background in science beyond the basics. I mean, I can build a table or wire a lamp or, I don't know, start up a Bunsen burner, but I'm not going to be able to offer much help with the actual science-y stuff."

"So you'll have the opportunity to learn, and I'll have the chance to teach." He pulled in a block down from my apartment. "I taught for many years in Germany, and have been missing it since my move here. It will be good for both of us." He poked his head out the window. "Your entrance appears clear. Fortunate."

"Yeah, they're still stalking GenCorp, I guess." I grinned at him. "Thanks for helping me make my escape."

"Let's get you inside before we celebrate."

Inside was just the way I'd left it, which meant pretty barren. My latest spare phone, now my new primary phone, was rattling on my nightstand, probably overwhelmed with messages. I stared at it unappealingly. "I have to check those."

"I'll look for a space for us to consider using for work," Ari said, and disappeared without another word. It was nice he hadn't made me ask him to leave.

Two from Ray, one from last night with him ordering me to pick up, one from this morning that was "a friendly reminder, big guy! Keep your nose clean for the next week!" One from Zane, weirdly hesitant as he said he hoped I was okay. Four increasingly frustrated messages from Memaw, demanding to know what was going on because it was her privilege as my grandmother, and why didn't I have them call her first when I got hurt? Who was going to take care of me?

Like she'd have a clue what to do if I needed help. I snorted and moved on. One from Jean, asking me to let her know I was fine "as a friend, not as a reporter, okay? I won't pass anything along. I have to make sure you're still breathing, you big idiot, so stop making me worry and call me back. If I hear you're okay from another network, I'm going to be so pissed at you."

The final message was one I'd been expecting, but was still nice to get. "Hey, Craig, it's your friend from down the street. I'm just calling to make sure you're doing all right, and see if there's anything you need. You should call Flower Pepper if you get hungry; they make a great spicy chicken soup, and they deliver for free. Talk to you later."

Okaaay . . . I stared at my phone for a moment. Edward knew better than most people how controlled my diet was. This was the first time he'd ever recommended a restaurant to me, which probably meant that it was a safer way of passing a message along than trying to call his phone. I could do that, but later.

I texted everyone else back, not in the mood to talk to them, then headed into my living room. Ari was standing at the door that led to the rest of the apartment, all the room I hadn't known what to do with and had left bare. There were no internal walls there, just load-bearing beams every ten feet or so. "I know it's not much to look at, but do you think it would work?" I asked.

"I think," Ari said slowly, "that you have an excellent space for a lab here. There isn't even any carpet to pull up. What was this before?"

"The whole place is a custom rebuild," I explained. "The original building was knocked down two years back, and when GenCorp gave it to me they said I could have the contractors do whatever I liked to it. It's not like I need much for myself, so . . ." I shrugged. "I had them leave that part empty."

"No car collection? No love nest? No extravagant display of your status through material goods?"

I couldn't quite tell if he was teasing me or not, but I grinned anyway. "Nah, you already heard what happens to my cars. A love nest would be a waste of space, and I don't need all that room for a home gym. The only thing I considered putting in there was an enormous fish tank, but my hours are so irregular that they might pay the price if I wasn't around to take care of them. And I don't want anyone to come in here without me, so that meant no pet sitters."

Ari raised one eyebrow again. "If I'd known what your privacy meant to you, I wouldn't have suggested invading your home in this way."

"If I'd minded, I wouldn't have said yes." We stared at each other in silence until my stomach growled. My cheeks heated up immediately. "Sorry, it's almost lunchtime, and I haven't even had breakfast yet."

"It's nothing to apologize for. Do you mind if I watch you eat?"

Uhm . . . "You mean join me in eating? Because I don't think I've got any food in the house other than my shakes."

"Lunch would be welcome, but I'm in no hurry. I really do want to watch you eat. I know the process, but I'm interested in the efficacy of the materials that are being used to penetrate your force field on such a regular basis."

I could think of something else I'd like to penetrate my force field. And oh god, my mind was crawling so deep into the gutter I'd be living with the alligators down there before long.

"Sure, yeah," I managed. "Kitchen's this way. Do you like Chinese?"

"I'll eat anything."

Flower Pepper had an online ordering system, which was convenient. I put in an order for the spicy chicken soup, hoping that whoever was watching would send me a message along with the food, and added pork dumplings and a green tea. Ari seemed like a tea guy to me. The *thank you* screen popped up with a thirty-minute delivery time estimate. "I can wait until it gets here, if you'd rather . . ."

Ari shook his head. "Don't worry about me. Please, eat."

He wasn't kidding about watching me, either. He sat across from me at the table and didn't say a thing while I took out a shake and chowed down. I was hungry, and a little self-conscious too, and downed it all in under a minute.

"Interesting. Do you detect any change in sensation when it first penetrates your force field?"

I thought about it for a moment. "Not really."

"May I take the straw, please?"

"Sure." I handed it over to him. He removed it from the canister and turned it over in his hands, bringing the tip close to his eye. He sniffed it, even licked the very end of it. I tried not to stare, and failed miserably, but he seemed too absorbed to notice me looking, thank fuck.

"Metallo-organic polymer," he decided. "I suppose the metal content weakens the strength of the force field the straw is imbued with so that it loses its potency more quickly. Or perhaps it's a stabilizing mechanism. The manufacturing lab has been slow with passing on their reports," he added for my sake. "These are things I should already know, but Dr. Wojciechowski has been rather territorial about her research." He said her name perfectly, with none of the stumbling I normally did whenever I saw so many consonants unfamiliarly smooshed up against each other.

"Yeah, that might be on me. I'm not her favorite person."

"Why is that?"

Right, he hadn't been around when Edward broke into GenCorp. I explained the incident to him, including how I'd been the Hero first called to the scene. I *didn't* explain how I'd let Edward get away with a bunch of protected information after he jury-rigged a way to touch me, just for a moment, but I did mention how Dr. Wojciechowski ended up with paper towels duct-taped over her eyes, ears, and mouth before I was able to free her. That, and Edward getting away from me hadn't been part of her plan.

"Ah." Ari nodded. "I can see how that might lead to some frustration, but what else could you have done? You were under Mastermind's control."

"Yeah." I shifted uncomfortably. "I was." Or wasn't, but there was no way I was bringing that up now. We sat in silence for a moment, and my discomfort grew. Should I say something else? Divert his attention? Like I could do that smoothly, but it didn't have to be smooth, it just had to *work*—

"Do you mind if we do a quick experiment?"

I could have melted with relief. "No, go ahead."

"It will involve touching you."

If I could have raised only one eyebrow right then, I would have. "How are you gonna manage that?"

He brandished the straw at me. "With this, if you don't mind. And nowhere particularly delicate, I promise."

What could I say? "Sure." To be honest, I hadn't thought of the straw as something that *touched* me for a long time. In my hands, it was just another part of me. But in Ari's hands . . .

He leaned in closer and gently ran the end of the straw over the back of my hand. I watched the cap trace my veins, winding up and down for a few endless seconds before Ari finally lifted it away. It was only then that I remembered to breathe again, air exploding out of my lungs in a choked gasp. It was nothing like being touched by another person, but it was probably the closest I was going to get at this point.

The nurses didn't count; everything they did was with a syringe and purely clinical, never tender, and never considerate the way this was.

Every inch of the path Ari had drawn tingled like it had been shocked, and my whole arm was covered in goose bumps. My hand was shaking. It was actually *shaking*, and I wanted to stop it, wanted to do anything but show how weak I was, but I couldn't bring myself to grab it and make it stop. If I did, I'd ruin the startling, wonderful way my hand felt.

"Craig?"

I looked back to Ari. His eyes seemed even larger than usual, and his face was oddly pale and shimmery. "Are you all right?" he asked quietly.

"I'm . . ." Why was my voice so hoarse? I raised my other hand to my face and felt water there. Tears. Oh no, fuck, *no*. I didn't cry. I never cried, especially not for something stupid like this. I was a Hero, damn it, and Heroes didn't cry.

"Fuck, I'm sorry." I stood up fast and wiped my face off. "Give me a minute." Then I fled to my bathroom and shut the door. Brilliant. Just brilliant.

I stared at my red-eyed reflection, then glanced down and groaned. "Oh my god, really?" One simple touch, from the end of one of my *straws*, and I'd gone hard? And Ari had to have seen that, of course he had. He was a fucking scientist; they were trained to observe, weren't they? Five seconds into his experiment and I was doing a great job of convincing him that this wasn't going to be worth his time. What would I do if he didn't stick around? I had a week of nothing coming my way, and the last thing I wanted to do was ostracize the only person who made me feel like I could be even a little productive during that time.

"Pull it together, you idiot," I told myself. "You're fine. You're fine." But goddamn, I'd never wished so hard that I could just jerk off and get myself back under control. I had special catheters to help with other bodily functions, but they weren't good solutions for coming. I could have a dry orgasm if I was careful enough and took a lot of time, but actually coming meant making a mess that wouldn't get taken care of until my next visit to the clinic, and that was gross. Which sucked, because I *really* wanted to come.

Instead I reached down between my legs and yanked on my balls, giving them a vicious twist that brought fresh tears to my eyes but got rid of my erection fast. Hopefully it would stay gone, and I could get through the rest of the day with Ari without embarrassing myself. I brushed away the last remnants of my tears as best I could. The eyes, well, there was nothing I could do about those, but at least my face wasn't the kind that got real blotchy when I cried.

I unlocked my bathroom door, completely embarrassed, and headed out to face the music. Ari was still sitting there, the straw neatly placed on my half of the table. He met my eyes immediately and opened his mouth to speak, but I beat him to it.

"I'm so sorry about that." Maybe if he saw how much I meant it, he'd give me a second chance. "It's been a long time since anyone's really touched me but myself—not that that's what I was in there doing." Why did I have to talk things back around to my inconvenient erection? "I mean— Shit."

Ari shook his head as he stood up. "Craig, I'm the one who should be apologizing. I didn't properly consider what your likely reaction would be. I should have taken more care with you."

"I'm fine," I insisted. "I'm not fragile."

"You've been locked away from the world in your force field for almost seven years. I don't think your reaction was one of fragility; I think it was the most natural, human way you could respond to such a stimulus." He came around the table and met me where I hovered by the door. Going slowly, he reached out and set his hands on my shoulders. Well, on my force field, but the intent was the same. His hands were probably going numb already, but he held on, and I let him keep me captive. I couldn't have moved if I'd wanted to.

"Everything we do together must be done with the understanding that there is no bad reaction you can have, and nothing to feel ashamed for. You're more than a scientific miracle, Craig, and you're certainly more than a Hero. You're a person: one I want to get to know, and someone who deserves to be treated with dignity and respect. I won't judge you, and I certainly won't forget that you're granting me an enormous favor by letting me into your home for the sake of my experiments."

I really didn't get this guy. Did I like the hell out of him? Yes, but I didn't get him. Arguing wouldn't get me very far, though. "Okay."

"Yes?"

"Yeah, fine. As long as you don't mind putting up with all of . . ." I waved my hand at myself. "You know."

"You speak as though it's a chore and not a pleasure." I started to blush again, and Ari backed off. I didn't feel him go, but I missed his closeness anyway.

"That couldn't have been the whole experiment," I said after a minute. "I mean, you already knew the straw could go through the force field."

"True. But I wanted to feel for resistance myself before moving on to phase two."

"What's phase two?"

Ari reached for the straw. "It's a bit more fast-paced, and possibly slightly percussive. However, I assure you I have excellent aim. I won't hit anything that might cause you pain."

"It's a straw; how could it hurt me?"

Ari smiled, and it was the smile I liked best. "My hypothesis is that it *can't* hurt you, not in the way I'm thinking about. If you'd let me throw it at you, though, we can verify that."

"Uh . . . sure."

"Wonderful." He took two steps back, and then chucked the straw at me like he was throwing a knife. I flinched when it passed right through the force field and hit me in on the chest.

I looked up from the fallen straw to Ari, expecting him to be disappointed—this was exactly what had happened the first time, after all. But he didn't appear annoyed. In fact, his smile had widened to a grin.

"Fascinating. I was sure that the kinetic component of the force field compound would prevent them from interacting at higher speeds, a sort of buttressing effect." He picked up the straw and examined the tip with satisfaction. "Clearly my hypothesis was incorrect. We'll need to do more tests to discover whether it's that I can't generate enough speed to reach the critical point, or whether I'm going in the wrong direction altogether."

"It felt like the right direction to me," I said.

"Let's verify." Ari threw it again, then a third time. Each time the tip of the straw bounced off of my chest after passing right through the force field. "It appears to remain permeable to anything generating a similar force field, regardless of speed. However, your force field is capable of causing varying degrees of damage to your surroundings based on how quickly *you* are moving. When you're standing still and you hit something with your hand, it's as if you don't even have a force field. Yet when you gather speed, the field channels the energy in a way that gives you far more destructive capability than a regular human being would have when, say, hitting a wall.

"It's a positively brilliant feat of bioengineering. I wish I could have spoken with its creator." He stared at the straw pensively, then shook his head.

"No matter. I'll get the materials necessary for some construction of my own, and then we can experiment with measuring the speeds at which the damage you can do changes, whether it affects the thickness of the force field in the direction you're running, that sort of thing. I hope you don't mind running."

I tried to tie it all together in my head. "So, if speed is part of what makes the force field do more damage, that might be why I keep breaking treadmills?"

"Yes! Yes, precisely." He looked at me with a pleased expression on his face, and my groin started to tighten again. "We'll make a scientist of you yet, Craig."

The knock on the door was a godsend. "That must be your lunch."

I headed over and began to undo the locks while Ari sat down at the table. I left the chain latched and opened the door just a sliver to verify that it was a delivery person. His head was down, but he had a Flower Pepper hat on. Good enough. I opened the door the rest of the way. "Hey, thanks."

"No problem." He lifted his head, and my heart almost stopped. At first glance he was an older man, shoulders stooped, heavy lines bracketing his mouth and fanning out from his lazy eyes. His hair was long and limp under his cap, and his nose was slightly red, like he'd either been blowing it a lot or drinking too much. At second glance, though, I'd seen this guy before.

In fact, I'd seen him more than I wanted to. And only *one* of those lazy eyes was real. I whispered, "What are you *doing* here? Are you crazy?"

Raul shrugged. "Edward was worried, but he's too busy to come himself. I thought I'd handle the delivery so I could see you and allay his fears. Is there a reason we're whispering?"

"Yes, because I have company and I don't want them to know that the Mad Bombardier is moonlighting as my delivery guy! Don't you have minions for this kind of thing? If it's important, I'll text, you know that." I didn't like to contact them directly if it wasn't an emergency, because I didn't trust my phones to be free of oversight. I knew Ray could access my messages if he wanted it, and I didn't want to say something wrong and be discovered consorting with a Villain.

"Company?" Raul glanced over my shoulder toward the table. "I didn't think you did that."

"Special circumstance: he's a scientist. Now, if you would—"

"Craig?" Ari called out. "Is there a problem?"

"Just arguing about the tip," I said loudly, glaring at Raul. I'd never wished for laser eyes so hard before. Seriously, laser eyes would be awesome, as long as they came with an Off switch. "I'm fine, no lasting issues, so would you please go away now?"

Apparently I'd managed the next-to-impossible, though, and dumbfounded Raul out of his smug. "You let . . . a scientist . . . into your home? A scientist from GenCorp? And you actually want him here?"

"He's a friend too."

"A friend." If Raul's voice was any flatter, it would be able to iron clothes. "You've made friends with a scientist at the very company that's holding your ability to touch hostage. How can you possibly trust him?"

It was a valid question, if you hadn't met Ari. Or maybe even if you had, but that wasn't the way I wanted to think right now. I shifted so that Raul couldn't see around me anymore; I didn't like the speculative look in his eye. "Anything else?"

"Yes. When are you going back to work? Your fellow Heroes are reckless menaces. If they keep moving into Z Street, we're going to have to go hard on them whether Edward wants to or not."

I grimaced. "Not this week. I'm benched until they finish filming for Mr. Fabulous's show."

"Hmm."

"Don't you *hmm* me; it wasn't my idea!"

Raul seemed ready to argue, but then his expression melted back to bland imperturbability. "C'mon, man, five bucks ain't too much to ask."

I hadn't sensed Ari's approach, but I liked the effect it had on Raul.

"Is there something else you need?" he asked Raul, every ounce of his Eastern European accent coming across like a cold breeze.

"Hey, I had to walk a dozen blocks, man, I don't think a little extra is too much to ask for the inconvenience."

"Fine." He pressed a five-dollar bill into Raul's slack hands. "There is your inconvenience fee." Then he shut the door firmly in Raul's face. "Rude."

"Some people," I agreed.

"Unless this soup is preternaturally good, I would suggest using another restaurant in the future."

"You'll have to tell me. They're new."

The soup, it turned out, was ridiculously tasty, in Ari's grudging opinion. "Hopefully we can ask for a different delivery person next time."

"Next time?" I asked hopefully.

"Tomorrow, I assume. A full day will give us time to set up your extra space as a basic lab. I'll provide the equipment if you can help me put it together."

"I can do that." I was good at that sort of thing. "And you could bring some food over too. Stick it in my fridge if you want. Then you wouldn't have to waste money on rude delivery guys."

Ari smiled like a shark, and I smiled back reflexively. "I'll do that. Thank you."

CHAPTER EIGHT

I get a lot of messages from people telling me that I'm ungrateful. They say it's shameful for me to criticize the things that make our city great, the very institutions that Panopolis is renowned for the world over. Our Heroes are a blessing, or a gift, or our rightful due for being at the bleeding edge of technology and taking the risks that other places won't. They say that anything other than my full support is a slap in the face to our city's protectors.

Let me make this clear: I care deeply about the Heroes in Panopolis. For both personal and professional reasons, I am dedicated to their welfare. I'm also concerned about the welfare of everybody else, though, from the Villains to the police to the everyday citizens who have to try to make a living in what amounts to a war zone at times.

You think I don't support the troops? I love the troops. I love them enough to ask whether or not they're being wasted.

Sunday, instead of being a mess of running to and from fights, wasting time in the clinic, and eating awkward dinners with Memaw, was spent assembling tables, rewiring the walls so they could handle more machines, and moving specialized equipment into the empty room, including a big stainless steel tub that was going to be filled with water.

"The timeline for how long you were able to go without air before you passed out is very loose," Ari said as he arranged plastic sheeting across the floor that would, I dunno, keep any spilled water from staining my concrete? I didn't tell him not to bother, but it seemed like overkill to me. "We have no definitive answer for how efficient it is at capturing and holding oxygen, or how quickly it exchanges carbon dioxide for regular air . . . there are many questions to be answered."

"So you want to dunk me."

"With a great deal of care and caution, yes, I do."

I shrugged. "I can handle that."

"I'm sure you can." Ari caught my gaze and held it for a long moment. "But I promise you, we won't be doing anything with this unless I can count on you to be perfectly honest with me, so don't try to tough something out it if *is* uncomfortable, all right?"

"Got it."

"Good."

I was ready to jump into experiments, but Ari had to go to work early on Monday, so instead I caught up on my phone calls and watched TV. The news was painful to watch, seeing things happen in Panopolis that I had no chance to help with. More painful, though, were the spots during every commercial break touting Zane's upcoming show with relentless enthusiasm.

"Each new day in Panopolis is a new chance for Villains to wreak havoc," the announcer intoned grimly. "The only thing standing between them and you—"

"Apart from the police and firefighters and emergency responders," I muttered to myself.

"—are the Heroes that make this city great. And the greatest of those Heroes is . . . Mr. Fabulous." The shot cut to a series of dashing images of Zane, running at blurring speeds, punching Villains in the face, grinning at the crowd. "Along with his Sidekick" —there were maybe five frames of Firebolt, who they didn't bother to name, in her ugly orange suit, blowing a plume of flame from her mouth— "he works tirelessly to keep the people of Panopolis safe. Where other Heroes falter, he stands firm. When others fall, he's there's to pick up the pieces."

"Or *not*," I snapped.

"For everyone who's ever wondered about the real, unscripted life of a Hero . . . for everyone who wants to see behind the myth to the man . . . for everyone who thinks they can handle the Truth"—I could *hear* the capital letter they slapped in front of the word—"this is the show you've been waiting for. The experience . . . of a lifetime!"

I shut off the TV to stop myself from breaking it, and then headed for the gym. I had some anger I needed to work off.

It was after eight at night by the time Ari got to my place on Monday. The line between his eyebrows was so deep I could've lost change in it.

"Bad day?" I asked, ready to commiserate.

"Frustrating." He set a sack of groceries on the table. I was pleased to see them; clearly he was taking my offer seriously. He sat down across from me and took his glasses off, rubbing on the bridge of his nose. "Very frustrating."

"How so?"

"Dr. Wojciechowski has refused to give me the manufacturing data for your implements. She insists they have no bearing on any research that I might do."

I frowned. "That's weird. Aren't you guys supposed to work together?"

"She has claimed that my research mandate relates solely to future improvements of Hero functionality, not tampering with things that already work as intended." Ari's scowl made me want to comfort him, even though I had no idea how. "I said I would take my request to the board of directors if need be, and she challenged me to do so. Which I did."

Shit, he'd had a busy day. "And, um . . . what did they say?"

"They don't meet again for another week, apparently. The issue has been effectively tabled until then, although she did give me a few samples to work with." He reached into the sack and pulled out a small plastic bag of straw tips. "I could reverse engineer these, but it will take more time and resources than I have here, and my department has been suddenly inundated with requests for some very specific Hero upgrades."

"Let me guess. Mr. Fabulous and Firebolt?"

Ari shook his head tiredly. "They've already been given new equipment from their sponsors; equipment that has *not* undergone the sort of testing it ought to before being deployed in the field. I have other Heroes and sponsors scrambling to catch up, and while GenCorp doesn't handle upgrades for every Hero on their books, they do have a say in what the majority of them are entitled to use in their missions. However, they've never micromanaged the process like this before, from what I understand. I spend half my time writing up reports and the other half double-checking my staff's work to make sure it's as good as it can possibly be, given the time scale we're working with." He frowned. "GenCorp seems overly anxious to create the next Mr. Fabulous all of a sudden."

I was feeling guilty. "You've got to be beat. You should have just gone home. We could do this tomorrow." Or the next day, or the next. I wasn't going anywhere, but he was clearly running around all over the place.

Ari looked at me. Even without his glasses, his eyes were luminously big in his thin face, the tired redness making the blue stand out even more. "Are you kidding me? This is the only thing that's gotten me through the day."

Fucking *blush*, I just couldn't get it under control. "In that case, um . . . do you want to stick me in the dunk tank and see how long I can breathe?" Worst segue ever, but Ari lit up as he pulled one of the tips out of the bag. It was a bit different from the others, with a tiny clip on the end.

"I took a few minutes to construct a basic pulse oximeter on the end of this straw, which will let me keep track of your blood oxygenation and heart rate while you're under. It also measures ambient oxygen content, so providing your force field extends for at least an eighth of an inch, I'll be able to measure the oxygen in the air surrounding you."

Wow, that was pretty . . . "Cool."

There, finally, was the sharky grin I was waiting for. "I think so too."

We filled the steel tub, and I stripped down to my underwear. My skin wouldn't get wet, of course, but I preferred not to have to shove my clothes in the dryer for the rest of the night. I didn't have many outfits, and getting into my suit would just be awkward. Besides, I definitely didn't mind the way Ari's eyes lingered on my chest and shoulders as I settled into the water.

He set the camera to record, connected the probe to his computer, then spoke into the microphone. "First immersion test, evening of Monday the eighteenth, subject Craig Haney, conducting researcher

Ari Mansourian. Can you detect the temperature change between the water and the air?"

"The water's a little cooler, I think."

"Interesting," Ari murmured. "I wonder how far your ability to detect ranges in temperature extends. You can't be burned, can you?"

"Nope." I'd been in enough fires to know that conclusively. "Even when I'm surrounded by flames."

"*Very* interesting. Another avenue of study in the future, perhaps. But for now . . ." He gently laid the clip against my chest. I shuddered when it touched my bare skin. "Please lie back. The moment you begin to feel any sort of distress, get out of there."

"Sure thing." I settled underneath the water, noticing that though the clip was in contact with me, I still didn't get wet. *That's an actual scientific observation*, I thought proudly as I breathed, slow and easy like always. I watched Ari through the distortion of the water, relaxed to the murmur of his indistinct voice. I couldn't remember the last time I felt so calm, yet so aroused at the same time. *Please*, I begged myself, *don't get hard right now.* Now I knew it was going to happen, it was just a question of how soon.

Thank God my oxygen ran out before then. I continued to feel okay, maybe a little light-headed, but the probe tip went away, and Ari sank a hand beneath my body, probably resting it against my back. I surfaced to him saying, "Two minutes before oxygen slipped to unusable levels inside your force field."

"Is that good?"

"It's informative," he said. "I can do calculations that will allow me to more accurately measure the volume of air contained once I get a baseline for your rate of respiration. And apart from a small spike in your heart rate, you seemed to handle it very well." He looked at me expectantly, but no, nope, we wouldn't be talking about that blip.

"Good."

"No issues with claustrophobia? Or aquaphobia?"

I chuckled. "What is that last one, fear of water?"

"Fear of being submerged in water, yes."

"Nah, I'm fine. It was just a little—" *A little bit of a turn on.* "—a little strange. I can't even remember my last real bath, and I don't work underwater, with a few exceptions."

Ari smirked. "Like the squid thing."

I rolled my eyes. "Yeah, the damn squid thing was one of them, but the tank wasn't that deep, so it doesn't really count." We stared at each other for a long moment before Ari cleared his throat.

"I'd like to do this test a few more times, if you don't mind."

"Knock yourself out."

"I think that's an idiom I'd prefer to have nothing to do with," he said, and a moment later I was underwater again.

Ari didn't leave until close to midnight, but he seemed happy about the work we'd done. Really, he just seemed happy with *me*, which was novel. And awesome. And not something I was ever going to complain about, even though I was worried he was working himself too hard.

He came over the next night too, and every night for the rest of the week. I did my part to make him welcome. I couldn't cook much, but I made sure there was a PB&J waiting for him when he got to my place, no matter what time it was. It was simple stuff, but he'd brought the ingredients over himself, and I liked seeing him make himself comfortable in my home.

For the first time since I'd moved here, it *felt* like a home, too. More than a place to fall into and out of between jobs. The equipment in the other room should have seemed cold and sterile, but I was there when Ari spoke to his machines like they were kids on the first day of school, coaxing them gently as they churned through the data he compiled. They were covered with sticky notes too, instructions for use that he'd put up for my benefit, all in neon colors. I couldn't do a lot of fine-motor stuff, but I could turn things on and off, at least, load the proper programs and handle some of the basic work on upgrading the probe tips depending on the experiment Ari wanted to do.

It was fun, maybe the most fun I'd had since high school. I didn't want it to end, but I was unlikely to be benched forever. Soon the filming would be done, Ray and Zane would have all the badass Mr. Fabulous footage that they needed for a season, and I'd finally be able to go back to work, doing what I did best. Heroing. I was even looking forward to it.

I didn't expect my lull to end the way that it did, though. It was late on Friday, and after an hour of work Ari had announced that his machines were all busy, and we'd have to wait to start a new test.

"You want to watch *Blue Planet*?" I asked, then winced internally. Ari was a *scientist*; he probably knew that stuff anyway. What was I thinking asking him to watch my beginner-level show?

"Is that the one about the oceans?"

"Yeah."

"I'd love to." He grabbed the plate with the sandwich I'd made on it, as well as a bottle of sweet black tea from the fridge, and sat next to me on the couch. His tie was gone, the top two buttons of his shirt undone, and his heather-blue sweater was pushed up to his elbows. He'd taken his shoes off too, and surprised me now by folding his legs up beneath him on the cushion. It made him seem younger. "I was always interested in oceanography, but where I come from the harder sciences were much more strongly encouraged."

"Back in Armenia?" I knew a bit of his history at this point, although he almost never offered anything on his own.

"In Armenia to begin with, and then in Moscow where I went to university. I got my first undergraduate degree at the National Research Nuclear University, which is well-known for its science programs."

"You are so crazy smart." I turned to cue up the Blu-ray, not wanting to get into a discussion of our relative merits again. Ari surprised me, though.

"I felt compelled to push myself as hard as possible in school," he admitted, staring down at his plate like the sandwich might hold the secrets of the universe. "After certain . . . incidents during my childhood, I was determined to know all I could about the challenges facing my home and my people. I became a scientist so I could learn to alleviate suffering. I . . . well." He shrugged. "I think my success is debatable."

"Not to me." How could it be, with everything he was doing for me?

Ari smiled, a soft thing, but I liked it as much as the shark smile. "You're very kind. Speaking of you, however, I made something that I think you might like to try. If you don't feel comfortable with it yet though, that's fine."

"What is it?"

Ari put his plate aside and got up, heading for his bag. "It's a— Hmm." For once he appeared more flustered than I was. "It's a means of connection."

Connection? I hadn't told him what Edward had done to touch me, what he'd managed using resources that we didn't have here, like a whole bundle of spare straws. It just seemed like too big a step to take, wrong when I couldn't tell him the truth about how it had happened. Maybe it felt extra wrong with Ari because I wanted it so badly. When he turned around, though, and I saw what was in his hand, my heart rate surged.

It looked like a gauntlet, and appeared to be made from the same silvery material as the straw tips. I stared at it for a long moment, and Ari stared at me.

"You could touch me with that."

"I could," he confirmed. "If you want me to."

If I wanted him to? I could have screamed, I wanted it so bad. I jumped up to my feet, ready to put the damn thing on his hand myself.

And then my phone rang. Not any standard ringtone, either; this was Edward's ringtone. Edward almost never called me from his cell phone; our code worked better via messages. This had to be something serious, but the timing was the worst ever.

I picked up, though. Of course I did. "Hello?"

"Craig! You have to get to Seventh and Z, *now*."

"What the hell?" I was already standing, heading for my bedroom and the closet that held my official uniforms. "What's going on there?"

"Mr. Fabulous is leading an all-out attack on us, that's what! He's less than three blocks from the clinic, and we've got people in there— people who aren't well enough to move without more lead time!"

"*Fuck*." I put the phone on speaker as I changed, making sure Ari was nowhere near the door. "You know I'm off roster, though; I'm not supposed to know what's going on there."

"Either someone gets out there and gets the Heroes under control, or there are going to be a hell of a lot of dead Heroes in the next few minutes." Edward sounded pained. "Not to mention Villains, and the people who live in this neighborhood. Raul is *pissed*. It's all I can do to get him to stick to percussive bombs and sound waves and not go straight to the heavy-duty stuff, and the rest of them aren't much better. I am barely holding them back, Craig, so you need to get out here and do what you do best."

"Be a Hero," I muttered as I pulled on my dark-blue gloves.

"*Save people*," Edward replied firmly. "Save them no matter whose side they're on. They need you, even if they don't know it yet. Come quickly." He hung up, and I stuffed my feet into my boots, slipped my phone into its pouch, then headed for the door.

Ari was back on the couch now, the special gauntlet nowhere to be seen. "I take it something has come up," he said.

"Yes." I wanted to stay, I wanted to so badly, but there was no way I could. "I've gotta go."

"That's fine. I can leave—"

"You can stay!" I blurted. "If you want to. I don't know how long this'll take, but I'd like it if you stayed."

Ari looked at me for a long, quiet moment before he finally nodded. "Then I'll stay. Be safe."

I gave him a half smile as I grabbed my car keys. "I doubt there's much chance of me being buried alive this time. I'll be okay."

Seventh and Z Street was part of what used to be a block of fancy shops back in the forties and early fifties. They'd been slummed out for decades, or so I supposed; I'd never been this deep into Z Street before, and I honestly wasn't sure what the fuck I was doing here now. I was downright *stunned* to see so many Heroes in the same place, though. And so many cameras too. It seemed like every major news organization was here, not to mention Mr. Fabulous's crew. They were staying back on Eighth Street, while down on Seventh, the battle raged.

When I said raged, I fucking meant it. There were at least five Heroes standing in the middle of the street, letting loose with whatever they had: Mr. Fabulous running around and hurling chunks of asphalt at whatever Villain was available, Keen sleek in her black-and-silver armor firing fléchette knives, Digger settling his roots in deep and grabbing anything that moved with them, Angelic floating above the fray like a golden ghost, calling down locations to everyone else, and Firebolt— She seemed like less of a bolt and more of a goddamn *wave* now: there was no weapon in her hands to direct the fire to, just sheets of white-hot flame pouring from her mouth in measured breaths. Her tank was bigger too, big enough to cover her entire back, and she tottered forward like a toddler under its weight, barely able to keep her feet.

The Villains weren't standing idle at this invasion, either. I didn't know them as well, but from the way the road cracked and broke beneath the Heroes' feet as they tried to move forward, I was willing to bet Vibro was on the other end of that maneuver. Digger resolidified everything Vibro broke apart, though, and didn't seem bothered by the bullets a four-armed kid fired into his thick, gnarled limbs. Smoke bombs came flying out of building windows, letting off a rainbow display of noxious gases, and Keen fell back to catch her breath. I grabbed her and pulled her behind me, in case the guy with the guns got any new ideas.

"What's going on?" I demanded.

Keen's eyes were red and swollen from the smoke, but she managed to peer at me incredulously. "Freight Train, what are you doing here? I thought you were *dying* or something!"

Dying? Who'd told her that? "I'm fine; just tell me what's happening. Why the push?"

"We're trying to reach Mastermind's lair. He's got hostages."

The hell? "What hostages?"

"The ones the police commissioner said he had! The clinic rumor is a hoax. He's been stealing people from apartment buildings along Z Street and experimenting on them in his lair— How have you not been told any of this?"

"Guess I'm behind the times," I said grimly. What the *fuck* was going on? "Have these buildings been cleared?"

Keen shook her head. "But they're all labeled commercial, not residential, so they should be empty this late."

She couldn't be serious. "Are you kidding me? You see any stores here? These are full of people, not businesses!"

To her credit, Keen grimaced and looked away. "We're not going to be able to clear them and fight at the same time, not without getting the police to help, and the mayor wouldn't let them come down here."

Thank God for that. "Then we need to stop fighting so we don't put more civilians at risk. We can handle the hostages some other way than fighting in the damn streets. You good to go?"

She took a deep breath and straightened up. The sharp silver blades painted across her dark skin were smudged, but she still looked every ounce a Hero. "I'm good to go."

"Backtrack, then. Only head into the places that aren't firing at you, but if you see people, you tell them to get gone, fast." She nodded and headed to the left, and I turned to the fight half a block down the street—

Just in time to see Angelic get blasted from the sky like a bedazzled comet.

"Angie!" Digger caught her before she hit the ground, but he had to uproot to do it. The next explosion hit right between his feet, and it blew him back so hard he left a broken groove in the street before coming to a stop a meter in front of me.

He was breathing though, and so was Angelic, and that was what mattered. I ran past them and headed for the front. "Mr. Fabulous! Fall back!"

"Freight Train!" He eagerly waved me toward him. "Perfect! You go first—take out the Mad Bombardier and open the path for me and Firebolt."

I stopped next to him. He was jittering so hard I could barely see his feet and hands. "We have to fall back. The buildings aren't clear. Not of civilians *or* of Villains. What were you thinking, coming down to this part of Z Street? You're gonna be surrounded if you don't get out of here!"

Mr. Fabulous shook his head. "We have to get the hostages!"

"*What* hostages?" I was pretty damn sure I'd know if Edward were keeping hostages in his clinic. He wouldn't lie to me about that, would he? "Zane—"

"Heroes!" A hidden megaphone blasted the word out so loud that none of us could have missed it. The voice was low and metallic, and sent familiar chills down my spine. "You have ten seconds to retreat. Otherwise, I will detonate the mines planted under your feet. *Ten.*"

"You don't scare us, Mad Bombardier!" Mr. Fabulous shouted. "And the more people you hurt, the more the tide will turn against you!" When I glanced behind me, the reporters and camera people were rapidly backing up, though.

"*Seven—*"

"Maybe we *should* go," Firebolt suggested from where she'd stumbled to a stop beside us. She was coughing so hard she was almost choking. "I'm having problems here. This new mix is too strong; it's starting to hurt my throat. I don't think I can keep this up for much longer."

It was the perfect out. "There, you see? You've got to take care of your Sidekick. Get her to safety, and I'll grab Digger and Angelic and—"

"*Four—*"

"Yeah, you'd love that, wouldn't you?" Mr. Fabulous sneered at me. "Stealing my moment in the spotlight. *Fuck* that. I'll go in by myself!"

He turned and darted forward just as the Mad Bombardier said, "*One.*"

A thick metal disk burst straight up from beneath the broken road under my feet. It might have broken my legs if I'd been hit with the impact of it, but as it was I sailed about ten feet in the air, then fell onto the ground. Those were the mines? Edward really was having a pacifying effect on Raul.

I couldn't see where Mr. Fabulous had gone, but I could see Firebolt lying on her front a few feet away. She sounded like she was choking. I crawled over to her. "Hey, Firebolt?" No response. Worried, I turned her over—

And got hit with a burst of flame straight to the face. My force field mitigated the worst of the heat, but I was blinded by the glare for a moment. "Hey, turn it off! I'm a friendly! It's me, Freight Train!" But the fire didn't stop, and neither did the choking sound. I rolled off to the side to get a better look at what was going on.

Firebolt's puffy orange gloves clutched at her throat, and I could hear fuel gurgling in her mouth just before the next wave of flame exploded from her mask. "Turn it off!" I said as I reached out to help her sit upright. "You've gotta turn it off!"

She shook her head violently, then motioned toward her pack. I leaned in and— What was that? Some sort of fuel pump, a mechanism that fed her flammable mix to her mouth. Was it broken? I leaned in close and heard the continuous rush of fuel. Yeah, broken then.

"Okay." Shit. She was drowning in her own fire-breathing mix, and spewing flames the whole time. "Okay, I have to get this off of you." But I didn't have super strength, not like Mr. Fabulous. I tried, but I couldn't remove the enormous pack from where it had been bolted to her uniform. *Shit.* "Hang on, I'll be right back!" I'd find something to puncture it, perforate it, and let the fuel drain out.

Firebolt shook her head again, so hard it looked like a convulsion. She reached for me, her arms closing hard over my shoulders. This close I could feel the heat like a second skin, see the flames rear up in the depths of her mask before they washed out over me. The flames . . . which were traveling down the tubes that led to the tank at her back. She'd been turned into a bomb, and I was the only thing standing between her and who knew how many people.

I didn't even think, just hugged Firebolt as tight to my body as I could. She spasmed in my arms one last time. There was a hiss as the fire connected to the tank, and then—

Then there was nothing but heat, and light so bright I went blind.

CHAPTER NINE

How many Heroes live to retirement? Does a Hero ever put in their time and then give up the good fight, and run off to spend their retirement in Aruba? How many, out of our enormous pantheon of Heroes, have successfully put Panopolis in their rear-view mirrors since the Spartan and his cohorts?

Two. Panopolis has had ninety-seven registered Heroes working its streets over the years, and the only ones who didn't end their terms of service in death or permanent disability were Bellaroque, also known as Bella and Rocco, the twin compatriots and best friends of Morpho Girl. You might remember them: Bella was the closest thing this city has ever had to a real psychic, and Rocco could snap his fingers and come up juggling fireballs.

After Morpho lost her marbles, the twins packed their bags and left, despite the mayor at the time entreating them to stay. They were subsequently pilloried by the media, and no one has heard anything about them since.

One can only assume that they'd had enough. They'd given their talents, their youth, their friends—everything they'd had—to Panopolis. And what had they gotten in return? Spite and hatred for leaving in order to preserve what was left of themselves. I don't know where they are today; I'm not sure if anyone knows. But wherever they are, I hope they've found the peace and happiness that they deserve. Because God knows, none of the rest of the Heroes have.

"It could have been so much worse."

That's what they kept saying. Everybody I ran into after the explosion had some variation of that to throw at me. People who would have shaken my hand if they could, people who were shaking so badly themselves it was amazing that they were still standing. "It would have been so much worse if you hadn't been there, Freight Train."

I got what they were saying. It *could* have been worse. The only person to die had been Firebolt, in the end. There were plenty of injuries to go around, but almost all of them dated from the fight up *to* that point. After the explosion, there was no fight. There was only me, crouched naked over the smoldering remains of another Hero, in the middle of a crater. Naked—great. Ray was gonna have a field day handling the new footage of my bare ass.

It had taken over thirty minutes for the blast zone to cool off so that people could reach me, and I hadn't moved for that entire time. It wasn't that I'd been hurt. I mean, okay, a bit of the heat had bled through for a few seconds there and I'd still been seeing stars, but that wasn't being hurt. It hadn't been enough to keep me down. It was more that I'd lost track of time. I hadn't opened my eyes, not until I'd heard someone yell my name in my ringing ear. *If I keep my eyes closed*, I'd thought dully, *maybe I can imagine that I'm not holding onto a shell. Maybe I can imagine that the last image burned onto my retinas isn't Firebolt's eyes, barely visible behind their protective heat screen, wide and desperate and so, so afraid. Maybe I can imagine that she didn't die in my arms.*

I didn't even know her real name.

That was the worst part, for me. Few people ever used my actual name, but the ones who did were important to me. Every time they said it, I knew they were seeing me as a person, and not just a Hero. Memaw might not always say it in a nice way, or Raul, but from Ari and Edward, it was like a pat on the back, or a kiss on the cheek. Hearing my real name was one of the most intimate experiences I could have these days, and I wondered if Firebolt had had that. Surely Zane must have used her actual name . . . right?

My part of the cleanup was easy. Too easy, honestly. I wasn't tired yet; I didn't hurt the way I ought to. But Ray didn't let me stay once he got to Z Street, and he didn't let me talk to the police or the media or anyone else. He handed me his own gym clothes and bundled me off to the clinic faster than I could blink, talking the whole time.

"That was— Well, shit, it was shit, but the *footage* will be amazing. Not that we can use it as it stands, since it doesn't show things in the best light for Mr. Fabulous," he rambled as he sped his Porsche through the streets, running red lights and getting no flack for it thanks to the siren he'd attached to the top of the car. "It's too bad; Firebolt was testing well with early audiences. We'll have to do— Hey, have you ever seen *The Apprentice*? Maybe a contest like that early next season, or even just for the show's promo since Sidekicks look like they're going to have a renaissance in this city."

"What was her name?" I asked dully, staring out into the darkness. Half the street lights in this part of town were broken.

"What, Firebolt's? Uhm . . . Belz. Sherry Belz? I don't know. Why, do you want to make a statement about her? Or did she pass something on to you in her last moments? Last words are always interesting to people." He turned north, toward the manufacturing district where GenCorp was headquartered. "There'll be a funeral. You can speak then. And that would be a really good time for you to announce your own show, big guy. Strike while the iron is hot; make it about protecting the city and helping raise future generations of Heroes to do the right thing. You would be unstoppable with a Sidekick."

We were getting close to my building. I wondered if Ari was in there, waiting for me, or if he'd gone home by now.

"Hey? Are you listening to me, FT? The news cycle never sleeps, and we're going to have to have something to announce by tomorrow. I'd love for it to be your glorious comeback."

"You should never have benched me to begin with."

"You can't tell me you're still sore about that," Ray cajoled. "Mr. Fabulous needed a chance to spread his wings and fly without Big Brother getting in the way! Now it's time for him to be set on the back burner for a while, though. He's oversaturated the market, and people are getting tired of him. It's time for us to focus on you." Ray turned his gleaming smile on me. "So, what do you say, Freight Train? Are you ready to take your career to the next level?"

My building was fast approaching. "Stop the car."

"This isn't the clinic, big guy. Your contract clearly states that—"

"Stop the *goddamn* car, Ray!"

I'd never taken that tone with my manager before. In fact, I could count on one hand the number of people I'd yelled at in the past year who weren't Villains, fellow Heroes, or civilians endangering themselves. It was enough to startle Ray into listening to me, and his foot slammed on the brakes practically at my front door.

"Hey, okay, so you're upset," Ray said, clearly trying for comforting but ending somewhere around overenthusiastic camp counselor. "I get that; I'm upset too. Firebolt was a great Sidekick, and Mr. Fabulous is gonna be devastated. Since you found her and brought her to our attention in the first place, I can see where you might be feeling a little guilty about the way it all worked out. But the show must go on, right? I can hold the media at bay for a few days, call it a mourning period maybe, but I'm going to need something from you to appease them."

I opened the car door, stretched my legs out, and stood up. Ray's bright smile dimmed. "FT? Come on, big guy, you've got to give me some play here. Even if it's just a sound bite for the masses. We can take care of the business stuff later, when things aren't so messy, but I need *something* from you."

"You want something from me, Ray? Here's a sound bite for you: go fuck yourself." I slammed his car door shut, turned, and walked up to my front door. I'd left my keys with my car, of course, but the biometrics should still work, or maybe I'd get lucky and—

The door knob turned smoothly under my fumbling hand. Lucky it was. I darted inside and shut it fast, bolting every bolt and latching the chain before I let my head rest against the metal. My eyes fluttered shut, and I sighed so heavily I could almost feel the condensation inside my force field.

"Craig?"

"Ari?" He was still here? Wait, naturally he was here; the door had been unlocked. I turned on my heels, punch-drunk, reeling as the adrenaline began to leave me. I felt empty in its wake.

There was Ari, solemn and concerned. He looked just like he had when I'd left, hours ago now, except that his feet were bare. I focused on them, the veined tops and the long toes, because it was better than staring blankly at Ari's face.

Those feet padded closer to me, finally stopping just in front of my own; I was in a cheap pair of foam sandals, all someone had been able to scrounge for me in the aftermath of the explosion. "I saw what happened."

I tried to smile, but my face didn't want to work. "It made the news already, huh?"

"Unfortunately, yes."

I sighed. "Do I even wanna know what they're saying?"

"By and large, they're extolling your virtues."

"Great." Positive air time. Fan-fucking-tastic.

"Craig." Ari's voice was so soft, I might not have heard it if he hadn't been close enough to touch. Or *not*, really. "You did the right thing for Shareen."

"Shareen." Shareen Belz. Not Sherry. "That was her name?"

"Yes. You didn't know?"

I shook my head, my throat tightening so fast there might as well have been a noose around it.

"Did you already go to the clinic?"

I shook my head again.

"I see. What can I do for you?" Ari paused for a moment, then said, "If you'd like me to go—"

"No!" I finally lifted my gaze, and the concern I saw in his almost floored me. I didn't want to be alone right now, and from the look of it, Ari didn't want to go. "Please stay. I'm not . . ." *Anything.* I wasn't anything. I had run out of air, of strength, of thought.

"Let's get you to bed, then." He led, and I followed him, magnetized, helpless to look away. He went to my bedroom and pulled back the comforter, fluffed the pillow for a second before turning to me, and I just . . .

I couldn't remember the last time I'd bothered to fluff a pillow. I didn't need comfort—I didn't need softness or warmth tonight, of all nights. I didn't *deserve* it, but here was Ari, staring at me with a quiet sort of hope, and I couldn't help wanting it. I wanted to lie down and forget all about today, forget every awful thing that had happened.

Tears boiled up out of the tension that choked me, welling in my hot, dry eyes and sliding down my cheeks before I could stop them. Tears, *fuck* no, I didn't cry. I never cried!

"It's all right."

I pressed my palms to my face even as I shook my head, trying to staunch the flow of those hateful things, but it wasn't working. They just wouldn't stop.

"Craig." I couldn't see him now, but his voice was there, straight in front of me. He wasn't running away. "Come and lie down," he said, and I obeyed. I stumbled forward until my knees hit the side of the bed, then tumbled down in the least graceful fall ever.

He maneuvered me over so that I was on my back, which . . . fine. Whatever. I couldn't stop the tears but at least I could keep them from collecting on my face. Instead they seeped past my ears and into my hair, finally coming to rest at the back of my head. I heard Ari get up and leave, and I was caught between relief that he wasn't going to stay and watch me break down, and horror that I'd driven him away. I breathed through my mouth, trying to make each inhale deep and slow. If I could get calm . . . if I could just see anything other than Firebolt's—*Shareen's*—face before it burned up, her eyes glassy and terrified, so terrified, then maybe I'd be able to calm down enough to ask Ari to stay. If he left now, I wasn't sure he'd ever come back, and I didn't want to be alone.

Something touched my shoulder. Something actually *touched* my shoulder! I was so stunned even my quiet sobs stopped, and I turned to stare at Ari, who sat next to me on the bed. He had pulled on the gauntlet, and his hand rested gently on my shoulder. He didn't say anything, just slid the cool surface of the gauntlet up my neck, then higher, his palm finally settling against my cheek. He thumbed at the wetness on my skin, wiping bitter tears away. I could barely breathe. I didn't want the moment to end, despite how my head ached and my eyes burned. Ari was touching me. Not a cold, clinical touch, not "maintenance," but touching me just to comfort me. Because he wanted to.

"Ari." My voice was awful, hoarse and guttural, but he just smiled. "You should rest."

"Stay with me." I didn't mean to make it sound like an order, but I wanted it to be. "Please."

"I will." He lay on the bed next to me, smoothing his fingers one last time over my face before dropping his hand down to my chest, careful to slide it under my borrowed T-shirt so I could really feel it.

If I'd been less tired, I wouldn't have been able to rest like that, but my nerves were shot for the night. Instead I relaxed against the weight of his hand, one touch in my otherwise untouchable world, and closed my eyes.

The tears kept coming, but I fell asleep anyway.

You know those dreams you have sometimes that are so vivid when you're in them, that you'd swear they were the real deal? When I woke up the next morning I experienced one of those moments, only in reverse.

I had rolled over onto my side in the night, and when I opened my eyes the first thing I saw was Ari. His gauntleted hand had migrated down to my forearm, where he was holding on to me so hard my skin was red around the edges of the glove. His glasses were askew, pressing against his nose in a way that had to be uncomfortable, and the line was back between his eyebrows, making him seem stern even in his sleep. It was probably good that Ari was bald, because his hair would have been a total mess if the wrinkles in his shirt were anything to go by.

He looked like the most amazing person I'd ever seen in my life. And he was here. In my bed. *Holding* me.

"Best dream ever," I slurred. Ari's eyes popped open a moment later, and widened slightly.

"Craig?" He relaxed his grip on my arm, and I protested, reaching for his hand. Which I managed to actually feel, because ha-ha, dreams were awesome.

"No, stay," I protested. "You should stay and kiss me." *And then give me a blowjob*, I didn't say, because I wanted to be polite to Ari even in a dream, but that was what I was hoping for after the kissing got underway.

"What?"

I shrugged. "That's how it always goes when I'm dreaming of you."

Ari's expression did something complicated, like it couldn't quite decide whether to be pleased or concerned. It settled on concerned. "Craig, you're not dreaming."

"I have to be." Because if I wasn't, then the other stuff flooding into my head might be real too: fresh memories of fire and heat and pleading eyes, memories I didn't want. They kept coming anyway, and I covered my face with my hands. "Oh, shit."

"It's okay."

"Um, no, not really." Because in addition to unwelcome thoughts, my body had also reacted the way it usually did when I had dreams about Ari. I slapped my hand over my face, which was tacky with dried tears, great. "I'm so sorry. I'll be fine in a minute, just—"

"Craig." Ari's voice was a lot closer than it had been a moment ago. "You have nothing to be sorry about. Honestly. And I'll leave if you'd like me to. It's no problem."

That was the *last* thing I wanted right now, to be left alone with the memory of my terrible yesterday. I couldn't remember the last time anyone had tried to comfort me like this. Maybe not since my parents. "No, stay. Please."

"Even if I can't kiss you?" His thumb rolled over the back of my hand, still touching me with the help of the gauntlet. It felt so good, and I was desperate to keep feeling good.

"You could do something else, if you wanted to," I suggested with a watery grin, lifting my hand to look at him again. If he took it like I was kidding, fine, but if he seemed interested . . .

"Hmm." Ari let go of my hand and touched the gauntlet to my chest, rubbing a small circle down my breastbone as he traced a path to my belly. "I certainly could."

Wait, what? "Are you serious?" I blurted.

"Do I not seem serious enough?"

I scrubbed my hand over my eyes and took a moment to examine Ari. He'd taken off his glasses, but he was close enough that I could see the way his pupils had started to expand. His mouth was soft and relaxed in an almost-smile, and his hand's path had stopped just above the waistband of my borrowed gym shorts.

"I would seriously like to touch you now," he told me, "but I won't if that isn't something you want."

"Um." Now that the prospect of sexy touching was actually on the table, a dozen different excuses popped up in my brain immediately. There were all sorts of reasons to think he wasn't really interested in this, in me, in anything physical between the two of us, but apparently that wasn't the case.

Ari didn't push, but he didn't back off either. He just waited, and eventually I managed to get enough blood back up to my lips to speak.

"I won't be able to— I mean, it's kind of a one-way deal."

"If you think I can't get myself off just looking at you, you're wrong."

Oooookay, then. There was covering all the bases, and then there was being stupid. I wanted his touch more than I could say, anything to keep my mind on him and off of Firebolt.

"In that case, please keep going." I swallowed hard. "Although I don't think I'm going to last long."

"You don't have to last; you just have to enjoy it." His hand crept under the loose fabric of my shorts, and I full-body shivered at the first touch of the cool surface of his gauntlet wrapping around my hard-on. It was as far from the feeling of my own hand as it could possibly be, not even close to the softness of skin, but his grip was gentle and determined, and I was so ready to go I couldn't even speak. Ari was the first person to touch my dick with intent in way too long, and it was . . .

I'd never gone in for the idea of orgasm denial as a means of pleasure; the pleasure was in the act itself, right? But I hadn't come for so long, and my senses seemed to have gone into overdrive. My skin prickled with every shift of Ari's fingers, and all I could hear was the satisfied hum he made as he moved closer to me, pressing so tight against my force field that I could almost imagine he was touching me everywhere.

When that initial indescribable shudder diminished to the point where I could open my eyes, I looked at Ari and found him looking back, and for the first time his smile seemed to touch his eyes, soft and pleased, happy and expectant. He clearly wanted this as much as I did, and *that* was enough to get me so hard I almost blacked out.

He started to stroke me, and every hair on my body stood on end. I clenched my fingers and toes tight enough to ache as all my muscles shivered toward the same climax. I tried to hold back, tried to let things build and enjoy the ride. This was less of a roller coaster and more like a cliff dive, but the anticipation was agony, so why wait?

I could barely breathe, my chest was so tight, and when Ari said, "Craig, come," I couldn't help but obey.

My body went through the motions, but that was almost secondary to the feeling of getting swept along in a rush, tingling and thrumming in a way I just couldn't replicate for myself. I arched so hard my hips left the bed, and by the time I slumped down again you could have wrung me out and used me as a rag, I was so limp. Holy shit.

"I agree."

Oh wait, I'd said that out loud? I would have said something else, but then Ari let go of me and carefully withdrew his closed fist from my shorts. He'd caught most of my semen inside the gauntlet's force field, which was awesome because there was a *reason* I didn't come often: cleanup was a bitch. He took the gauntlet off, then sat up and quickly but methodically undressed. I watched him reveal his body piece by piece: broad shoulders that my legs would fit over real well, a chest covered with dark curls leading down to a lean waist, and a long, slim cock that made my mouth water just looking at it.

"What can I do?" There was so much I wanted to do: suck him down like I was underwater again and he was the only source of air, touch him the way he touched me and watch him fall apart, spread my legs and pull him into my body so that maybe, for once, I wouldn't feel so empty.

"Just watch," Ari said, and before I could stop him he slung a leg over my hip and settled on top of me.

It had to hurt. It had to *really* hurt; his balls were flush with my hips, and the force field apparently felt like pins and needles, a crawling pain that got worse the longer you were in contact with it. But if Ari was in pain, he wasn't bothered by it; given the way his cock perked up in his fist, red and already leaking from the tip, he might actually be enjoying it. Who knew someone could get off on something like this? He stroked himself slowly from root to tip, groaning as he ground down against me, and I didn't have to feel that to find it stupidly sexy.

Cautiously I set my hands on his hips, and the result was awesome: he fell forward, one hand on my chest, the other working his cock a lot faster now. I traced my fingers down his thighs, and Ari groaned again; said, "*Fuck*," in a low, desperate voice; hitched his hips; and came across my stomach. It rolled right off, of course, and wow, I was going to have to change my sheets in the first time in forever, which was *awesome*. Just watching Ari get off was enough to make my own dick start thinking about resurrection.

No, I told it firmly, because Ari seemed totally spent. He'd shifted off of me and settled onto his back, panting wordlessly.

"I can't believe my force field does it for you," I said after a moment, because hey, coincidence.

Ari shook his head. "It isn't that," he said, a bit breathlessly. "I'd certainly never say no to a little pain with my pleasure, but it isn't the force field itself. It's the fact that it's you."

"I don't get you," I told him honestly.

Ari shrugged. "You don't have to get me, as long as you accept what I tell you as the truth."

I must have looked stricken, because he held my gaze for a long time, even opened his mouth to speak once or twice before finally shaking his head. "I need to shower, and I'm starving."

Ah, nice subject change. I could deal with that. "Yeah? You want breakfast?"

"Lunch would be more appropriate, I think; it's almost noon."

Noon. It had been almost twelve hours since Shareen had died. The weight of remembrance settled in my stomach like lead. "We can do lunch." Because life might be the weirdest combination of awesome and awful right now, but we both still had to eat. "I can order something in. What do you want?"

"Chinese would be nice. That soup from before was excellent." He got out of bed, and I watched him collect his clothes and head for the bathroom, because it was nicer than thinking about talking to Edward and Raul. Last night's fight was the kind of event that would either make or break our partnership, and the whole thing with the hostages . . . what had that been about?

There was only one way to find out. I got up from the bed and changed into a pair of my own sweats, then grabbed a new cell phone off my nightstand—seriously, I needed a telecommunications company to sponsor me so I could stop spending thousands of dollars on new phones—and placed an order at Flower Pepper for soup.

"And the quicker the better, please." If I could have this conversation while Ari was in the shower, that would be ideal.

The knock on the door came fifteen minutes later. I jerked it open, ready to yell at Raul for his reckless fucking mines, only to find a shorter, slimmer man on my doorstep. One whose messy hair was only partially concealed beneath the restaurant's cap, and who had two very concerned eyes looking in my direction. Ari was still in the shower, so I ushered Edward inside and locked the door behind him. "What the fuck? What happened last night?"

"I don't know!" he snapped back. "Why don't you tell me? I thought you were supposed to keep us in the loop when your people decide to marshal full-scale assaults on the Red Zone!"

"I've been benched for the past week, you know that. The first I heard of them doing this was from *you*."

He grabbed on to his hair and tugged so hard I worried he'd pull a chunk of it out. "Why, though? Why wouldn't they tell you about something so important, when you're the best Hero the city has?"

"Maybe for the same reason you didn't tell me you were holding on to hostages."

Edward shook his head. "I don't know where that rumor came from, but it's not true. All the names they've cited in the media are people who went missing from a residential area four blocks out of Red Zone territory two nights ago, but I have no idea where they've gone. I reached out to enough of the Villain community about it that I'd *know* if someone there had something to do with that. The only people in our clinic right now are Red Zone residents; none of them even have any special powers! Clearly it's an excuse that your people came up with to justify what they did next." Edward's shoulders slumped. "Are they *that* crazy for ratings?"

"I don't . . ." Something was wrong with that. If there honestly weren't any hostages, then there wasn't any pressing reason to mount an incursion into Villain territory. It was expensive, dangerous, and risky, and Ray was a lot of things but he wasn't the type to jeopardize his star performers needlessly. "I don't know why they did it. But I'm going to find out."

"Good." Edward set the soup he was holding down and eyed me critically. "Are you okay?"

"Not really."

"Well, no," he allowed with a grimace. "Obviously you wouldn't be after what happened to Firebolt, but do you think you will be?"

"Yeah. Probably." I heard the bathroom door open. Time to wrap this up. "Okay, let me pay you."

"It came already? That was fast." Ari came into the kitchen and looked at Edward curiously. "You're not going to argue about the tip as well, are you?"

Edward took one glance at Ari, paled, and darted forward. Before I could stop him he took Ari's hand. A second later Ari's curious expression melted away, and he turned around and walked into the living room without a second glance. That was the first time I'd seen this new development in Edward's power, and it worked scarily well.

"Eddie, what the *hell*?" I whispered furiously as Ari settled silently on the couch. "Why did you mind-whammy my boyfriend?"

"For the millionth time, it's not mental, it's emotional— Wait. He's your boyfriend now?" Edward gaped at me. "When did *that* happen? Do you even know who he really is?"

"Yes." I knew . . . not everything, but enough. "He's Ari Mansourian, double PhD, medical doctor, educated in Russia, worked in Germany—"

"Educated in Russia, yeah. Raul recognized him eventually. Hang on." Edward grabbed his phone and pulled up a picture. "Do you remember this?"

I glanced at the photo. It was in black and white, and the caption was in Cyrillic. I did recognize the photo, though: it was famous. A small group of men and women in white lab coats stumbling off a train, staring to the side in complete horror at something not in the picture. "Yeah, that's from the Siberian explosion, right?" I'd only been a little kid then, but I remembered it being in the news.

"Look closer," Edward said grimly. I frowned but humored him, taking the phone and enlarging the photo. Person, person, person . . . person who maybe could have been Ari. Only much younger, and with hair. Ari had worked on the Soviet Super program?

"So what?" I said at last. "So he spent some time in Russia's Super lab. What does that matter? It's his area of expertise."

"It matters because something happened there that was apparently so horrible, the details have never been brought to light," Edward said. "You know that area is still fenced off fifty miles in every direction? It's patrolled night and day to keep people out."

"So they're keeping people *safe*, what's wrong with that?"

"How about the fact that one of those scientists, who was never identified after the fact, went on to work in some of the top Super labs in Europe? And that the projects he worked on led to several of the most frightening technological innovations in the twenty-first century? The majority of Dr. Mansourian's research is classified, but the few papers I could dig up? Listen to this." Edward went to a new article. "'Practical applications of optical refrigeration accompanied by spontaneous anti-Stokes emissions.' He made a real-life *freeze ray*, Craig! Or this one." Edward swept to another screen. "'Creation of sonic black hole analogue in a Bose-Einstein condensate.' It creates a black hole that works on sound instead of light. Think about all the potential for abuse for *that*. And he could pose an even bigger danger than we know. It turns out that at each of his research posts, Heroes have gone missing."

"What the hell are you suggesting?" I asked, trying to keep up my bluster but the ground was dropping out from under my feet. "That Ari's some Hero serial killer? That he's a mad scientist or something? He's done nothing but help me!"

"He's helped you figure out weaknesses. Your vulnerabilities." Edward suddenly looked tired. "Just consider, please, that there might be more motivating him to research your weak spots than trying to help you conquer them. You're the best Hero Panopolis has to offer. What would strike a greater blow to the city than taking you out for good?"

"I think you should go," I whispered.

"Craig..."

"Really. Leave. Leave right now."

"Okay." Edward heaved a sigh and gave me his puppy-dog eyes, but I wasn't going to cave. I had things to say, but none of them were to Edward. "Just be careful."

"*Leave*, Edward!"

He finally scooted, and I locked the door behind him, more exhausted than ever. What had I gotten into? What was going on? My life used to be simple: Be a Hero. Save people. Now I didn't know friends from foes.

"So that was Mastermind."

I whirled around and saw Ari standing in the doorway, a distant expression on his face. "His is a fascinating power," he went on. "One minute I was thinking about lunch, the next I wanted nothing more than to get comfortable on the couch and turn the television up as high as it would go. Fortunately for me . . ." He smiled thinly. It wasn't one of his good smiles. "I've got experience with that kind of emotional manipulation."

"How'd you know it was him?"

"I've seen pictures of Edward Dinges before, Craig. I was familiar with his face. And when I put him together with the last delivery man's unfortunate ocular issues, it simply made sense." The false casualness melted out of his voice, replaced by iron. "What I don't understand is why Panopolis's most notorious Villains are delivering Chinese food to your door. What does the city's greatest Hero have to do with people like that?"

When cornered, go on the offensive. "Well, I don't understand why someone with a reputation for making *weapons* is giving me the time of day, unless you're planning on getting rid of me the way you have other Heroes."

Ari's frown was deeper than I'd ever seen it before. "I haven't been getting rid of Heroes."

"But you have been making weapons?"

"It's not what you think. I never intended for my research to—"

"Why are you here?" I was one step away from a complete meltdown, and Ari knew it if the way he held up his hands was any indication. "Why are you *actually* here with me? Why are you giving me the time of day? I *knew* there had to be another reason for it, I knew it. There's no way I could be enough for you, so what is it?"

"Craig—"

"*What is it?*" I screamed.

"I want to help you," Ari said firmly, although his hands shook slightly. "That's all I've ever wanted: to help Heroes. That's what

I came to Panopolis to do. But I don't just want to help make you into a better Hero, Craig. I want to give you the option to *stop* fighting, if that's what you choose."

My rage came to a screeching halt. "There's no way."

"There are ways. There are always ways, if someone bothers to look for them."

"No." I shook my head. "That's not how it works. You just keep going until—until you can't keep going anymore."

"I swear to you, that's not true. I do know about the Heroes who have gone missing. I did associate with several of them, but I didn't *kill* them, Craig. I helped them discover methods of minimizing their powers, or in one case, get rid of them completely. I gave them back the lives they thought were lost to them." His mouth twitched irritably. "And in some cases that has meant developing technology that could potentially be used to make weapons, but there was no other way my research would get funded. Ending a Hero's career isn't a very profitable business decision. Most of them have had to go into hiding to avoid further exploitation, much as I had to change my identity in the end and seek employment on a new continent."

"So . . . the freeze ray?"

"Miniaturized and multiplied, and placed in the home of a former Hero who spontaneously burst into flame on a regular basis. She couldn't touch her husband, couldn't hug her children without worrying she would damage them. Within the confines of her home, though, she doesn't flame. It isn't a perfect solution, but she was grateful for it."

"And the sonic black holes?"

"Is that what the press has called them?" Ari sighed heavily. "*Science* writers, always dying to turn legitimate inventions into doomsday devices. That particular technology was created for the Mole Man of Minsk. His hearing was so sensitive he could only relax within the walls of a heavily insulated panic room. He now wears one of the devices as a necklace, and it strictly controls the frequencies that come into his range. He can go to a concert; he can drive a car; he can live a more normal life, which was all he ever wanted in the first place. Not everyone asks to be a Hero, Craig. You know that even better than I do." He slowly lowered his hands. "Will you sit down with me now? So that we both can explain ourselves better?"

It was that or keep throwing a fit, and I was just too tired. I wanted to listen to Ari; I wanted what he said to be true. "Okay."

We sat down at the kitchen table, the soup in a plastic Flower Pepper bag between us. Ari glanced at it, and I saw the question in his face.

"My turn, then?" I rubbed a hand over the back of my neck. "So, you maybe know that I knew Edward before he became Mastermind."

"Indeed. You dated briefly."

"No." I shook my head. "I wanted to date, but he was already seeing Raul then. Edward lived next door to my memaw, and after things went south between us—because I was a pushy dick, not to mince words—he ended up getting arrested and sent to the Abattoir."

Ari nodded. "I know all of this."

Hah. "Yeah? Did you know that he was tortured there? That that's how he got his powers? Did you know that he could have ended up in the same boat as me, unable to touch anybody, if Raul hadn't been looking out for him?" My throat tightened, but I forced myself to keep speaking. I had to finish it, had to tell the whole thing even if it meant giving Ari some serious leverage against me. Was it any worse than what I had on him, though? Maybe not, but I wanted to be honest with him. *Please don't turn me in after this.* "When I helped him escape from GenCorp after he broke in, I did it because I wanted to, not because I was being mind-controlled. He's got to touch somebody's skin for his power to work, and, well." I chuckled, but it was too weak to be a real laugh.

Ari stilled for a long moment. "Ah," he said at last.

"That's all you have to say? 'Ah'?" I demanded.

"I'd rather not assume anything until you tell me why you helped him. I'm sure you had a reason for it."

Well, yeah. "He was being forced by another Villain to steal information from their computers. It was the only way he could save Raul. Said he'd check into my stuff too, find out why GenCorp's lying to me about my force field. I know they've been lying, I'm just not sure what about. It's taking time to decrypt what they got, but he gave me a formula of some kind a couple of weeks ago that's linked to my name."

Ari leaned forward. "A chemical formula?"

"Yeah, I think so."

"A formula for the compound that creates your force field?" he pressed. "Because that is one piece of information that I haven't been given access to. I can create a facsimile of your straws with the information I get from a mass spectrometer, but it's incomplete, and therefore incorrect. Having the original formula would allow me to make much faster progress on the issue of your force field."

"Why do you care?" Ari opened his mouth, but I beat him to the next line. "And don't tell me it's because you like me. You've said that. I want to know why you care at all. People—doesn't matter if they're regular Joes or scientists—*love* Heroes, because of what we can do, not who we are. Why are you so interested in getting Heroes to be something less than that?"

Ari folded his hands on top of the table for a moment. His thumbs made slow circles around each other, probably a stall tactic, but I didn't call him out on it. After a few seconds of silence, he said, "I was born in a small village in the Ararat province of Armenia. My parents were farmers. Our neighbors were farmers, or they worked in the state-run chemical plant nearby. The closest school was a single building for over a hundred children of all ages. By rights, I should have been a farmer myself. At most, perhaps gone to university for biology or veterinary studies.

"When I was ten years old, my best friend's father was in an accident. He fell into a vat of one of the chemicals while it was being transported through the plant—a new type of fertilizer. It caused unrestrained and toxic growth in his cells. The manager of the plant didn't know this at the time, though. He sent Yevgeny's father home with an admonition to rest. The results of the exposure hadn't yet started to be seen, you see. They thought he was lucky." Ari sounded more bitter than I'd ever heard him before.

"He went home at midday. His wife and my mother were there, and he kissed them both on the cheek before he went to lie down in his bedroom. By the time my mother came home, her cheek was bright red, like she'd been slapped." Ari didn't look at me, just kept staring at his hands, which was good, because I didn't want him to see my horror. "Yevgeny and I played together after school, and my mother sent us outside because she felt unwell. When it was close to dark, he returned to his home, me to mine.

"I called out for my mother, but she didn't answer. I found her in the bedroom, lying on her side, with pink foam coming from her mouth. Her entire body was red, so red. It was a good thing I didn't touch her, for she was highly contagious at that point. She was also very dead."

Holy shit. "Ari—"

He held up a hand. "You asked. Now listen." I shut up. "I ran for my father in the field. By the time we both returned to the village, word of a plague was spreading. Officials from the plant were already in the square to direct us toward the buses that would take us to quarantine locations. I wasn't allowed back in my home. We were never able to claim my mother's body, and I never saw Yevgeny again. I assumed his whole family had died as well. Only they hadn't."

"The Red Death," I breathed. The most famous of Russia's Heroes. The man who could spread poison with a touch, and who seemed immune to it himself.

"Yes, Yevgeny's father, Piotr, was the Red Death. Piotr Panossian was the reason I decided to dedicate myself to the science of superheroes. I didn't realize it was him until I got to Siberia, but once I was there—"

"That *was* you!"

"Mastermind showed you that picture of me, then?" Ari nodded. "It was before I had learned to better guard my face. I was an undergraduate then; I had been awarded a position in the facility's work-study program. It was only two months after I arrived that it came to an end, though.

"The event that occurred in Siberia was an object lesson for me in what could happen when a Hero is pushed too hard. They were trying to make more people like Piotr, you see, trying to re-create his abilities. The doctor in charge was a German, Heinrich Schlimmer, who had created some of the most fearsome Heroes in post–World War Europe. The Soviets brought him for Piotr specifically. Hundreds of people were sacrificed in the pursuit of another Red Death."

"Holy shit." My stomach roiled. "How could you help with that? Especially when you *knew* him, when he killed your own—"

"I didn't help with it. Not directly. I was a work-study student, but in the Siberian facility that meant far more work than study. I cleaned floors, I archived old data, I assisted the kitchen staff when they needed it. I never even entered the Red Death's laboratory, just worked on side projects." His voice sounded hollow, and he stared at his clasped, trembling hands. "Not that that erases my culpability." He shook his head.

"The day came when Piotr had finally had enough. I was cleaning one of the vacant labs when it happened. The evacuation alarms sounded, but before we could leave, the televisions that the administrators used to make announcements with came on, and Piotr was there. He said that he was tired of being sent out to kill people, that all he wanted was to die. Then he said we had half an hour to vacate the facility, or we would die with him."

"You made it out."

"I *barely* made it out," Ari corrected me softly. "Most of the workers were bused in, and the buses weren't returning to the site. There was a drastic shortage of vehicles available, and close to a thousand people died. Untold numbers of test subjects. Military, guards. That wasn't the man I remembered, the father of my friend, who loved his wife and children more than anything. That was what he became because he was *forced* into a role he had no desire to play. That was a decade of use and abuse, finally breaking the soul of a man who should never have been forced to play Hero for his nation. And look at the Hero they made him be." Ari's voice was thick with loathing. "A killer. Nothing but a tame terror made to inspire obedience. That was when I knew that, more than anything, I wanted to understand not only how Heroes were made, but how they could be *un*made."

"Craig." He reached out toward me, and I let him put his hands on top of mine. I wished so much that I could feel it. "If I could find a way to remove your force field, wouldn't you want that? Isn't that part of what you were hoping your friends would discover for you?"

Passing something through my force field was one thing. Having no force field at all, though . . . "I don't know if I want that or not. I'm not . . . smart, like you are. I don't have a lotta other options. I'm good at Heroing. I don't have to be smart to be Freight Train."

Ari's frown returned. "You could do many different things."

"Like what, go back to being a cop?" I snorted. "Watching Villains get away with shit when I could be stopping them instead? Or working construction; there's a lot of call for that, what with the way buildings keep collapsing. Or any of a dozen jobs that'll embarrass my memaw, not to mention void my contract with GenCorp, if I even survived being de-Heroed long enough to get into that fight." I was under no illusions about the number of people who might come after me if I lost my power.

"That's what you retain legal counsel for: to handle your professional relationship with GenCorp."

"Yeah, but Ianthe's sick. I don't want to overwork her."

"Craig." Ari sounded exasperated, but there was a note of kindness in there. "You're allowed to put yourself first sometimes."

"That's not what a Hero should do."

"But it might be what Craig Haney should do," Ari said gently. He pulled away from me. "Just think about it, please."

"Sure." I probably wouldn't be able to stop thinking about it now.

"Will you at least consider giving me the formula at some point in the future?" His eyes stared at me bright and earnest. "I swear, I only want to provide you with options. I would never take away any part of you without your permission."

"You can't tell anyone where you got it." I had to be clear about that. "If someone found you with the formula, you couldn't tell anybody where it came from. If people learn that I'm working with Mastermind and the Mad Bombardier, I'll be tried and sentenced before the day is done, Hero or not." I knew that like I knew my own name, and I didn't want to be forced into giving up Raul and Edward's safe houses. "Not to mention I'm supposed to help cover for them."

"I have no interest in incriminating you or your friends."

He sounded genuine, but . . . "Why not? They're the bad guys, after all. They don't trust you, that's for sure." And were prepared to expose him if things got messy, it seemed.

"True. But they're trying to help you, so in some sense that makes them the good guys too, at least to me." He shrugged tiredly. "I have no association with them directly, and I cannot prove anything about you if asked. You don't need to worry about me giving you, or them, up."

His eyes were huge with worry, but they didn't waver from my face. "I want to help you. I want to *free* you, if I can. That's all I've ever wanted from my work, and with you, well . . . it's more than work, Craig. I hope you believe that."

It might have been stupid, probably was—I could hear Edward's warnings ringing in my ears—but I believed Ari. I might not be the smartest guy, but I was pretty good at telling when someone was full of shit, and Ari's story smelled like a rose. A dead, chemically mutated rose maybe, but a rose all the same.

"Hang on." I got up from the table and headed for my bedroom. The thumb drive was in the drawer of my night table, right next to the most expired condoms ever—how had I not thrown those away in seven years? I took it back to the kitchen and held it out to Ari.

His eyes were so wide they could've fallen out, and his mouth had gone slack. "That easily?"

"I just had sex for the first time since I became Freight Train, because you made a custom metallo-organic glove to touch me with," I said with a wry smile. "I'm hoping that's a sign that you've got my best interests at heart."

"I do, I just . . . I thought it would be harder to convince you of that."

I shrugged and dropped the drive into his hand. "We might not have much history together, but you haven't been working at GenCorp for long either. I've got no reason to think you knew about any of this before, and besides . . . I want to believe you. I really want to, because I like you, Ari. Maybe way more than I should. Please don't make me regret it."

"Never." He closed his fingers around the drive and clenched it to his chest. "I never will. I swear it." We stared at each other in silence for a long moment before the beep of an incoming message had him checking his phone. "I'm being called in to the lab. The scraps from Firebolt's fuel harness need to be evaluated per GenCorp guidelines before final consignment."

"What's that mean?"

"It means they want to figure out why it failed the way it did before the last of the evidence is disposed of." Ari shook his head. "It will go into a report that no one will ever reference again after next week's board meeting, and then the problem will be forgotten. Nevertheless, as it was made by our labs, if not by *my* lab"—he scowled—"we must follow protocol."

"Sounds like a long day."

"And possibly a long night," Ari agreed.

"You should come back here when you're done."

Ari's eyebrows raised at the invitation. I was surprised at myself for offering it, honestly; our interactions had been all over the place lately, and my life was only going to get busier as the day wore on. Ray would only be able to deflect attention from me for a while. But that only made me more determined to get Ari back here again, soon, where both of us could think about something other than GenCorp for a while. "I mean it," I said.

"I could be very late. It might not be until tomorrow, even."

"Tomorrow is fine. Stay long enough and I can drag you out to dinner with Memaw." There was no way she'd let me miss another Sunday, and after last night I was looking forward to her cranky normalcy.

"How irresistible," Ari said dryly.

"Yeah, I could be a lawyer, huh?"

"I think you could be almost anything, actually."

Well, damn it. There he had to go messing up my bad attempt at humor with solemnity. The faith was nice, even if it was totally misplaced.

"Go to work," I told him. "I'll hold down the fort. And take the soup with you. You didn't get a chance to eat lunch."

"Don't forget to eat yourself."

"Cannibalism isn't my thing, thanks."

"Ha-ha." Ari took the soup, checked for his wallet and keys, then walked with me to the door. I opened it up for him, and he stood beside me for a moment, close enough for our shoulders to touch, before heading out into the sunshine.

CHAPTER TEN

There are a lot of opinion polls floating around Panopolis these days, especially on the subject of Heroes and what you think of them. We're as quick to demonize as we are to proselytize, it seems, always casting our guardian angels in new and exciting roles. This week, let's make them Lucifer falling from grace! Next week we'll reconfigure them as Judas, selling out one of their fellows for personal gain. Then it's back to being our savior in another month or two.

I wonder sometimes whether or not they do the same thing with us. It's got to be something that all celebrities experience to a certain extent, right? The wish to turn the tables on the crowd that perennially watches them. "Would you classify your fans as: (a) bloodthirsty harpies, (b) bleating sheep, or (c) adoring minions?"

I'd like to get a bunch of Heroes drunk and ask them that, actually.

I locked the door behind Ari, then checked my own phone, where I had . . . no messages? That couldn't be correct. I stared at it, then made sure I'd brought it up-to-date. Sometimes I went through cell phones so fast it took a while for everything to transfer over. But no, I had saved texts from earlier in the week, and messages from yesterday, and evidence of Edward's call to me last night. Then after that, nothing. Which could only mean that I was being blocked.

"Fucking Ray." I called him and, shockingly, he picked up immediately.

"FT! Hey there, big guy, how are you doing? Feeling better after yesterday? You're being inundated with requests for interviews, so I want you to think about who you want to start with. I know you and Jean go way back, but she's got a tougher rep than some of the late-night hosts, so maybe instead you should consider—"

"Ray," I interrupted. "Why aren't I getting any calls?"

He didn't even try to deny it. "Security issue. You're Panopolis's number one hot topic today, man. It's all I can do to get the police to maintain the perimeter around your place."

"A *police perimeter*?" I glanced out the nearest window and didn't see anything unusual, apart from a total lack of traffic. "Where are they?"

"A block out. I wanted to keep things nice and private for you before we do a big reveal, maybe on Monday. Don't worry," he said, "Dr. Mansourian has been added to the inner circle list, and they won't stop him getting through."

He knew about Ari. Of course he did. He probably read my text messages, the damn voyeur. "Ray, you can't control my phone like this."

"I think you'll find that according to the contract *you* signed, I can," Ray said, his voice going cold. "It's a sub clause under media representation during extreme circumstances, look it up."

"I'll get Ianthe to do that for me, thanks."

"Oh, speaking of Ianthe, I think you're gonna want to consider finding a new lawyer. She tried to call you via Saint Street this morning. That's a bad sign." Saint Street was an exclusive private hospital where a number of Heroes who weren't associated with GenCorp got their care.

"Goddamn it, Ray."

"Hey, it's just business," he said. I could picture the way his sculpted eyebrows were probably lifting right now, the way his pearly teeth were gleaming. "You know corporate's got more than enough lawyers to take care of you."

"Yeah? How well did they do for Firebolt?"

"Let's not bring up the past again, okay? What's done is done, isn't it?" Ray's tone went from confident to tentative. "Although, speaking of that . . . if, um, Mr. Fabulous shows up at your door, do me a favor and humor him, okay? He's going through a rough patch right now."

I had no doubt of that, but really . . . "Did you pimp me out to Zane to be his babysitter?"

"On the contrary. I told him to leave you alone, but he was in a *mood* this morning, and said I couldn't tell him what to do." Ray sounded disgruntled by that, which seemed like a good mood to leave him in.

"I want control of my phone again. I'll contact Ianthe if I have to, but I'd rather you do it for the good of our working relationship, Ray."

There was a long silence, then, "Personal contacts only. No media, not yet."

"Fine."

"Good. Later, FT." He hung up, and I resisted the urge to slam my phone so hard into the table that it would get consigned to the dead-phone pile, because I was an adult, damn it.

I tried to call Ianthe, but got her canned message. I left her a quick, "Sorry I wasn't available earlier, Ray is an asshole, let's talk" and then moved on to Memaw, who happily didn't pick up her phone. "Sorry to miss you, Memaw, I'm fine, see you tomorrow." Duty done.

The last thing I wanted to do now was watch more television, especially since it was probably going to be mostly a bunch of bullshit about Heroes versus Villains and nonexistent hostages (or totally existent hostages who'd been captured by someone else or something; I didn't know, but I was giving Edward the benefit of the doubt). I didn't want to see footage of the explosion played over and over: watch it be dissected in slow motion so that viewers could see "the very moment of ignition!" That was just the sort of sick thing the networks would do, too. Nope, nope, nope.

So instead of plopping down on the couch, I grabbed a shake and headed into the lab. There were still a few tables I could put together for Ari; two of his computer monitors were resting on the bare floor. *Or you could go into the bedroom and jerk off . . .*

Tempting, but no. I'd rather get off with Ari if I was going to. The thought made me smile as I reached for my Phillips head screwdriver. If only my twenty-year-old self could see me now. Actually, if time travel were possible and I could go back and talk to my non-Heroed self, I'd tell him . . .well, I wasn't quite sure. I'd been honest with Ari when I said I didn't know if I would get rid of the force field, even if I could. I might bitch and moan, but then things like last night happened, and I was reminded, pointedly, of how much I could accomplish as a Hero. I hadn't saved Shareen, but I had saved other people. *I'd* done that, me, Freight Train. What could Craig Haney do that would ever compare?

I don't know how long I spent in there, but by the time I heard the banging on my door I'd assembled two tables, a chair, and refreshed the water in the dunk tank, because who knew, maybe we'd do more work with that soon. It had to be Ari; I couldn't think of many other people Ray would consider "inner circle," the fucking jerk, but the banging was erratic, unsteady. I grabbed my stuff and headed for the door.

It wasn't Ari. It was pretty much Ari's polar opposite standing there, out of costume for once, one hand raised to knock, the other wrapped around a bottle of what looked like very expensive vodka. Zane smiled crookedly at me. "Hey, Craig."

"Did you drive drunk to get here?"

"Calm down, old man," he scoffed, pushing past me into my apartment. I frowned as I let him go by; I wasn't *old*, I only had a couple freaking years on Zane. "I didn't drive, I ran. Only clipped, like, one or two cars. Three, max."

"Uh-huh." I shut the door but didn't bother locking it; I was in no mood to put up with Zane on a bender. "And what are you doing here?"

Zane held up his free hand and extended his index finger. "I am here to get *you* drunk, Craig."

Oh wow. He must be completely wasted if he was bothering to use my first name. "I don't think that's a good idea."

"Why not? Why? Because you're the golden boy now, you're too good to hang out with me?" Zane snapped. "Or what, are you finally lis'ning to the bullshit Ray throws around? Thought you didn't care what he says."

"He hasn't said anything to me about you."

"And he shouldn't! It's none of his— Not his fucking—" Zane slumped down in a chair and set his bottle unsteadily on the table. "He pretends like he knows what's goin' on out there, but he *doesn't*. Ray doesn't know *shit*, Craig, so don't listen to him. He'll just fuck life up for you."

Now *that* talk was unusual from Zane. He and Ray were generally closer than Siamese twins, especially since they'd been working on his show. "Yeah?"

"Yes! That's why I came here, y'know? To talk to someone who understands these things. Because you're the only one who does." He stared at the vodka like it held the answers to the universe. "The only one. Couldn't go to my folks, they won't talk to me right now. Ray doesn't want to listen. There's just you, Craig. But I can't *tell* you anything unless you drink with me. 'S'fairer that way."

The last time I'd gotten drunk had been almost five years ago, after a particularly bad night on the job. I'd sworn I'd never do it again. But Zane was here, speaking to me like a person and not a persona, and I couldn't deny that when it came to commiserating, I might be his best bet. "Fuck. Fine." I handed over my empty shake container. "But not too much."

"Excellent!" It took him a few tries to unscrew the cap, but he managed it, and poured way more vodka in there than I was comfortable with—I'd have to sip slowly. He passed it over to me, then hoisted the bottle. "Cheers, man."

I didn't know what we were toasting to, but I clinked with him and took a sip.

Okay, so—an hour of drinking vodka on a mostly empty stomach when you haven't had alcohol in five years? My head spun so hard I could barely get the bottle to my lips without missing. It tasted so bad, but it was sooo good too, and I had to put my phone aside to keep from drunk-texting Ari. Vodka was maybe the best thing ever, and Zane was totally right, drinking together was the best way to open up the floodgates of honesty. I let him go first. It was only fair.

"It's been a fuckin' nightmare," Zane moaned from his side of the couch. We'd moved to the living room after he'd tried to balance a kitchen chair on two legs and fallen over instead. "Everybody calling me, shouting at me, blaming me for fucking it all up. Like it was *my* idea to send Firebolt in there with that fucking tank on her back. That was the production people. They wanted more flames with fewer breaks to refill her. It cut way down on her mobility but they figured I was mobile enough for both of us, so why not?" He took another pull on the bottle. "Why the fuck not? Give us enough gas to burn down a fuckin' building, why not?"

"That *was* you, then?" I mean, I'd assumed, but . . .

Zane bit his lower lip and glanced at me. "Yeah. Firebolt was kind of on edge that night, and Vibro kept doing this thing to the ground that kept me from running in a straight line, and we ended up— Yeah. I'm glad you came out of it okay, though."

"Me too." And I'd been the only one injured, in the end. "It could have been worse. At least they got me out before I suffocated."

"Hah. It fuckin' *has* been worse," Zane muttered. "I'm not s'posed to tell you this, but fuck Ray." He took a deep breath. "There weren't any hostages in Z Street."

I opened my mouth to say I already knew that, then remembered why I wasn't supposed to know that. "Are you serious?"

"Yeah. I mean, there were people missing, but—" He drew in a shuddery breath. "They were already dead. From a car accident. That I caused."

"You . . ." I didn't know what to say. I'd been in fights where civilians had gotten hurt, of course—what Hero hadn't? But I'd never directly harmed any of them that I knew of. "How?"

Zane laughed wetly. "It was for a *promo* shoot, if you can believe that. The producer wanted a video of me running next to a car, like we were drag racing or something. He got this group of fucking *teenagers* together, handed them a bimmer, and told them to drive down an empty stretch of street with me. It was close to Z, the road was pretty rough, and—"

He shut his eyes. "I tripped. I fucking *tripped* in the middle of the goddamn road, and the car would have run over me if the kid who was driving hadn't jerked it to the side. Only he went too far, he pulled it over too far, and he ended up smashing into a lamppost. None of the kids survived the collision. It was—it was messy. It wasn't good, Craig. It really wasn't good."

"Shit." At least the vodka wasn't making me loq—loq—talkative or anything. "That sucks."

"You have no idea." Zane took another pull on the bottle. "None. But we couldn't just out and tell their families what had happened, right? It would have spelled the end for my show. So Ray came up with the hostage idea, had the bodies put on ice and figured that after we broke into the Villain's lair, we could say we found the bodies there and blame it on Mastermind and the Mad Bombardier. I mean, it's the sort of shit a Villain would do. Nobody would know any better."

"That's an asshole move," I said before I could stop myself. "I mean, yeah, old-school Villains, maybe. But Mastermind hasn't killed abynody—aby . . . he hasn't killed regular people."

"But he *could* have!" Zane persisted. "It's a Villain thing! They, you know, they do that shit. That's why we fight them!"

"Dude." I looked him straight in his bleary eyes. "*You're* the one who killed those people."

"I know," he whispered after a moment. "I know. I can't stop thinking about it. Four of 'em, and they were fucking kids, man; they were my little brother's age. And then that stuff with Firebolt happened, and you had to save the motherfucking day *again*, and I just . . ." He slumped even deeper into the couch. "Sometimes I hate you. I was always going to be a Hero, you know?"

"Because you were born that way." He had been born the perfect Hero; everybody knew that.

Zane shook his head. "No, because I was *designed* that way. I'm the result of my parents collaborating with Dr. Steuben to make the perfect Hero, straight from the womb." He bit his lip and glanced over at me. "It's part of my shtick, right? No side effects, no downsides—the perfect Hero from the start. But really, I was made in a test tube, Craig. I've had over fifty operations since I was born, all of them to shore up the parts of me that didn't improve the way they were supposed to in utero. *Fifty*.

"And every time I fuck up out there, my dad tells me what a disappointment I am. He and the board at GenCorp can't wait to replace me with Philly. That's my brother. They did a better job with him; he's only had, like, twenty operations so far." Zane stared at his bottle, which was mostly empty at this point, and smacked his lips. "Shit. This stuff's makin' me stupid."

"You want a snack?" I asked, because I was pissed at Zane but I was also finally seeing that a lot of the things I hated about him had maybe been, very literally, bred into the poor fucker. "I've got apples, stuff for PB&Js, crackers—"

"Ugh, no. I've got brutal food allergies. I have to be careful what I eat, or else—" He made a little explosion sound. "Boom, bad news for me. I can't even have chocolate. What kind of fucking life is this, when you can't even eat chocolate, or peanuts, or fuckin' bread, even?"

"Um, one a lot like mine?" I shook my mostly empty shake container at him.

"Oh, yeah." He looked caught between commiserating with or condemning me. Condemnation won. "But you still suck. You're, Jesus Christ, you act like a fucking idiot sometimes and your power is so one-dimensional, but you get shit done and everybody loves you. Why can't you just retire?" He poked me in the shoulder and winced at the tingle. "Wouldn't you like to retire? If you could? I'd do it, if I thought I could."

My heart started beating faster. "Maybe we both could. Retire, I mean."

Zane blew a raspberry. "Mmkay, now I know you're drunker than me. You're being crazy."

"No, I'm serious. You know Dr. Mansourian?"

"The new lab guy?"

"Yeah." I wasn't sure if I should share or not, but Zane seemed so miserable . . . this might be my best chance to tell him without him automatically shutting down his ears. "He's done a lot of research on superpowers. He's trying to figure out ways to, um . . ." *Here we go.* I took a deep breath. "To get rid of them. Or at least, to minimize them so people can live normal lives. He's already working on how to do it for me." Not exactly, but Zane didn't need to know that.

Zane's jaw dropped, literally fell wide open. It was like watching a cartoon in real life. "He can get rid of your force field?"

"Not yet, but he's working on it. All that stuff in the other room?" I waved toward the lab. "We've been experimenting on my force field, testing the limits. He could do the same thing for you. He *wants* to."

"What the hell does that mean?"

I drew back a little. "Nothing, just . . . think about it. Ari's a genius, man, he's done this for other Heroes in Germany. He could help you live the normal life you want."

Zane's pupils had shrunk to tiny dots. "You're serious."

"Yep."

"He can un-super Heroes."

"Well, it's not like he'd do it without your permission, but yeah."

"Holy shit." Zane sounded *scared.*

"Look, you can ask Ari about it when he gets back, if you want," I consoled him. "He'll probably be here soon."

"Why is he coming here?"

My face started to heat up. "Because we're . . . maybe . . . dating?"

"You're shitting me."

"No."

Zane shook his head once, then set the bottle down. "You're dating the guy who can turn us into normal people. Wow. And you really like him?"

"Yeah, he's great."

"God." Zane ran both hands down his face, digging his nails into his cheeks. "How is this even happening?"

"Shit, don't hurt yourself." I batted his hands away from his skin.

"Right. *Right!* I wouldn't want to do that." He put them on his knees instead, tapping out a tempo that got faster and faster. "I think I would like to talk to him, actually. You said he'll be back soon?"

"He should be, yeah."

"Then I'll wait." He looked from the bottle to me. "More vodka?"

I shook my head. "Nah, I'm drunk enough. You?"

"Think I've hit my limit for tonight. I need to sober up if things are about to get serious."

"I don't think Ari will judge you for drinking, but I get it."

"No." Zane stared at me solemnly. "No, Craig, I don't think you do."

I frowned at him. "What do you— Oh." The handle on the door turned. "He's here."

Before I could stand up, though, Zane was already off the couch and over to the door. He met Ari coming in, grabbed him around the neck with one hand, and dragged him inside, then slammed him against the wall so hard he dented the drywall.

"Fuck, Zane!" I got to my feet and immediately staggered to the side, cursing internally. "What are you *doing?*"

"He has to die," Zane panted, holding Ari at arm's length. Ari's face was turning red, his hands clawing at Zane as he tried to dislodge the grip. "I can't let him take away my powers. I'm nothing without them!"

"Then he *won't*!" I finally reached the two of them and added my hands to Ari's trying to drag Zane back. I wasn't super strong, though; without getting up some speed I couldn't force Zane to move. His grip loosened enough for Ari to draw a breath, though. "Jesus, he won't make you do anything! It's just an option, Zane!"

"And how long will it stay an 'option' when the board finds out they can get rid of anybody they want without having to worry about us turning Villain?" Zane demanded. "How long will my *parents* want me around when Philly's waiting in the wings to take over as Mr. Fabulous? They won't even see me anymore, not after I fucked so much stuff up lately." Zane's whole body was trembling so much I was sure it would start vibrating in a moment. "If they know this guy can take away my powers, I'm *done*. I've worked too fucking hard to be done, Craig!" He tightened his grip again. "I'm sorry."

"Zane, please, don't *do* this, *don't*—" My pleas were interrupted by what looked like a white balloon suddenly popping into existence from the front of Ari's watch, smashing Zane right in the face as it exploded outward. It knocked him across the room as Ari collapsed to his knees, gasping for air.

"Fuck, Ari!" I wanted to make sure he was all right, but Zane was already getting back on his feet. I had to put him down for good before I could do anything else. I took a few steps back, then lunged forward as Zane put on another burst of speed, and tackled him around the waist.

The force of it sent us bursting through the kitchen wall, straight through the bedroom, and ended up sprawled out over the lab. Zane kicked me off of him, but I charged again before he could try to get to the kitchen. We ended up grappling on the floor, me on top, and I rained punches down with as much force as I could get.

"I'm doing this for you too!" Zane screamed at me. Blood seeped out from what had to be a broken nose, making a mess of his pretty face. "You're nothing if you're not a Hero! You'll be *nothing*!"

I slowed my punches, then stopped them altogether. "I'd rather be nothing than be a Hero like you."

Zane's face twisted with rage. "Then I'll have to get rid of you as well." Before I could react, he bucked his hips up, slithered out from under me, grabbed me beneath the arms, and threw me headfirst into the far wall. I hit hard enough to crack a joist, then fell straight down into the tub of water. Before I could sit up, Zane was there, both hands pressing down on my chest as he held me underwater.

He knows how to kill me. I'd told him I'd almost suffocated; he knew he could drown me. Shit. I punched and kicked; I managed to dent the tub, but Zane was too strong and my range of motion was too limited to push him off. I couldn't get up the speed I needed to do real damage, and I was breathing hard. How long had I been under here? Thirty seconds? A minute? I'd lasted about two during the immersion tests, but I'd been calm then. Now I was frantic, panicking, and I knew my air was almost gone because those stars floating across my eyes were a bad thing, they were really bad. I was *dying*, and then Zane would kill Ari and it would be all my fault. All . . . my . . .

I only noticed being dragged out of the water when my vision slowly started to clear. My ears were ringing, but after a minute or so I could hear Ari hoarsely chanting my name. "—aig! Craig! Look at me, come on, focus on me." After a few more seconds his face swam into focus, no glasses to be seen, and a handprint around his throat already turning purple. "Oh, thank God," he said as we made eye contact.

"Where— Zane?" Shit, I felt dizzy. Still, I tried to push myself to sitting. If Zane was here, or about to wake up from whatever Ari had done to him, I needed to be ready to go.

"He's dead."

I couldn't have been more stunned if Ari had managed to smack me with his balloon-watch thing. I glanced to the side and yeah, there was Zane, lying on his back. His face was smeared red and brown, and oddly swollen. It felt like I was underwater again, drowning all over. "What did you do?"

"Anaphylactic shock." Ari spoke in a monotone, not looking over at the body. "He had a severe peanut allergy. I forced him to ingest peanut butter. It was the only way I could think to get him off of you."

"You're lucky he didn't turn on *you*."

"He— It happened very quickly. I could have tried to find an EpiPen on him, but you were still underwater and, well. That wasn't a difficult decision."

"Oh shit." Zane was dead. "*Shit.*" I could hear sirens outside; naturally, because my block was surrounded by cops who'd probably heard us banging around.

"I'll take full responsibility, of course," Ari went on.

"The *hell* you will! You'll be thrown in the Abattoir faster than you can blink!"

"But once we explain it was self-defense—"

"That won't matter." I knew that as surely as I knew my own name. "He's a Hero. Everyone will assume he had a good reason for attacking you, and even though I can tell them otherwise, they'll put you in prison for the interim. You are *not* going to the Abattoir, Ari, no fucking way." I wouldn't do that to another person I cared for. I still hadn't dealt with my guilt from Edward. There was no way I was compounding that by letting them put Ari away. "We'll say it was my fault."

"None of this was your fault!" Ari exclaimed. "He tried to kill you!"

"Sure it was. I opened my big mouth about what you might be able to do for me, and Zane took it as a possible threat to himself. That's why he went after you, Ari."

"He was clearly unbalanced," Ari insisted. "There must be some way to indicate that, someone who will believe the truth. You're the city's greatest *Hero*; you don't belong in a place like the Abattoir."

"Better me than you. I'm untouchable, remember? You're not, even if your watch does a nice double duty as a boxing glove. I'll say we got into an argument about Firebolt or something, and then it came to blows. It's better this way, Ari, trust me." If I was sent to the Abattoir, I doubted I'd be there for long.

I was a fucking Hero, after all.

CHAPTER ELEVEN

For everyone who's been living under a rock since the fifties, Abbott's Penitentiary, otherwise known as the Abattoir, is the world's largest confirmed prison complex that houses people with superpowers. There are plenty of rumors about Russia's infamous Zlodey Gulag, and widespread suppositions about similar holding areas and forced work camps in China, the Central African Republic, pre-war Syria, and Colombia, among others, but when it comes to cold, hard numbers, America's Panopolis takes the cake. Over half of the prison population are Supers, and the other half probably wishes they were.

Thirty percent of the people who are transformed, accidentally or otherwise, into Supers in this city end up in the Abattoir. Some of them are there because, true to the propaganda we're all fed, they jumped on the Villain train and wreaked havoc with their new abilities as soon as they had them. That group, though, is actually the minority of the Abattoir's prison population. Many of the people existing in that place—because can we really call it living?—are Supers who never set out to be Villains but didn't have the chops to make it as a Hero. And that's not allowed. Haven't you heard? You're either one or the other when you're no longer "normal"; you don't get to abstain.

And once you're in the Abattoir, full-frontal assaults excepted, you never get out again.

Word of my arrest got out fast. That wasn't surprising—this story would probably feed the news mill for weeks. I expected that the police would want to get me into the system and out of the public eye. After I made my one phone call to Ianthe—hopefully she'd get out of the hospital soon, since I didn't want a court-appointed lawyer—I figured it would just be me and a bunch of cops trying to work out the processing.

Um, no. Nope. Apparently when you had a Hero in disgrace sitting in your jail, everybody wanted a piece of the action. The first person to stop by was, of all people, Mayor Wright. He was dressed in a dark-blue suit and tie, both slightly shiny. He looked like an upscale car salesman, or an oilier version of Ray. I'd never liked the new mayor, and I wasn't disposed to chat with him when he sat down across the interrogation table from me.

"Freight Train." He shook his head sorrowfully. "What on earth happened? I thought you and Mr. Fabulous were the best of friends!"

I stared stoically ahead, not quite making eye contact. "With all due respect, I'm not talking to anybody until I've spoken with my lawyer, sir."

"Come on now, Freight Train, that's no way to be with someone who might be able to help you out of this. One of the *only* people who could do so, in fact." When I didn't say anything, he went on. "Nobody wants to see you go down on murder charges, son. You're our city's greatest Hero! Our biggest attraction! Tell me your side of the story, and we'll see how we can spin it into something manageable." He paused, then continued in a stiffer voice. "I don't want to believe the accusations against you, but if you don't try to help yourself here, then I may have no choice. I'm hearing that not only did you kill Mr. Fabulous, you did it because you two fought over what happened to Firebolt. Just the kind of ugly love triangle you read about in the tabloids."

I glared at him. "I'm gay."

"That doesn't have to mean anything, under the circumstances." The mayor's face hardened, his eyes narrowing to tiny slits. "Maybe you weren't trying to save Firebolt when she went up in flames, maybe you had something to do with killing her. Maybe Mr. Fabulous had left you for her, and he came to your place looking for revenge. Maybe Dr. Mansourian was just in the wrong place at the wrong time, or maybe . . . maybe *he* was the jealous one, and found a way to kill Mr. Fabulous himself."

That was way too close to the truth. "That's ridiculous!" I protested.

"Is it?" Mayor Wright countered, then put on his friendly face again. "I'm not saying I believe any of that, Freight Train. I'm just saying that it's the sort of thing that *might* be said about you if you don't speak up, and soon. People will believe the loudest narrative, son, and if you're not shouting yours, someone else will shout a better story and then, well . . ." He shrugged. "Things get messy."

"Volume shouldn't trump the truth."

"Tell me the truth, then. I'll help you make it palatable for the public."

Oh, I bet you would. Nothing I could've said then would have been sacred, and I hadn't needed my words twisted any more than they already had been. I'd gone back to staring straight ahead. "I'm waiting on my lawyer. Sir."

Mayor Wright wasn't the last one to try to pry a statement out of me. The police commissioner, who was as incompetent as I'd thought he would be, let a whole parade of people interrogate me at that damn table. I put up with fifteen minutes of Ray alternately pleading with me and yelling at me next. He was a complete wreck, like he'd been up drinking all night and then resorted to drugs to keep himself on his feet. Once it became clear that I wasn't going to give him anything he staggered out, and the next supplicant took his place. I saw a reporter—not Jean, that wasn't surprising—two more politicians, and a representative from GenCorp before they finally brought in someone who startled me.

"Memaw?"

"You!" Before I could react, she had thrown her purse at me, straight at my face. Used tissues and mostly empty tubes of lipstick scattered across the table as it fell away, upside down. None of it touched me, of course. But it felt like a slap across the heart. "You *bad* boy! How could you do this? How? I thought I raised you to do the right thing, Craig!"

"I did," I told her softly. I could hardly make myself speak. "It was the right thing, you'll see. It'll all be explained, Memaw."

"Murder is never the right thing, Craig!"

"It was self—" I cut my words off before I could say anything incriminating. "How about you wait until I tell my side of the story before deciding I'm wrong?"

Memaw pulled a fresh tissue out of the sleeve of her cardigan, and dabbed at her eyes. "There should never be any doubt! Not with a *Hero*, you should know that. You know how a Hero is supposed to act."

Be good, be strong, be brave, do the right thing, be, do, be, do . . . Yeah, I knew what everyone expected me to be. And I also knew nobody could live up to that standard, not all the time. But I wasn't going to convince Memaw of that.

They escorted her out after another five minutes of shouting, and then my jailers proffered a waiver that would authorize them to keep out everyone except for my preapproved visitors—Ianthe and Ari. I gratefully signed it. It took another few hours, but then, *finally*, they brought in someone I wanted to see. "Your doctor is here," my doorkeeper said, and a second later Ari was let inside. It was all I could do not to jump across the table and try to hug him.

He looked as tired as I felt, his eyes only halfway open behind his glasses, which were taped together along one earpiece. His black turtleneck covered the mess of bruises that circled his throat, but I could hear the damage done as he said, "Drink this," and passed me a shake. I took it with an unsteady hand.

Ari leaned across the table and spoke quietly. "Our lab space in your apartment has been emptied. Everything is gone: the computers, the equipment, everything. I don't know who has it now." A warning if ever I'd heard one. "I'm on record as your personal physician, and GenCorp is exercising a lot of pull with the police commissioner, which is why I'm being given access to you at all. I intend to do everything I can to keep that status. I'm not going to leave you to weather this fallout on your own. You have friends, Craig," and the way his lips turned up briefly made me hopeful, "and we're not going to abandon you. Do you understand me?"

"Yes," I murmured. "Are you okay?"

He shrugged. "As well as can be expected. I'll recover fine. It's certainly not enough to keep me from working."

"Don't work too hard, Ari."

His mouth thinned. "I will work without pause until I put this situation to rights. There's more going on here than you know—"

"Time's almost up," the guard called.

Ari sighed. "Drink that," he said pointedly. I did, even though I didn't feel hungry, and he took it back once I was done. "I'll see you very soon, Craig."

My stupid throat tightened as he stood up. "I hope so."

"I will. I swear." Ari stared at me for a long moment, then turned and stalked out of there like he was king of the castle. Watching him go felt a little like being held underwater again, like my vision wanted to blur.

Finally Ianthe came, pushed in a wheelchair by Viv. Ianthe looked even worse than Ari, and this time I did shoot to my feet. "Jesus Christ, what the hell happened to you?"

"My body has decided that now is the perfect time to be difficult," she said with a grimace. One of her shoulders was hitched oddly high, and her left side seemed slack. "My immune system has been a touch disrupted, but the inflammation is slowly going down. I'll be fine. Let's talk about you. Viv, if you'd set up the recorder and then give us some privacy?"

"Sure," she said. Once she'd completed her task and left, Ianthe reached across the table to me. I blinked hard—no crying, *no* crying, damn it—and gently touched the back of her hand.

"Tell me what happened," she said.

I did. The whole sordid tale took over an hour, with plenty of interruptions from Ianthe to clarify details. By the end of it I felt like my tongue was going to fall out, and Ianthe was frowning fiercely at the tabletop.

"Okay, well. Obviously we're going with a not-guilty plea which is *true*. Honestly, Craig, are you sure you don't want to let Dr. Mansourian take responsibility? It was his choice."

"It's not a choice he would have had to make if I hadn't spilled the beans to Zane. I'm not letting him go down for this."

Ianthe's lips tightened, but she nodded. "Fine. We'll stick with a self-defense plea. Will Dr. Mansourian at least be willing to speak for you?"

"Yeah." I was positive of that.

"Good. I can make a case that Mr. Fabulous was extremely unbalanced by the recent tragedies in his life, which is also the utter truth. There's more than enough footage of what happened in Z Street the other night to prove that you're the responsible Hero, and apart from your brief interlude with Edward Dinges, your record is almost flawless. There's so much evidence in your favor, actually, that what's going to happen next shouldn't happen at all, but as you know," her mouth twisted unhappily, "the law never moves in a straight line in Panopolis. GenCorp's lawyers have submitted that until your trial, you need to be sequestered to Abbott's Penitentiary, as they're the only institution capable of containing you."

I blinked in surprise. "But I'm not gonna run."

"I know that. I already put in a motion for house arrest, but it was denied without explanation. I'm going to work this out, Craig, but I'm afraid I can't do it fast enough to keep you free of that . . . *place*."

Shit, she sounded like she was ready to spit nails. "Hey, it's okay." I tried to smile. "What can they do to me, huh? Nobody can touch me."

"That doesn't mean they can't make your life a living hell. You'll be surrounded by people you helped *put* there, although I'm insisting on protective custody. I hope I can get you into solitary for the whole stretch of your stay; that would be best since you're not going to be there long, but I can't guarantee it."

"Eh." I shrugged one shoulder. "What can you do? I'll be fine."

Ianthe didn't seem convinced, but I honestly wasn't that bothered about going to the Abattoir. Yeah, it was filled with bad guys, but the only person who could touch me was Ari. And if there was one guy I didn't have to worry about, it was him.

Finally, close to midnight, I was loaded into a transport and taken off to the Abattoir. Even though it was late, the sidewalks around the justice center were teeming with people, shouting and holding up signs. Some of them said stuff like, "Justice for Mr. Fabulous!" and "Freight Train Lies!" but the majority of them were, surprisingly enough, real supportive of me.

"Let Freight Train Go!"

"Real Villains=Politicians!"

"FT Is Innocent, MF Is Insane!"

One sign, with glittery blue letters that made me smile a little: "Don't Lock Up the Only Hero Who Can Be Bothered to Get Off His Ass and Do His Fucking Job!" Not that I'd been doing much of my job for the past few weeks, but it was nice to be appreciated.

"This is fucked up," the cop sitting in the back of the van with me said after half an hour or so of uncomfortable silence. The prison was in an isolated location out by the lake; getting there would take time. I'd recognized her: it was R. Flanders, the one who'd been upset about Mr. Bubbles turning into a Villain a few weeks ago. "How can they arrest you? You're our best Hero!"

"I'm really not, but I appreciate the sentiment," I said.

"You're the only one who always, *always* stuck it out at crime scenes to make sure things got done and we stayed safe, you know? Mr. Fabulous never did. And you don't have to talk about it," she said seriously, her eyes red around the edges, "but if it came down to a fight between you and him, then I'm glad you won. You believe in the greater good."

"Thank you." Her assurances made me feel a little better, and anything helped at this point. "I appreciate your faith in me."

She might have said something else if there had been time, but at that point we pulled up to Abbott's Penitentiary, an enormous concrete building surrounded by three layers of walls, each one sporting a different type of defense: barbed wire, electrification, and some sort of ultrasonic cannon that could fire in every direction, including straight down in case of tunnelers. The structure was lit with white and red lights, and I reflected as I stepped out of the back of the van, that those colors were a poor choice. It made it seem like the place had been drenched with blood.

I'd brought Villains in often enough to know what would happen next. So I wasn't surprised when a pair of black-garbed prison guards met me and my escort at the front gate. They looked bigger than I remembered. Maybe that was the effect of being on the other side. "We'll take it from here," the one in front said to the cops.

"That's not proper procedure," R. Flanders retorted. "We don't do the handoff until we get him inside, seated and prepped for intake, and sign off on the transfer."

"Procedure's changed."

"Oh yeah? Then why hasn't your supervisor sent the department a memo informing us of the new change?"

The guard scowled at her. "Hey, I don't make the rules, I just enforce them. And the rules state that no outside security is allowed into the facility. That includes cops, bodyguards, and private security contractors. It's not only you. You can still sign off on the transfer."

He handed over a tablet with the document already pulled up. I glanced at it as my escort took it and began to read. Yep, there was my name . . . my call sign . . . there was more, but after a moment R. Flanders's partner grabbed the tablet out of her hands and scrawled his name across the bottom of the touch screen. "There."

"Tom!"

"We've got better things to do than escort a *traitor* to prison, Rommie!" The look he shot my way almost froze me solid. A Mr. Fabulous supporter, then. At least I knew what the *R* stood for, now. "Our shift ended half an hour ago; don't you want to get home to your kids? Come on, hand him over."

The staring match between the two of them was quite a sight, but eventually Rommie folded. "Fine." She turned to the guard. "His advocate should be by soon. I hope you can be bothered to let *her* in the building."

"Sure, sure." He reached for me, then stopped when it became clear he'd have to either shove me from behind or try to grab my force field, thanks to my short sleeves. "Um . . ."

"I'll just walk beside you, how 'bout?"

"Yeah, that'll work." He chuckled nervously. "No funny business though."

"No funny business." I looked over at Rommie. "Thanks for the lift, Officer Flanders." Her partner was already hustling her away, although she glanced back more than once on her way to the van. I turned to the guards. "Lead on."

For all the weirdness outside, the next part was pretty standard. A new mug shot, fingerprinting (which, ha, nope), being issued a number that would be part of my identity here. After that, though, things got strange.

"Normally you'd be meeting with Dr. Steuben for your physical now," my chattier guard said. "But he was called into the city for a meeting, so that'll have to wait until tomorrow. Your paperwork says you're supposed to be in protective custody, so you'll get a cell to yourself. The doctor can reassess your needs when you meet in the morning."

Whatever that meant. I'd met Dr. Steuben a few times, and always thought he seemed a few colors short of the full rainbow.

He'd certainly managed to fuck up Edward in short order, but I was probably pretty safe.

Ten minutes later, barefoot and clad in an orange prison suit with the designation *A-10* stamped on my chest, I was led down a long hallway lined with metal doors, each with a small slot cut in it at about chest height. I could hear people shift behind them, see eyes appear as I walked by.

"No, no," one person muttered. "It's the end days; they're finally here. The apocalypse has come at last."

The guard banged his baton against that door. "None of that, Flix," but the guy was just hitting his stride.

"End days. End days! When the greatest in society are cast down from their mighty towers! The end days, my brothers and sisters, the end days are here!"

The guard sighed and tapped his earpiece as he unlocked the very last door in the hallway. "This is it," he said to me, and waited for me to step inside.

For a second, I considered refusing. If I got a little space and ran, I could bowl this guy over like he wasn't even there, smash through the door at the other end of the hall, and take off for the front gate. Concrete was tough, but with enough momentum, I was practically unstoppable. Ultrasonic cannons, electrification, every one of their defenses: I could run through all of it, run and find somewhere to hide, somewhere that wasn't the Abattoir, and then . . .

And then I'd be a fugitive, and my only option for help would be Edward and Raul, who didn't need that sort of shit storm right now. So I stepped into the cell, and the guard locked the door behind me. A minute later the lights were out, and I was alone in a six-by-eight-foot cell with a narrow bunk to sleep on, a toilet, and a sink. No catheter, though. Good thing I didn't have to pee right now.

"End days! End days!" Flix went on and on, alternating between a shout and a whisper, but no one else on the block seemed inclined to tell him to stop.

As lullabies go it wasn't a good one, but I was so tired I fell asleep anyway.

Dr. Steuben's lab was deep inside the prison—maybe beneath it, I couldn't quite tell, but given how deep the elevator was going, I wouldn't have been surprised. I remembered his old lab here; I had visited it during a promotional thing that GenCorp wanted to do, showing its Heroes in close connection to the security of the Abattoir. We weren't, of course; we hadn't been allowed anywhere near the place except during emergencies, like when Raul bombed his way into the facility last year to retrieve Edward.

The point was, I'd been shown into the original lab so promo shots could be taken, and it had been a ground-level place with lots of windows. This seemed like something out of a first-person shooter game. I almost expected the neon lights to start flickering at any moment, obscuring the zombies or aliens that would then jump out at me. The door at the end of the hall resembled the entrance to a vault, opening into a big room that was so familiarly geeky I felt a pang of homesickness.

"Mr. Haney!" Dr. Steuben met me at the threshold, a welcoming smile on his Santa Claus–like face. He had gold-rimmed half-moon spectacles and a thick head of hair despite his advancing age. His white lab coat covered khaki pants and a cardigan, and I hated him in that moment for being so obviously a scientist, but not *my* scientist. "Welcome to Abbott's, welcome, welcome! I must confess I never thought I'd get the chance to have you in my care. It's almost enough to give me faith in God, to have my wishes come true."

"Um—"

"But I'm babbling! You must be ready for a trip to the lavatory. Here, here." He handed me a catheter that I was actually able to feel. "The restroom is right through that door. Before you go, though—" he held up a tape measure "—may I measure your ankles?"

"I guess so."

"Lovely!" He measured quickly, then walked over toward a table. "Meet me here when you're finished, Mr. Haney."

If I prolonged things in the restroom, it was because I really needed to go, not because I was avoiding Dr. Steuben or anything. I disposed of the catheter in a hazardous waste bin on the wall—what kind of person kept a hazardous waste bin in their bathroom?—and went back into the main lab, where Dr. Steuben was hovering over what looked like a plush arm chair.

"Good, good! Do sit down."

I sat. The chair molded against my body, enveloping me around the middle a bit like a cocoon. It didn't touch me, but it wouldn't be easy to stand up. "What's this for?"

"Hmm? Oh, to hold you still while I attach these." He smiled amiably as he displayed a pair of thick, ring-like cuffs in each hand, keeping them as far apart as he could. "A precaution against your wonderful abilities, Mr. Haney; we are a *prison*, after all, not a rehabilitation facility. There is no deciding you want to leave halfway through your mandated stay." He leaned over and, before I could react, snapped the cuffs around my ankles.

And I *felt* them. They clamped down against my skin, which was disconcerting to say the least. Dr. Steuben must have felt me stiffen, because he tutted as he straightened up. "Mr. Haney, I am the man in charge of GenCorp's Hero clinic. Did you think I wouldn't have access to the materials needed to construct an appropriate restraint?"

"*You're* the doctor?" The mysterious doctor that I'd never even met before? I guess I knew why, now. He was too busy running the Abattoir to deal with the functional Heroes.

"I am indeed! And *these*," he reached down and patted the cuff around one ankle, "contain a pair of very powerful magnets. The closer your feet rest, the more you will have to resist to keep them from snapping together. Running will be out of the question if you want to avoid falling flat on your face, and given where you are going, that's certainly a behavior to shun. Do endeavor not to overtly display weakness, and you'll last much longer here. Now, as for your wrists—"

"I'm not going to be here that long." I don't know why I blurted it out like that, but in less than ten seconds of listening to this guy, I was more scared than I'd been when the mayor had threatened me at the police station. Maybe it was the way he said everything so matter-of-factly, like it was obvious that I would be here until I was all used up. "I'm just waiting for trial."

"Hmm, yes, you'll face trials indeed." Dr. Steuben sighed. "I don't anticipate having you for very long, but haste doesn't necessarily have to make waste of science, thank heavens. I've done more with less time, and you are a truly exceptional specimen for this sort of experiment.

Truly, I wish you to understand that. I haven't had someone like you at my disposal for decades."

"*What* experiment?"

He wagged a finger at me. "Ah-ah, Mr. Haney. I can't simply tell you, that would mar my results! Anticipation can result in false positives, and although in your case the results will be self-evident in due course, I'd rather not risk it."

"You're not allowed to—" *Experiment on me*, I was going to finish, but then, actually, he could. I knew that. Dr. Steuben had carte blanche from the city to experiment on his prisoners, as long as the process was neither cruel nor inhumane. Given what had happened with Edward, he was clearly using a loose definition of those words. "Does this experiment have to do with these cuffs?"

Was he going to give a set to every bruiser in the Abattoir and tell them to have a field day? Had he made something more insidious that someone might be able to use against me: a shank, a garrote, something small but subtle that I wouldn't see coming before it was too late?

"Not at all! No, no, the cuffs are merely to keep you safely contained," Dr. Steuben assured me. "I won't be giving anyone in the prison population the means to get through your force field, which would certainly destroy the chance for the experiment to come to proper fruition." He clasped a second set on my wrists, and even with them a few feet apart, I could feel the pull of the magnets. "There we are. Very nice. Is it a good fit? No chafing?"

"These are unnecessary," I said as calmly as I could manage, which wasn't as calm as I'd have liked. "I'm not going to run."

"Oh, my boy, I've heard those words far too often to give them any credence. But if it helps," he added brightly, "I do think you mean it more than many. Now!" He clapped his hands together. "The cuffs also contain handy monitors that will broadcast your vital statistics to my laboratory, most helpful, so I'll be able to check on you at a moment's notice. If you remove the cuffs, an alarm will sound on my personal computer. A self-destruct will also go into effect if they are removed, and they will explode five seconds later. Given that they are made of the only material that can penetrate your force field with its own, I would suggest that you consider the shrapnel implications of that, and not try to remove them. Besides, I have more pairs."

God, how long had he been preparing for my incarceration? "How many more pairs?"

"As many as it takes." He headed over to a stainless steel fridge and pulled out a familiar shake bottle. "Breakfast!" He actually held the straw up to my lips. "Finish this one here, and I will ensure you are given another tonight."

I was pissed off enough that I wanted to refuse, but I was pretty hungry too. As I sucked, he kept speaking.

"Do you like your quarters? They should suffice for the protective aspects of incarceration that your lawyer has requested. During the day, of course, you'll join the rest of the inmates in the central room of the penitentiary. I think you'll find them diverting."

I was going into the general population, hobbled by cuffs, the subject of an experiment I knew nothing about. *Fuck.* My stomach turned, and I stopped sipping.

"You didn't finish," Dr. Steuben chided me, then shook the bottle. "Close enough, I suppose, but I expect you to drink all of the next one. We don't want your baseline statistics to change any more than they must, for the sake of accuracy. Now, let me get a guard, and you can begin interacting with your peers. I'm sure it will be quite the experience."

Yeah, it probably would be. Especially with me shackled like I was. My top speed with the new cuffs on? About half of what the guards wanted me to walk at. The escort was impatient, and when they tried to get me to move faster, *snap!* My ankles clacked together, and I went down like a shot of tequila. It took the three of us almost a minute to pry my feet apart again, which was useful insofar as I figured out that the last thing I wanted was to get put into a position where this happened again. Despite what Dr. Freaky had said about the cuffs not being part of his experiment on me, I didn't trust that he couldn't be bribed to give away bits and pieces of the material just to see what people would try to do with it.

Eventually they released me into the central room of the two-story prison, where inmates ate meals and congregated when they weren't required to be elsewhere. I might not know what my future held, but as soon as the heavy steel door shut behind me, I knew what my present was going to consist of: a big fucking fight.

"Freight Train?" The first person to say my name was a small-time Villain, Jimmy the Edge. "You gotta be kiddin' me. Dey're puttin' front-page mooks like you in here now?" He snickered and snapped his sharp teeth in my direction. Had Jimmy the Edge become a crook because he'd been shunned due to his piranha-like mouth? Was it a deliberate surgery, like the Villain Corvid had been infamous for, to build his reputation in Panopolis's underworld? Nobody knew for sure.

"Lookit dis guy, Rhino," Jimmy went on, casting his beady eyes worshipfully up at the hulking creature sitting at the table behind him. "Freight Train was so big an' tough, an' now he's in here wit' us."

"How the mighty have fallen," the Sapphire Sultana added. I barely recognized her without her sparkly costume. She was another thief, a much better one than Jimmy, but not good enough in the end. I'd put her here. I'd put Jimmy here. The guy they were kowtowing to, though . . .

I hadn't had anything to do with Rhino. He'd been put inside years ago by Morpho Girl, one of her last big collars before her breakdown. He was the only prisoner to escape without outside assistance since then, by using another prisoner as a human shield to help him hop the barbed wire fence back when prisoners were allowed to be outside. Returning him had taken half a dozen Heroes.

The second time he'd escaped, he'd snuck out with dozens of other high-profile Villains in the aftermath of Raul's revenge. Rhino'd been returned shortly thereafter, courtesy of Mastermind; he'd actually walked up to the front gate and turned himself in, dazed and compliant.

"Freight Train." Rhino eyed me up and down, and I could almost hear the sound of everybody's eyes following him as he rose to his huge, leathery gray feet. His nose was practically flat from being broken so much over the years, and his face was covered in dozens of tiny scars. This guy was a brawler, and I— Shit, I wasn't going to be able to do much if I couldn't get up momentum.

"Rhino." I said it as calmly as I could, but didn't seem to fool anybody from the way his crew started to laugh.

"Big Hero, thrown down to Hell." His hands clenched almost spasmodically. "You look *slow*, boy."

"Looks aren't everything."

"Sometimes they are." He came over and hunkered down so he could stare me in the eyes. "Sometimes they're everything. Let's see how far you've fallen." Before I could dodge, Rhino ducked to grab my left foot, hoisted me into the air, and slammed me against the door I'd just come through. My force field left a crumple in the metal, and I had to fight to keep my limbs starfished while being held upside down by this asshole.

"Hah!" Rhino laughed and swung me again. The dent I left this time was bigger. I couldn't free myself—he had his hand clamped firmly over my cuff, which meant he probably wasn't as bothered by the buzz of my force field as he should be. "From a freight train to a bowling ball!" With the next swing, he actually did let me go: he chucked me right down the middle of the mess hall. I sent tables and chairs and a few Villains flying as I careened through the crowd, and it was all I could do not to hobble myself. I felt dizzy, and I could hear Rhino heading my way, his heavy feet kicking debris aside to the tune of dozens of jeering voices.

I might not have the advantages I was used to, but I'd learned to be good at making what I did have work. There were lots of ways to win a fight, and sometimes the best way was to take a weakness and turn it into a strength. Rhino was strong, but he wasn't as strong as Zane. He might not even be as strong as me and two other guys. That would be nice.

I got to my feet just as he reached me. He opened his mouth to start monologuing—and wow, it *was* a thing; did I do that too? Anyway, fucking obnoxious habit, but useful because it gave me time to leap forward, right between his arms, and clasp my hands behind his neck. And then I locked the magnets together in front of his throat with a *click*.

My grip was tight, but not that tight. If he'd thought of it, Rhino could have thrashed until he got his head out, and we would have been back at square one, only my wrists would still have been bound together. But Rhino didn't think of that—he was a brawler, not a tactician. Instead he wrapped his massive hands around my waist and pulled.

He tugged until the exertion made his gray skin go pink. My hands seemed pretty solid, but I didn't want to wait for something else to go wrong, so as soon as the distance seemed right, I planted one foot on Rhino's gut and swung the other one as hard as I could straight down into his crotch. Funny thing: in all the people with super strength I'd ever tangled with, none of them had been any stronger where it counted.

Rhino groaned and dropped my middle in favor of grabbing for my legs, but he was slower now, and I had time to swing myself around to behind him. That put my hands in a dangerous position; with enough time, he'd eventually be able to pry them apart. But they were also tight against his throat now. I hiked my knees up into the small of Rhino's back, braced them there as securely as I could, and heaved away with my upper body.

Rhino's head tipped up, and he made an angry, choking sound and slapped backward with his hands for a few seconds before he figured out he wouldn't be able to grab me. Then he went after the cuffs, but I could feel him weakening. I'd been choked unconscious a few times before I got my force field, once on the playground, once by a guy robbing a liquor store. It had taken about thirty seconds with me each time, though I hadn't had the thick skin that Rhino did. I held, and held, and his grip on me got weaker and weaker. His whole body jerking, Rhino went after my cuffs with one final squeeze. I felt my right one start to bend, and I knew it wouldn't last much longer.

And then Rhino collapsed, tumbling both of us headfirst onto the ground. He hit hard, bouncing off the edge of a table before we rolled to the side. In my first lucky break since I got to this place, the impact of hitting the table forced my cuffs apart. I stood up carefully, straddle-legged, keeping my arms firmly away from each other.

"Anybody else wanna try making me their bitch?" I asked breathlessly. It wasn't the best line, but I was tired, and angry, and the more of an asshole I seemed, the more these people would take me seriously.

"Are you laying claim?" the Sultana snapped.

"Claim to what?"

"Rhino's place, moron."

Oh, jeez. Prison hierarchy. "Nope. I just want to be left alone."

"*Good.*" She darted across the empty space and pulled a shiv from the front of her shirt faster than I could blink. I staggered back as she rammed the thin, sharp blade right into Rhino's open mouth, stabbing deep. Rhino jerked awake, but he was still out of it, and now he was choking on his own blood.

I should do something. I was supposed to protect the people that needed it, even when they'd just tried to hand me my head. Jimmy jumped on Sultana before I could get there, though, sinking his sharp teeth into the back of her neck and shaking her. She shrieked and turned the blade on him, and from there, well . . . people started picking sides.

I'd been in riots before, but I'd never been in a *prison* riot before. And I'd certainly never been in one where a bunch of Villains whose powers had been curtailed went after each other with such abandon. I think I saw somebody's hand go flying past my face—just their hand, nothing attached to it—before the guards gassed the place. A minute later, I was the only one standing when the guards waded into the unconscious fray, gas masks firmly in place, and started kicking people apart and cuffing their hands behind their backs.

"The hell, Freight Train?" one of them demanded of me. It was the guy who'd met me at the gate last night. "First you bring us picketers, now you're inciting riots?"

The latter wasn't strictly correct, and as for the other half . . . "What picketers?"

"The ones making it hell to move anything in or out of this place," he replied. "What, our lives aren't hard enough already looking after you assholes?"

"Sorry." Not that I could do anything about it, but I was. The guard flipped his middle finger at me before going back to cuffing prisoners.

I spent the rest of the day back in my cell. A guard brought me a shake and another catheter, and waited around for me to use both and give them back before he'd leave. A few hours later—I guessed it was a few hours, I wasn't that good at telling time when there was nothing around to tell the hour with—the lights in the cell block dimmed, and

I figured it was time for bed. Not that there was any way I was falling asleep.

It wasn't the fight. I was used to fighting, as shitty as this situation had been. I could handle the adrenaline dump, the physicality of it, even the aftermath, where there had been so much violence so quickly.

Part of it was the bunk. Last night I'd been able to squeeze myself onto it, but now that I needed to keep my hands and feet apart, there was no way I'd be able to lay there. I ended up flat on the floor instead, my limbs as spread apart as I could manage them in the tight confines of the cell.

The other part of it was I was *intensely* aware of my wrists and ankles. The cuffs weren't too tight, Dr. Steuben had been okay about that, but I wasn't used to feeling something against my skin like this. As soon as I even thought about the possibility that they might itch, suddenly it seemed like that was all they did. They itched like *burning*, and I spent a few futile minutes trying to dig my fingers under the edges and soothe my wrists.

It didn't work. I ended up staring at the ceiling, frustrated and angry and unable to stop flexing my hands and feet. I'd rub my skin raw on the edges of the cuffs if I didn't quit it, but I just couldn't. They felt so wrong, invasive in a way even the catheter didn't. At least that I could put in myself. These had been put *on* me, no choice, no nothing.

After everything that had happened in one single day at this place, I felt guiltier than ever about the people I'd stuck here. I'd seen them attack each other during that riot with more ferocity than most of them had shown me on the outside, and yet they had so much less to gain here. Was it because they'd been feeling this way for so much longer? Like they had an itch they couldn't scratch, a sore that got worse and worse every day until there was nothing to do to appease it but claw and rend?

Plenty of these Villains were murderers. Lots of them had hurt people, and all of them had used their powers to enrich themselves at the expense of the city at large. I'd never thought I'd have anything in common with them. I'd never thought I'd have any reason to commiserate with them.

Looked like I'd been wrong.

CHAPTER TWELVE

How have things changed so fast with regard to Freight Train? What happened to the protests, the signs, the cries of outrage and anger? What happened to the media coverage? What's the status of the investigation into Mr. Fabulous's death? What's happening with this case? Do you know?

Probably not, because it's only been a few days since Freight Train was arrested, but now no one *is talking about it in the media. Not the picketers who were cleared out last night, or the reporters who are turned back at the Abattoir's gate, not the politicians whose schedules have suddenly filled up with time-wasting minutia, not the police who refuse to comment over and over and over again. There's no news, and in this case, no news can't be good news, folks.*

And you know what? I don't accept silence as a response.

When I woke up the next morning after maybe two hours of sleep, the first thing I saw once I'd rolled the kinks out of my neck was a mouse. I thought I might be dreaming: it was the kind of stereotypically cute mouse that you'd expect to see in a dream. It was tiny, and sitting less than a foot from my head.

"Hey, little guy," I murmured.

The mouse cocked its head, twitched its big round ears, and then without any further warning leaped right at me. I *may* have shouted a bit as I backpedaled into a sitting position against the wall. The mouse kept coming though, smacking itself into my force field again and again as it gnashed its teeth.

"What the *fuck*?"

"That's enough, my friend," someone cooed. The mouse stopped its tiny, ferocious attack, turned, and ran straight up my door, squeezing its body through the slot and vanishing into the hall. "That's enough. Good, yes, come back to me, come back. Rest up for next time."

It couldn't be. No, wait, it *had* to be. "Zena?"

"He knows my real name! Isn't that special? Special boy, this one, a very special boy. You're the best of the murdering bastards, for sure."

"What are you talking about?"

"I'm talking," her voice went from sweet to growly in the space of a single syllable, "about my *friends*! All of my friends, my precious friends, and you burned them to death!"

The rats. Riiight. "I didn't burn your friends, Zena. That was Firebolt."

"But did you stop her? No! You sat back and watched as she destroyed everyone I loved."

"You set them to attack people."

"Only so that they could be free!"

Okay, there was an inherent problem with arguing with a delusional person. It didn't matter how I protested; nothing was going to change her mind. So I changed tactics. "I'm sorry that they died. I never intended it."

"Doesn't matter what you intended, only matters what you did."

"I can see why you'd think that," I said cautiously. "But why bother holding on to a grudge now? Your mouse can't get through my force field. It can't hurt me."

Zena laughed. "Oh, Freight Train. It doesn't have to touch you to hurt you. You haven't been imprisoned before. Give it time. Time and repetition, over and over and over, and if you kill this one I'll send another, and another, and another, until you're surrounded by mice and have nowhere to go to escape them. Nowhere but deep inside, with nothing but your own agony to look at, your loneliness, your failure." She sighed. "It will be beautiful."

Holy shit. That was disturbing to hear first thing in the morning. Fortunately our conversation ended then, as the guards came and took me back down to Dr. Steuben's lab. It managed to be even creepier today than it had been yesterday: there was a hand—presumably the one someone lost yesterday—in a glowing container on a countertop, its stump attached to a series of tubes that made the fingers move in sync. It looked like it was playing the piano currently.

"Mr. Haney! Excellent, come, sit, sit." He ushered me back over to the recliner, helping me keep my feet when I stumbled. "You seem distracted." He followed the line of my sight. "Ah! A little souvenir, kept from the ravages of decay by a stasis field of my own invention. I told the man who lost it that if he's very good, I might give it back to him once I've taught it to play Mozart. Now." He folded his hands. "I understand you were the cause of yesterday's troubles?"

As in the fight that started an enormous riot? "You could say that."

"Indeed, so I have. It was quite interesting, sociologically speaking. I have video of it, of course. It will make for some good entertainment times as I review it. Perhaps I'll fix myself some popcorn." He chuckled to himself as he put on gloves and grabbed a needle attached to an empty syringe. "But your cuff was damaged. Not enough to set off the alarm, but I wouldn't want to tempt you, so I'll fix that while you're here. Please stay still now."

He carefully drew my blood, tutting at the state of my wrists. They were bright red around the cuffs, and crusty with blood in a few places. "Mr. Haney, you need to learn self-control! We can't have you damaged before time. If you continue to fight your restraints, I'll be forced to chemically subdue you."

Oh, hell no. "I'll be more careful."

"Good, good. We must be cautious over your health, yes? I want nothing to interfere with the experiment." He put some of the blood into a test tube, which he then inserted into a machine I didn't recognize. It started to whirr as he set the syringe aside and handed me a shake. "Breakfast." He watched me drink with a paternal smile. "Very good. Ari would be so pleased with you."

I choked on my next sip. "Ari?" I gasped. Ari was in on this? "What do you mean?"

"Oh, never fear, never fear," Dr. Steuben assured me. "Ari Mansourian has no idea what is happening within these walls. He would like to, I've no doubt; he's already petitioned to be allowed to see you under the guise of giving medical care. Fortunately I, as the head of GenCorp's clinic, have the authority to refuse his petitions."

My relief at hearing that Ari was trying to see me, that he hadn't been working with Dr. Steuben this whole time, was almost enough to make me black out. Ari hadn't lied to me. Dr. Steuben was just a fucker.

"I also have access to *all* of his research," the doctor went on. "He's done some wonderful work with you, and his latest attempts at cracking the formula of your force field are positively inspiring! He is quite close to an answer. It's a shame I can't share my own knowledge with him, but . . ." He shrugged. "It's better he doesn't know who I am. I wouldn't want to drive him to do something rash. Besides, I'm curious to see what he comes up with next. He always showed excellent initiative as a student."

Before this, I'd thought "mind-boggling" was just a turn of phrase, but now I actually felt my stupid thoughts trip over themselves. I was almost too stunned to speak. "You know him?"

"Oh, I've been following his career with great interest, Mr. Haney. Great interest. So many wonderful publications. I believe that in the realm of deconstructing superpowers, he may be even more accomplished than I!" Dr. Steuben chuckled. "But no one, I think, is more accomplished in their creation. It's a shame that so much of my research must remain classified, including all that pertains to you. The regrettable price of my situation, I fear."

"Why are you telling me this?" I asked, because when a Villain started to monologue, it meant one of two things: either they were trying to distract you, or they were supremely confident. I wasn't getting a distracted vibe from the doctor.

"Who else can I tell? Only the subjects of my experiments can truly empathize with what I'm striving to accomplish. You will understand once my work comes to fruition. Possibly not for long," he added regretfully, "as it will almost certainly necessitate your death."

"I want to see my lawyer." The words slipped out before I could stop them. "I want to see her *now*. You can't keep her from visiting me."

Dr. Steuben nodded. "True. Fortunately, Ms. Delavigne again became indisposed after her visit to you downtown. She is back in hospital, and unlikely to leave anytime soon. The simple reality of the situation is that legally, we are only obligated to allow her in to see you. Not a proxy, not a representative: *her*, and only her. We have you on record as preferring it that way. Or did you think that refusing to speak to anyone but your lawyer and Dr. Mansourian when you were in holding wouldn't have consequences?

"In fact," he continued brightly, "we have been given permission to turn away any and all visitors to the prison or its grounds during your settling-in period, and to set up a blockade and checkpoint a mile down the road. No more picketers. The only people who are getting within viewing distance of this place are the staff. That is the nature of Abbott's status in Panopolis, and given that you started a riot yesterday, our latitude with regards to your treatment has only increased."

Wait, no. "I didn't start that riot."

"You were the catalyst of it. I believe anyone would agree that it would not have occurred without you." The machine dinged, and the doctor leaned over the tablet attached to it. "Ah! Right on schedule. We have an exciting week ahead of us, Freight Train."

"You can't kill me," I said, desperate now. "You can't just kill me; there are people who care about what happens in here. I'm not just another prisoner!"

"Oh, Mr. Haney." Dr. Steuben shook his head. "Everyone who comes here believes that at first. They think that they're important, that they have too many friends or too much notoriety. But Abbott's Penitentiary has disposed of scores of inmates over the years. There is always a way, and I can always find it. No one can stop me in my pursuit of knowledge. *No one.*"

He looked at me intently. "Do you have friends, fans, interest? Oh yes, yes, you do. But you are less powerful than your reputation would suggest, and even the inmates know it. You can be hurt. You can be damaged. You can be *killed.* And accidents do happen inside these walls. Investigations, on the other hand? Those will never happen while I am in charge here. The mayor, the police commissioner, the board of GenCorp—they answer to *me.* And I only answer to my calling.

"Surrender yourself to the inevitable, Mr. Haney. You are here for as long as I want you to be here. If you see your lawyer, if she recovers in time, it will be because I am interested in analyzing your mental distress, not because she will be able to free you."

He smiled then. "But I know you don't believe that, which is why I don't think you need a suicide watch! Hold on to your hope and your fire, it will make life far more exciting for both of us. Now." He released me from the chair and handed me a catheter. "Please feel free to use the restroom before you go about your business."

The only thing I could say about the rest of my day was that I was left alone for most of it, which was good. I felt numb. I wanted to be hopeful. I wanted to be the stupid optimist that I was used to being, but the fact that Dr. Steuben had been so frank with me led me to one undeniable conclusion: I wasn't gonna get out of this alive.

Nobody except for Edward had ever gotten out of the Abattoir and stayed out, apart from the people who'd fled in the aftermath of Raul's break-in, then sworn their allegiance to the new order of Villains in the Red Zone. After being here for only a couple of days, I could see why the escapees weren't the ones who were reoffending now. Nobody who'd been in here and managed to escape would risk getting sent back.

I worried about Ianthe and I worried about Ari, and it was a nice break from worrying about myself. That was ever-present, a nagging pressure in the corner of my brain that threatened to swoop in and run off with my thoughts if I didn't carefully control it. I managed to, for the most part. One day turned into two turned into a whole week, and they all went the same: morning meetings with Dr. Steuben, who gleefully updated me on Ianthe's health and Ari's persistent petitions to enter, all of which were shot down. Blood draws and a shake, then off to the main floor of the prison, where I was pointedly ignored by the leaders of the new cliques. Rhino hadn't survived Sultana's power play, but no one else had quite risen to the top. The hierarchy was fractured, and fights played out daily, but a lot of them had been restrained like me, their powers curtailed in some way. There was no more major damage done, and no one ever approached me for support, or to attack.

Every night Zena sent a mouse into my room. I got pretty used to ignoring them, even when they tried to get through the force field. They were never gonna make it, and I could ignore them pretty well. On the seventh night of my stay, I fell asleep with my wrists aching and my stomach churning and my mind unsettled.

I woke up the next morning and saw a mouse sitting on my chest.

"*Fuck!*" I shot upright and sent the critter tumbling off my body and onto the floor. Instead of running at me, though, it ran up the wall and through the door almost before I could blink. Zena started to laugh.

"Something wrong? Did my friend frighten you?"

"N-no," I stammered. Oh shit, the floor was cold. I could feel the temperature of the *floor*. I wasn't completely without my force field; my clothes still weren't touching me where I wasn't sitting on them, too light to penetrate it maybe, but I shouldn't be feeling *anything*. What had happened?

The experiment. This had to be what Dr. Steuben had been testing me for. How had he managed it, though? Nothing had changed here, and he'd only taken blood, not injected me with something new. What was different now?

My heart was beating so hard in my chest it might dent the inside of my rib cage, and my vision was blurry. I bent over and pressed my head against my knees, and now I could feel the cloth of my jumpsuit. It was rougher than I'd expected.

"Hey!" A guard banged on the door. "You sick?"

"No." I had to pretend to be okay. People would think I had my force field as long as I pretended it was still there. As long as I was careful, I'd get through this. Ianthe would come as soon as she was better, and I could tell her what was happening to me, and she could . . .

Do what?

Nothing, said a voice that sounded suspiciously like Dr. Steuben's. *There's nothing she can do. You're here, and you're going to spend the rest of your very short life here. It's just a question of who figures out your secret first.*

Fuck that voice. I wasn't going to make it any easier on my enemies than I had to. "I'm fine," I said, raising my voice.

"Doctor wants to see you anyway. Something about vital signs." The guard opened the door and motioned at me with his baton. "Come on, then." He didn't try to touch me; good thing too, since now he might be able to if he gripped hard enough. I shuffled out, careful to keep my feet and hands at the proper distance apart, and followed him down the hall.

"End days!" Flix shouted from his cell the moment he saw me. "The end days are here!"

I was uncomfortably certain that he was right.

Dr. Steuben was even more pleased than usual to see me that morning. "Seven days exactly! Not that I didn't trust my calculations, but this is the first time we've been able to take you all the way from full power to the beginning of true diminishment. The radioactive compound in your beverages has a precise half-life, but there are always challenges when one is experimenting in the flesh, so to speak."

"The shakes." *Of course.* Oh my god, of course. The sound of my own blood rushing through my ears almost drowned out the rest of Dr. Steuben's explanation.

"Yes, the shakes. Made by GenCorp, infused with the same ingredients that gave you your marvelous properties to begin with. We have been maintaining your force field ever since you were first doused in Mr. Ward's brilliant concoction."

He patted my hand where I sat bound in the chair. His skin was too warm; it felt like a brand. Not the touch I wanted, but why should he care about that? My body thrummed with impotent energy, and I had to bite the inside of my cheek to maintain any sort of control over my mouth. If I opened it, I might scream, or worse, beg for this sadist to save me.

"Don't take that to mean that you aren't special, though," Dr. Steuben assured me. "You *are* special, regardless of the fact that we can take your power away. I tried to re-create the circumstances of your creation a dozen times, and no one else's body could handle the systemic changes required to generate and maintain a force field. Mostly it stopped their hearts."

"Great," I managed to grit out between clenched teeth.

"Yes," he sighed. "It is. I can't wait to do a proper dissection!"

Oh . . . boy. The temptation to surrender the last of my dignity and start begging and pleading for my life was so strong it made me tremble. I didn't quite break, but it was a close call.

"But!" Dr. Steuben finished taking blood from me and handed over a shake. I took it with numb hands but didn't drink. "Your lawyer has finally recovered enough to request a meeting with you. If you get through today unscathed, I will allow her to see you tomorrow morning. A gift to reward your efforts."

"And what then?" I asked. "You'll kill me if I tell her what's really going on in here?"

"Oh no, Mr. Haney." Dr. Steuben shook his head. "I'll have *her* killed. She's fragile these days, in and out of the hospital, barely able to keep her rapid mutations under control. It wouldn't be terribly unexpected for her to pass on suddenly."

"I don't understand." This was the part that got to me the most. "I don't see how you can get away with all of this. I just— Why do they let you do these things? It's so illegal. It's so *wrong*." Somebody had to know what he was, what he did—why hadn't they put a stop to it?

Dr. Steuben sat back and looked at me thoughtfully. "I learned at an early age, Mr. Haney, that the primary driving mechanism of humanity is self-interest. With enough power over the self-interests of those in nominal control, you can get away with almost anything. The Nazis managed it, and they would have continued to do so perhaps even into the present had they not overstepped with their wars. The Russians were experts, until they underestimated their greatest asset's determination to die. I warned the KGB, but my warnings were dismissed." He shrugged tiredly. "So much for my one attempt to preserve life.

"I learned then that it wasn't enough to own the science; I had to control the politicians as well. When I immigrated to this country, Panopolis was ripe for a guiding hand. I ensured that that hand would be mine. It took time, but it was worth it. There's no one to challenge me here now, and I plan to keep it that way."

No, there had to be a light at the end of the tunnel. There had to be a chance for me in there somewhere. "What about Edward? You didn't plan on him."

Dr. Steuben's contemplative expression drained away, to be replaced by coldness. "Drink quickly if you're going to, Mr. Haney. I'm done with you for today."

You know that feeling you get sometimes, a prickle across the back of your neck like someone is watching you? That was the feeling I got the instant I stepped into the central room of the Abattoir. Not just that I was being watched, because people invariably glanced my way when I joined the crowd in the mornings. It felt more like I was being evaluated this time, like just by looking, somebody was gonna be able to tell that my force field was down. It didn't work that way, but it would be so easy for me to slip up. All I had to do was brush up against someone, or let them bump into me, and my secret would be out. I couldn't have that, not now. Not like this. Hobbled as I was, I wouldn't be able to defend myself for long.

I went to my habitual spot along the wall—it was crazy to think that I'd already laid claim to a "spot" like I was a lifer, but I guess everybody here was a lifer—and settled in to wait out the day. Most inmates were careful to give each other space as they passed, but they kept at double the normal distance for me. Nobody talked to me either, and that was how I wanted it. If I could make it through today, then I could make it through tomorrow. I could do it.

Sultana was the only one who wasn't circumspect about her stare. She'd cut Jimmy the Edge's throat shortly after he attacked her, but apparently committing two murders wasn't enough to warrant solitary confinement. Killing Rhino had made her his de facto heir, and I didn't like the way she was looking at me.

I was getting better at telling the time in here. With ten minutes to go before we were sent back to our bunks, Sultana approached me, stopping two feet away and mimicking my spread-legged stance. "You've been quiet today."

"Like every day."

"More quiet than usual. You usually find better things to stare at than your feet."

I didn't reply, and her gaze sharpened. "You seem nervous, Freight Train. Bad news from the good doctor?"

I snorted. "Does he ever hand out good news?"

"Oh, I don't know." She smiled beatifically. "Getting his confirmation that Rhino wouldn't be back was pretty good news, don't you think?"

"He wasn't an insurmountable problem."

"Not for you, maybe. For the rest of us? Well . . . my people are grateful you took care of him, but that gratitude only goes so far. What do you want out of this place, Hero?"

"I want to leave it."

"But you don't get to leave it." She tossed her long, dark braid over her shoulder—she almost certainly wore it that way as a red herring.

Grab me, her hair whispered. *Grab and pull, I'm the perfect handhold.* There were probably razor blades in it. "So you have to live with it instead. What would make that easiest on you?"

"What's your proposition?" I countered. There were less than five minutes before the siren sounded and I'd be escorted out of here.

"I'm big enough to admit that I could use a little help subduing the worst of the worst. They're having a hard time handling change," she said with a laugh. "You come out publically on my side, and that'll go a long way toward convincing them to do the same."

"I'm no good for fighting, not with these cuffs on."

"Maybe not, but you—" Sultana glanced down, and her breath caught in her throat, her eyes going wide. I followed her gaze and finally saw what I should have noticed before this.

A mouse. There was a mouse sitting on my foot. *Oh, fuck.*

I shook it off with a massive shudder, and immediately stepped away from Sultana, who looked at me with a slowly dawning smile. One of her hands twitched toward her shirt, undoubtedly reaching for her shiv. I brought my hands up into a defensive position, fighting the pull of the magnets even as I realized that there was no way I'd be able to stop her for more than a second. This was it. This was—

The short, barking siren suddenly blared through the prison. Sultana glanced around, and then slowly relaxed.

"Tomorrow will be better anyway," she muttered. "More people to watch when I take you down. Killing you will be even better than recruiting you." She seemed gleeful at the prospect, backing away from me. *Sleep well,* she mouthed before heading to her own cell.

I don't know how I forced my legs to return me to the solitary ward. Autopilot, I guess. I was done. I was gonna die at the hands of a second-tier Villain who'd figured me out because of a fucking *mouse.* Goddamn Zena anyway, I had no idea how she got that little fucker to follow me all the way from my cell. Regardless, I was screwed.

"Did my friend find you?" she asked once the guard was gone. "He says he did. Secret's out, hmm?"

"Fuck off!"

"Aww, poor Freight Train. Does it hurt, getting a taste of your own medicine? Staring down your own mortality?"

I didn't say anything, just stuffed my blanket in the slot in my door and crammed my pillow against the crack at the base of it.

I didn't *think* a mouse could get through there, but I wasn't going to take any chances. One more rodent and I'd lose whatever was left of my mind.

I hadn't even lasted one day without my force field. Even now, my clothes were settling down on my limbs as if the last of my superpower had dissipated, leaving me just . . . me. Craig Haney, the least special person in any room, average in all ways except for a freakish ability to survive a radioactive contamination. And now that ability didn't matter, because I wasn't going to get my force field back. Dr. Steuben wasn't going to change his mind and start giving me normal shakes. He was going to let me die and study my remains, and Memaw probably wouldn't even get my body to bury. I'd never be able to spend another night with Ari figuring out how to touch each other, and I couldn't tell Ianthe anything or I'd be signing her death certificate too. I was dead. So dead.

I could have killed myself. My room was pretty bare, but I had the sheet and something to tie it to, and now that my skin wasn't inviolable, well . . . hanging wasn't pretty, but it wasn't the worst way to go. But I wanted to see Ianthe, even if I couldn't tell her anything. I wanted to see a friend, *any* friend, one last time. I didn't expect a miracle, but maybe it wouldn't hurt so much going to my death tomorrow if I got to see someone I gave a damn about first. Or maybe I was just scared, too scared to kill myself. It didn't matter. It wasn't going to happen.

I didn't sleep a wink all night, fruitlessly pacing the length of my cell. The next morning, when I took my blanket out of the slot, it was chewed full of holes. Well, at least I'd been spared the company of Zena's pets on my last night on Earth. That was a bright spot. And pissing in the toilet for the first time in seven years without having to use a catheter—that was pretty awesome too.

The guard didn't bother to take me to Dr. Steuben that morning. Instead we headed back toward the entrance, where there was a single room set aside for visitors. He opened the door and pointed me toward the far chair. "Sit."

I sat, and the door closed. There was a camera in the corner, and I gave it the finger. My nervous feet tapped away, and I barely remembered to keep my hands from twining before they were close enough to lock together. This was it: the last time I'd see a friendly face. I didn't want to fuck myself over by needing the guards to help unstick me, thus using up my time with Ianthe.

After a few more minutes that might as well have been hours, the door opened again. Ianthe rolled herself in, pausing to pat the guard holding the door for her on the arm as she murmured, "Thank you."

There was no Viv to help her this time; I guessed she hadn't been cleared to come inside. The door shut behind Ianthe, and as she rolled to a stop I almost did a double take. "Ianthe? I thought you'd been in the hospital." She didn't seem like she'd been sick. In fact, this was the healthiest I'd seen her in ages: her skin rosy and her eyes bright. She winked at me.

"It looks like I recovered in the nick of time." She gave me a once-over. "Ari told me today was the last day we'd be able to pull this off; I'm glad the timing worked out so well."

My heart leaped. "You've talked to Ari? How is he?" Then my brain caught up. "Pull what off?"

"Your daring escape, of course!" She tapped the face of the watch she was wearing. "We've got five minutes before they start destroying the outer defenses, so we've got to hustle." A second later, Ianthe was up and out of the wheelchair, pulling it expertly apart.

"You— That—" *Wait.* "You're not really Ianthe, are you?"

When she met my eyes again, it was Viv's face staring back at me. "Now you're getting it, Freight Train. She's safe at home, in bed."

"You . . . We're . . ." I wasn't doing a good job of being coherent today. "We're being recorded," I said at last, pointing at the camera.

"The chair emits a low-level disruption field. It should blur the image enough that we'll have time to get underway without alarming too many people." The frame of the wheelchair was being reconnected into a rectangle, and the seat unfolded and plugged into it like some sort of battery. "Not that we won't attract plenty of attention holding on to this, but if you take one end and I take the other, I think we can make it look official."

There were too many questions I wanted to ask, so I narrowed my list down to the ones that were immediately applicable. "Official how? You're not supposed to be here, and nobody will believe you're Ianthe at this point."

"True." A few heartbeats later and Viv had vanished, her sleek suit giving way to the black uniform of one of the guards. She grew about seven inches too, and bulked up as well. "And now I'm your man on the inside," Viv—Ianthe—*whoever* it was announced with a grin.

There was only one person I knew of who could do this kind of shifting. "Morpho Girl?"

"Close, but no cigar. Let's stick with Viv, huh?" He popped one of the handles off the new contraption and placed it on the table. "This'll keep the disruption field up in here. There's another attached to our gear that will cover us on our way out. And *now* for you." He came around the table and looked me over. "Anything I should know about that might keep you from making a break for it with me?"

"My cuffs are magnetized. They'll stick together hard if I don't go slowly and carefully."

"That's fine; we can just break them off—"

I shook my head. "They've got an alarm that will go straight to Dr. Steuben if they're broken. And, um, it makes them explode too."

To her—his—credit, Viv just nodded. "Definitely something we want to avoid. Our ride's waiting with a few extra fail-safes beyond the gate. We brought a reporter too. She might curb Dr. Steuben's worst impulses."

"Jean?"

"Yeah. We promised her the story of a lifetime if she followed us to the Abattoir." Viv's grin came back. "She already made Mastermind sign off on an interview. Come on, let's get going."

"Hey, Viv?"

"Yeah?"

I stood up and took his hand. "Thank you."

He looked from my hand back up to my face, eyes widening. "Holy shit, Ari was right. Your force field is gone. No wonder he said it *had* to be today; he was ready to haul Ianthe out of the house if necessary. Raul wanted to wait, said you'd be under less scrutiny in a few weeks. I think Ari might have jumped him if Edward hadn't stepped in."

Ari must have worked out what GenCorp was putting in my food. I was so glad I'd given him that damn formula. "Ari's a smart guy."

"Yeah. Yeah, he is." Viv squeezed my hand, then turned and grabbed half of the frame. "Ready to get out of here?"

I shuffled over and picked up the other half. Damn, this thing was heavy. "Yeah."

The hallway we entered was empty, and we made it all the way to the small entrance hall of the prison before we were challenged. "Hey, Rodriguez!" It was the burly guard from my first day here. "You're not cleared to take that prisoner out of here."

"He's on work detail," Viv/Rodriguez called over as we staggered along.

The guard puffed his chest up. "I happen to *know* that this prisoner isn't on work detail. Only low-level prisoners get pulled for work detail, not Tens." He gestured to the number on my chest. If only he knew how far I'd fallen. I was more like a Zero now.

"Sir, I— Hang on," Viv said irritably, setting down his half of the frame. "Lean that against the wall," he snapped at me, adding under his breath, "Make it *flush*, we've got less than a minute," before turning to face the guard. "Sir, I think there's been a mix-up."

I listened to them argue with half an ear and a pounding heart as I leaned the frame against the wall, then pushed it so that was completely upright. The frame seemed to seal to the wall with a *squish*, and the bottom of the seat-battery blinked red for a moment, slowly shifting to orange.

"Let me see the work order!"

"It's in my locker in the break room. C'mon, man," Viv/Rodriguez whined. "Lemme finish this, and then I'll go get it for you." The light was blinking yellow now.

"Not good enough. I'm going to write you up on—"

All of a sudden the lights in the front hall went out. At the same time, metal panels slammed down over the door in the distance, and in the entrances to the other halls.

"Power's down," the guard said, sounding nervous. He picked up his radio. "Hansen, what's the status outside?"

"Looks like a blown transformer, sir."

"Nothing major, then," the guard sighed. "The backup generator's already come on in the doc's office. Once it reaches full power the gates will lift again."

"No, sir, I mean the transformer has really been *blown*, sir. Like, it's so blown I can't even see the power line it was connected to anymore."

"But that won't stop the backup generator," Viv/Rodriguez said helpfully. "Which is why my friend and I can't afford to wait, so if you'll pardon me—" He swung his wrist up, pressed a button, and a familiar white balloon burst violently into existence. It hit the guard in the stomach and hurled him into the nearest wall. He collapsed in a heap.

"Airbag watch!" Viv said gleefully. "Ari has the best ideas, huh? Is that light green yet?" Viv stole the guard's radio. "Because we need to get past the electrified fence before the backup generator starts working, and that means we have . . ." He checked his watch. "Approximately three minutes to get past it."

"Yeah, it's green," I said dazedly.

"Great. Now, stand back a bit," he said, pulling me behind him. "We're about to make a hole in this wall."

I didn't mean to be a killjoy, but . . . "It's five feet of concrete. How are you gonna blow it without knocking the hell out of both of us?"

"Oh, this isn't an explosive." Viv reached for the tag, which now that I looked closer was actually a pull tab. "This is a laser grid attached to a *gravity* trap. Which is majorly cool, but Ari already said he didn't have much time to test the prototype, so let's hope it works."

"It'll work." Ari wouldn't have sent Viv in here with one of his inventions if he wasn't sure it was going to work. We were getting out of here.

"Let's see if you're right." Viv took a deep breath and pulled the tab. The wall lit up with a bright red glow, and I could hear the concrete start to crumble. None of it fell, though. The gravity trap—frame—whatever it was, held all the bits and pieces in place. "Awesome. Now help me push it through." He leaned on one side of the frame and I leaned on the other, and we pushed.

The frame skidded a little against the floor at first, but we kept a slow, steady pace through the thick wall. After another thirty seconds, we hit the end of it. The sunlight felt wonderfully warm on my skin, and I wasted a moment blinking in the brightness as Viv pulled the tab again. I could feel *warm* now, really warm, without having to sit through a face full of fire. For a second all I could do was bask in it.

"You can sunbathe later, buddy," Viv said as he deactivated the trap. A heavy pile of rubble fell onto the ground as his watch beeped. "And— Yep! Perfect!" He pointed ahead. "They cleared us a path." True enough, a section of barbed wire fence had been ripped from the posts holding it up and flattened into a tangle on the ground. The section of electric fence inside of it had been torn apart, and as for the sonic cannons perched on the turrets between the fences . . .

Spread across the grass beyond the Abattoir were a series of what looked like gigantic gramophones with their enormous black horns pointed straight at the prison. And beyond those were four very familiar faces.

"They're all working together to get me out?"

"I'm as surprised as you that Raul and Ari haven't killed each other yet," Viv said. "Good thing Ari was the one to find your phone and go scrolling through your contacts, by the way. You didn't hide your association very well."

"How do you *know* all this?" I demanded. "Who are you really?"

"I'll explain once we're out of here. C'mon." Viv led and I followed, too slowly and carefully to break into a run, but I managed a jog. We made it through the electric fence, but the tangle of barbed wire required awkward maneuvering.

"You couldn't cut it out of the way?" Viv shouted to Ari.

"It's not your typical barbed wire," he shouted back. "The laser cutter I brought wasn't strong enough to get through it, so we settled on this."

"I'm surprised you didn't try to blow it up, given your company," I said with a pointed glare at Raul, who shrugged. And then Ari looked at me, straight at me, and for a moment I was so overcome with genuine happiness I almost didn't hear Edward yell, "Craig, look out!"

The barbed wire beneath us flexed suddenly. Viv tripped and scrambled to his feet, but by the time he reached back toward me, the wire had already risen as high as my knees. I wasn't gonna be able to jump it in time, and Viv wasn't gonna be able to pull me out of it without getting caught himself. And that didn't make any sense.

I shoved Viv's chest hard, sending him falling away onto his ass even as the barbed wire began to jerk me backward. It brought the magnets in my cuffs too close, and before I could stop it, they snapped together with a noisy *click*. But that was the least of my worries at the moment, given that I was caught in a tangle of barbed wire that could *perforate* me. And did; I heard the tiny spikes rip through the cloth of my jumpsuit right before I felt them stab into my skin as they pulled me back toward the Abattoir.

"Oh my god!" Jean Parks yelled from the sidelines, narrating to her tiny handheld camera. "The rumors are true! Freight Train has somehow been stripped of his force field!"

"A necessary evil."

My heart stopped for a moment as Dr. Steuben's warm, cozy tones carried across the grass. I craned my neck to see him. He looked the way he always did, so friendly it shocked me a little more each time he hurt me. The only change in his appearance were the heavy-duty metal gloves covering his hands that seemed almost to glow.

"Freight Train is a highly dangerous prisoner, and precautions had to be taken to ensure the safety of his fellow inmates."

Ari stepped forward, his mouth twisted in a snarl. "You *dismembered* him. You took away something that had been a part of him for seven years in seven *days*! How can you think to justify that?"

"I don't need to. And you, Dr. Mansourian, are associating with known criminals."

"And *you*, Dr. Schlimmer, *are* a known criminal!"

"Ah." Instead of angry, the doctor sounded pleased. "So you figured that out."

"Who is Dr. Schlimmer?" Jean demanded. "Why is that important?"

"Because he's also known as the Butcher of Berlin," Raul told her. "Among other things."

Jean gaped for a moment, but rallied nicely. "Dr. Steuben! How do you respond to these accusations?"

He shrugged, and the barbed wire I was caught in rippled with the movement. I winced, biting back a groan at the pain. "My employers know who I used to be, but all the evidence of any crimes committed under that name were lost to the explosion in Siberia. Therefore you cannot prove anything, and I am within my rights to defend my prison. Indeed—" He turned to me and smiled as the upright sections of the electric fence began to hum. "It seems the generator has caught up with us. Therefore I will be giving your avenging cabal a taste of my cannons. Don't worry," he added. "After the first thirty seconds or so, you won't even feel your brain liquefying."

Everyone tensed, but they stood their ground. The cannons charged with a low, intensifying whine, and then released with a massive boom of ultrasonic sound. I expected to see everyone bowled over screaming, but instead, the energy . . . dissipated, I guess is the closest term. Just vanished. Dr. Steuben frowned.

"I didn't realize you had modified your research in sonic black holes to cover ultrasound."

"Good thing I did," Ari said grimly. "Now release Craig Haney to us."

"You have no grounds to take him."

"We have evidence of severe misconduct based on the fact that he is *bleeding* right now," Ari ground out. "He came to you incapable of being injured in such a way. Now release him to us!"

"With no warrant?" Dr. Steuben tilted his head. "And no police here to back you up? The commissioner wouldn't send them, would he?" He smiled. "Bringing along a civilian in their stead was, in some ways, a clever move, but you assume I don't care to harm her. The reality is, I don't care."

Jean Parks's mouth dropped open. "I'm getting all of this on camera."

"And your superiors will control it for the same reason everyone's will. I know things about them, their owners, their sponsors, that they wouldn't want to be exposed to the greater public. In exchange, they will not allow me to be exposed there. No matter what you say, I am inviolable here."

"Are you sure?" In one smooth motion, Raul pulled a gun out from under his trench coat, sighted, and shot. The bolo bullet should have wrapped around Dr. Steuben's neck, like it had with Mr. Bubbles, but instead it bounced off. I covered my head with my hands as it exploded a moment later somewhere to the right of us.

"Very direct, Mad Bombardier. I appreciate that about you. Fortunately for me, I have been taking quite a lot of blood from Freight Train on a daily basis for the past week. It still retained the protective properties of the chemicals he ingested, their potency carefully maintained in a stasis chamber in my laboratory. I was able to make a very effective injection out of it."

I had to force myself to speak up, to interrupt. It didn't make sense. "My blood should have killed you. You told me no one else could handle the chemicals." I might not know much science, but I remembered when someone said I was exceptional at something, even if it was just surviving dumb shit.

"Well, yes, it took a while to identify the biomarkers that allowed you to metabolize the chemicals and not die, but a few human experiments helped me discover which ones I needed to enhance in myself. And as you can see," Dr. Steuben indicated his unexploded state, "I am putting it to good use. Nothing any of you have will be able to hurt me now." He smiled. "I do like to prepare for all eventualities. And while you may have countered my cannons, I believe that the electricity is now working just fine." He lifted his gloved hands into the air, and my barbed cage rose with them, with me caught in the middle of it like a bird whose wings were broken.

"Sympathetic metamaterials." Ari sounded shocked. "You're controlling the wire through your gloves."

"The same compound, the same properties, carefully linked," Dr. Steuben agreed. "Ah, Dr. Mansourian. I was so hoping that you could be used; your intellect is second only to mine."

I didn't know what any of this conversation really meant, but I didn't care at the moment. The barbed wire was pulling me closer and closer to the electric fence and my impending doom. My breath came in huge gasps, but stars still flickered across my blurring vision. I didn't even have my hands free to try to tear my way out, although the cuffs had loosened quite a lot thanks to the slippery blood dripping down my arms.

Actually, maybe I wasn't *completely* screwed . . . as long as I could work fast enough. Raul would probably do something fancy like dislocate his thumbs to make this happen; Viv would just shift to smaller hands. My only option was to pull as viciously as I could, bracing my wrists on the nearest piece of wire and jerking hard. My wrists slid back and forth in a pool of blood and raw flesh, straining to free my hands. I was close . . .

Dr. Steuben didn't even seem to have noticed. "Now, either you surrender yourselves to me, or I will be forced to kill your friend."

"You wouldn't be able to keep us," Ari said, clearly trying to sound sensible while he eyed me anxiously. "Not all of us. Jean at least: she's a reporter, you'll have to release her—"

"Perhaps. Perhaps not. That would be up to the courts, and what do you think they would say?"

"No, listen to me; just *listen* to me, Heinrich. This isn't the way to get what you want. You're only causing more trouble for yourself, trust me."

Ari was going to try to reason with him? Really? I gritted my teeth and pulled harder. My left one was almost through . . . I needed to catch up with the right, though, because the damn things were stuck together, and if they stayed that way I'd still get blown up.

"It is *you* who is causing trouble for me. And I'm tired of arguing with you." Dr. Steuben moved my cage, nearer to the fence. Oh, god no. This was it; how could this be it? I had come so close, I was *so* close, Ari was there, and all I wanted to do was grab him and I *couldn't*. I wrenched my hands hopelessly. There was a snap and sizzle, and as I hurtled the last few feet into the taut wires, I thought Ari screamed. Or maybe that was me.

Whoever it was, it stopped after I hit the fence and bounced off. I didn't get a shock, not even a tingle. If I'd had anything in my stomach, I would have vomited I was so fucking relieved.

"Oh, thank goodness."

Ari rounded angrily on Edward. "Why did you cut it so close?"

"My mind-controlling ability isn't exactly a science!" he argued. "I had no way of knowing *when* Rodriguez would reach the generator."

For the first time since this encounter began, Dr. Steuben looked dumbfounded. "You . . . What did you do?"

"Raul and I paid a visit to one of your employees this morning," Edward said. He smiled coldly. It was a surprisingly Villainous expression on him. "This one, in fact." He pointed at Viv, who gave a bow. "And I gave him something to deliver to within twenty-five feet of your generator. I wasn't sure when it would make it there, or even if the order held, but apparently it did."

"A bomb?"

"EMP," Raul said. "If I wanted to bomb this hideous place again, I already would have."

"Your defenses are down," Ari told Dr. Steuben. "No one is coming to help you. Surrender to *us*, and I'll see what we can do to keep you out of prison yourself."

Dr. Steuben's face contorted, all Santa-esque traits vanishing under a layer of fury that stripped his softness away. "I hold your Hero," he snarled. "And no matter what happens, I can keep *you* from having him again." He made a twisting motion with his hands, like he was wringing someone's neck, and the wire closed more tightly around me.

"No!" Ari began to run forward. I had to get these off before he got too close.

Now or never. I gritted my teeth against the pain and heaved, and the cuffs finally came free as a solid, blood-soaked unit. I almost dropped them, but managed to turn far enough to toss them over my shoulder at Dr. Steuben.

I'm not sure if he even noticed what I'd done. But Ari did. He skidded to a stop ten feet in front of me, his eyes so wide, so blue and beautiful and afraid. "Craig!"

A barb hooked my cheek, filling my mouth with blood. I was punctured all over, and squeezed so tight I'd surely die, but I had the breath for one more word. "Duck."

I stayed conscious just long enough to see Ari hit the ground, and then the world burst apart, everything flaring brightly for a moment.

I might not be special anymore, but at least I can be a Hero, one last time.

My vision went black.

CHAPTER THIRTEEN

I've heard many different people over the years say that larger change must start with the individual. Like attracts like, positivity springs from positivity, basically a bunch of pithy sayings that would have us think that all we need to do is be kind, and kindness will result from it.

I never used to believe that. Maybe I'd learned too much about the darkness that lives in our city, which hides in offices and laboratories and lingers behind closed doors. Maybe I'd seen too much of our mob mentality to believe that one single person, making a difference in their own life, could make a difference for all of us. The chains of power have always rested firmly in the hands of the wealthy corporations, and when they'd lose one piece on the chessboard, they'd simply buy another. Down a pawn? They'd just pay to replace it with a knight, always increasing their holdings in the mind and heart of Panopolis.

What happens when a knight decides to become a pawn, though? When he doesn't slink away to the loony bin or prison, when he doesn't go down in a blaze of glory or a haze of ignominy? What happens when he, against the odds, thrives as a pawn?

Maybe then a true revolution can start with one person.

When Jean Parks's footage from the showdown outside of the Abattoir went live, people lost their freaking minds.

City officials tried to stop the broadcast, of course. Her camera was confiscated as soon as the cops caught up to us in the aftermath of the fight, but she'd already uploaded the footage to a private server. Her station was refused permission to air it, and threatened with lawsuits from the city if they released footage that was, as they put it, "part of an active investigation."

So rather than release the footage herself, Jean somehow managed to get her video to SuperTruther instead, who immediately posted it to his blog. The authorities tried to shut it down, but SuperTruther always stayed one step ahead of the corporate hackers trying to take him out. The more people saw the video, the more the outrage spread. It was decried by the media as a fraud, evidenced by the fact that "known Villains" helped in the escape, but me being laid up in a hospital, notably *sans* force field, didn't go unnoticed.

Yeah, I was in a hospital for a couple of weeks after the big breakout. Apart from the damage done from the barbed wire and the cuffs, which was extensive, the mini explosion I'd set off to kill Dr. Steuben had *also* sent plenty of shrapnel winging my way. I'd come away from the whole thing with plenty of perforations, lacerations, and a head injury that kept me out for a solid week. So I missed most of the drama that occurred at my bedside, thank God.

The night nurse, Stacy, had been *more* than ready to fill me in when I woke up though. She was a former fangirl, and could keep a running patter going even while changing my sheets and checking my vitals.

"There was a huge fight between GenCorp's lawyers and yours over whether or not you should be treated at the company's clinic," she confided as she replaced my IV one night. "The company wanted to move you out of the public eye, but Ms. Delavigne told them that there were clauses in your contract that *specifically* ruled out corporate interference if you were to somehow lose your powers. As soon as you were designated a civilian instead of a Hero, they lost their hold over you. She was super fierce!" Stacy's eyes gleamed with admiration. "Add that to the new info coming out about the shit that was going down in the Abattoir under their watch, and I bet their lawyers have better things to do than fight about who should be taking care of you. Which, for the record, is us." She patted my hand, beaming as she did so.

"Your doctor's been all over the news," she added with a wink. "He's pretty persuasive, that guy. You know they're putting him in charge at the company? I think he'll do a great job cleaning up GenCorp."

Ah, right. That was the other side of having to cover their asses: cleaning house and putting the one guy who worked for them and could be seen doing the right thing into a position of power before federal regulators stepped in and took charge. Ari wasn't impressed, I knew, but he *was* determined not to leave a job half-finished, and right now there was too much information that he felt might be useful at GenCorp to leave it in some other scientist's hands. He told me about the turmoil in the company every time he visited, which was mostly late at night, looking more exhausted than I'd ever seen him. Stacy kindly turned her eyes the other way when Ari broke the rules about visiting hours, and he was the only person I didn't mind waking me up, including Memaw.

"It is all they can do, with such clear evidence of malfeasance," Ari explained a week in as he slumped in a hard-backed plastic chair next to me, holding my hand. I'd first woken up to find Ari doing just that, in fact; for a second I'd thought I might have died and gone to heaven, but there was no way the afterlife would hurt as bad as I had when I initially opened my eyes.

"Abbott's was raided, and Dr. Steuben's laboratory destroyed, of course, but there's no denying the proof that exists in you. Add to that SuperTruther's very public outing of three of GenCorp's board members, and their statements confirming that they knew Dr. Steuben was actually Dr. Schlimmer with a new name and some plastic surgery, and they're in a great deal of trouble."

"So they're putting you in charge."

"Only for a short period of time," Ari assured me. "I won't accept a more permanent posting as GenCorp's new CEO; it comes with too many restrictions from the board. I might be the only scientist public opinion cares to trust these days, but I'm still a scientist, not a businessman. Besides, I would rather end my association with the company altogether."

"What will you do if you don't work for GenCorp?" I asked as his fingertips stroked over the base of my wrist. Swear to God, if I hadn't been on so many painkillers, I'd have been hard as a rock. Being touched was *awesome*.

"Anything that will allow me to research more ways to reduce or remove unwanted powers. Perhaps form a partnership with Abbott's Penitentiary and look into rehabilitation for the inmates there."

"Seriously?"

"How many others must have suffered as you did?" Ari said softly. "As soon as chance afforded Steuben the opportunity to study you with no regard for your safety, how long before he used his technology to take you apart? The thought of stealing your ability for himself and leaving you with nothing must have delighted him. How many others must have died at the hands of that madman? How can I forget about them, when no one else is willing to remember?"

I smiled at Ari, a broad, loopy smile. "You're a nice guy, Ari."

"I have my moments." He smiled back at me, that sharky grin, and my heartbeat sped up on the monitor. "I'm perfectly willing to demonstrate how *bad* I can be as well, once you're out of here."

"Yeah?"

He raised my knuckles, scraped and bandaged though they were, to his lips. They were thin but soft, so soft, and I sighed happily. "Absolutely."

Not that getting out of the hospital was easy. There were plenty of curious doctors anxious for a chance at me, reporters desperate for an interview, and lawyers trying to stick me with a gag order. Plus there were the gawkers, the people who'd seen the video and wanted to verify that I was a regular guy again with their own two eyes, or more offensively, with their hands.

One of them even tried to sneak into my room through a vent in the ceiling. Stacy was there when he tried it, though, and she moved me behind a privacy curtain, and then used a fire extinguisher on the snooper once he dropped down, all cat burglar–like. Security escorted the guy out covered in foam and swearing a blue streak, to which Stacy shouted back, "You want a piece of this? Bite me, bitch!"

I got out in the end, though. I even avoided staying with Memaw. Hers would have been in some ways the natural place to go, considering she was my only relative and my own place had been thoroughly destroyed in the fight with Zane, but neither of us were comfortable with each other right now. My notoriety was high but my power was gone, and Memaw was having a tougher time with that than I was.

She'd cried when she'd first seen me, then cried harder when she cupped my cheeks in her wrinkled hands and smoothed her trembling thumbs over my stubble. "Oh honey," she'd sobbed. "Oh honey, oh no. Oh no, no, no."

Once she'd calmed down a little, we'd been able to talk almost like normal people. "I'm glad you're getting better, of course," she'd said, "but what will you do now? What on earth will you do if you don't— Are you sure you don't want to get your force field back?"

"Yeah, Memaw." Boy, if I was sure of anything, it was that. "I'm positive. And I'll find something to do. Don't worry about me."

"I'm your memaw; it's my job to worry."

I'd shaken my head. "Don't. I'll be fine."

I was looking forward to having my own space again, filled with things that I liked, that I could *touch*. I'd have to think about things like thread counts and memory foam; I'd have to consider what kind of detergent I wanted to use, whether my shoes had proper arch support. Normal, everyday stuff that I hadn't done in years.

Not quite as exciting as my own space, though. Especially since the apartment I'd picked was right below Ari's. He'd managed to salvage most of my furniture from the wreckage of my last place, and Ari assured me the new apartment was livable, it just needed feathering. I'd get him to help me. It seemed only fair, since he'd probably be spending a lot of time there.

Ari had already suggested living together, and I'd been tempted, though the practical side of me had said that might just be the result of going through such an intense time together: feelings were always more overwhelming under tough circumstances. The romantic side of me said nope, I was in love and it wasn't likely to change, but that didn't mean I was ready to pick out china with the guy. I needed somewhere I could relearn how to be normal without an audience, even a well-meaning one.

Besides, I could more than afford a place on my own, as Ianthe had told me when she came to visit me in the hospital. She picked me up the day of my discharge too, citing "paperwork you can't fall asleep to avoid dealing with anymore, Craig." She'd taken me back to her place, sat me down in her kitchen, and made me a cup of coffee. It was the first real cup of coffee I'd had since I lost my force field; the colored water they'd offered me in the hospital didn't count.

I sipped, and almost choked on the bitterness. "Shit, that's strong!"

"It's not, really," Ianthe said from where she sat with her own cup. Her smile was tired but genuine, better than the last I'd seen on her. The *real* her, at least. Viv was nowhere in sight today. "It's just been a long time since you've tasted something like this." She chuckled at my dismayed expression. "There's cream in the fridge."

After adding what was probably way too much cream to my cup, I had to admit it was better.

"I wonder what else isn't gonna be like I remember it." Once I used to be almost religious about drinking my coffee black. Back then I'd liked licorice too, and Tabasco sauce, and both of those had already betrayed me.

"I'm sure plenty of things will be different, but that's not only because of the force field. You're seven years older now; your tastes would have changed regardless. Besides," her lips quirked, "I'm sure there will be plenty of things that are *much* better than you remember to make up for it."

I rubbed my hand over the back of my head, already feeling my blush coming on. "Uhm . . . yeah."

"How are things going with Ari, by the way?"

"They're good. He offered me a job once he's done at GenCorp." That had been more than a little strange, but he'd sold it well.

"Doing what?"

"Research assistant." Doing science. Me, doing actual *science*! Even though I didn't have the background for it, apparently a lot of science was just making sure your machines kept running and your equipment didn't fall off the walls. He'd ended up accepting a job at Abbott's, offered up on a silver platter by the city council and Mayor Wright, after he'd wrangled a guarantee of third-party oversight. He had to finish out a month-long tenure at GenCorp first, though, to complete the overhaul of their management.

Many of the company's board members were being investigated by the FBI now, and facilitating swift and systemic change in the city's biggest black eye would be one small step toward their redemption. No private company ever wanted to let outsiders stick their fingers into the corporate pie, so to speak, but right now, GenCorp didn't have a choice. It was better than being broken up into parts or going into bankruptcy, which had been the other options on the table.

Ianthe nodded. "And did you accept the job?"

"Not yet. Not because I don't want to, but I don't want it to be because he feels . . . guilty, I guess? And I don't want to jump on it because I have no other options, either."

"Well, you shouldn't worry about options. It's not like you need to work," Ianthe said.

I frowned. "What?"

"Haven't you checked your bank statements lately?"

"Why would I bother?" It wasn't like I'd ever had much of a reason to go on a spending spree. I knew I made enough to cover my occasional purchases, and that was good enough for me.

Ianthe blinked at me, then sighed. "Oh my god, you haven't even looked? Craig! I told you before that you didn't need any extra income! You've got over two million dollars in the bank."

Wait, *what*? "You're fucking with me."

"No, I'm not. In your initial contract, we guaranteed a percentage of your income be saved in an actual bank account, not folded back into the company or in the form of them covering your expenses." Ianthe grimaced. "The percentage was regrettably low, but you've been the most popular Hero in Panopolis for years and your merchandise is flying off the shelves faster than ever. You don't need to worry about running out of money, as long as you manage it properly. You've been paying *taxes* on this income, Craig, how could you not know about it all?"

"Mostly I just signed stuff?" I said weakly, and Ianthe groaned. "Hey, I was busy!"

"And now you're not, and you're also not hurting for cash, even without the payout you're going to get once the lawsuit we've filed against the city gets resolved."

That part still didn't sit real well with me. "Was that necessary?"

"Necessary? Perhaps not. But was it a way to drag some of the city's worst abuses into the light and ensure that there's more oversight in the future? Yes. And I don't care what you do with the money, Craig. You can set up a charity with it, hand it out to the families of cops killed in the line of duty, build a giant wicker statue of Ray with it and then burn it in effigy, I don't care. Do whatever you want now; that's the *point* of this newfound freedom, isn't it?" Ianthe set her cup down and pointed a finger at me. "You paid a hard price, but there's nothing and no one that can force you to do anything you don't want to now. So work where you want, or don't work and spend all day sitting in flannel pajamas eating chocolate ice cream, it's totally your call."

"Wow. I'm . . ." *Stunned? Shocked?* I shouldn't have been. I smiled sheepishly. "I should've known all this, huh?"

"Yes. But you'll learn it. You've got time for that now."

"I couldn't have gotten this far without you." I decided to break down the last wall between us. "Or Viv. Who isn't Vivian, I don't think."

"Ah." Ianthe looked down at the lace-covered table. "No. She isn't."

Thought so. "But she's not your mom, either."

"No, I'm afraid not."

"But she's got your mom's powers." Somebody with the ability to morph, who could sneak into places with impunity, who had the benefit of complete anonymity because no one would ever consider them for the role, because they weren't supposed to be alive anymore. Somebody connected to Ianthe, maybe connected to a lot of people who didn't even realize who they were talking to.

I couldn't think of a better cover for somebody like SuperTruther.

Ianthe's shoulders stiffened. "Craig . . ."

I shook my head. "I'm not gonna ask. Just . . . tell Julian thanks for me, okay?"

"I don't know what you're talking about," she said, but she was smiling now. "Don't you have dinner plans?"

"Are you trying to get rid of me?" I was already pushing back my chair though, because she was right.

"Just trying to facilitate your chances of getting your handsome doctor alone for a while." She had a point there; life had been busy for both of us, to the extent that we hadn't . . . There hadn't been time to . . .

I was sick to death of third fucking base, is all I'm saying. And third base was about as far as we'd been able to go while I was in the hospital and hooked up to more monitors than I could shake a cat at. Not that I'd been upset about getting what was probably the most fantastic blowjob of my life at one in the morning after making sure that Stacy was on the other side of the ward, but I was greedy. I wanted to do *more*, and ideally, to last for longer than the thirty seconds or so it had taken me to come.

Ianthe's driver took me to my new apartment; my Humvee was still impounded in the police lot, and I wasn't looking forward to picking it up. It was too big, too bright, to much a part of who I used to be. Maybe I'd sell it, get a Prius or something.

No, a Prius was too far in the other direction. Maybe I'd split the difference and get a Camaro.

The door to my second-story apartment was unlocked. Not a surprise; I'd given Ari a key to the place as soon as he'd offered to help move things in while I was laid up, and he'd told me he was going to make a welcome-home dinner when he visited this morning. I let myself in and toed my shoes off next to Ari's, hung my jacket up in the closet, and followed the smell of warm food into the kitchen. Ari was there, dressed for work even though it was a Saturday, but his cardigan was slung over the back of a chair, his sleeves were rolled up, and his feet were covered in pale-pink socks. He was lifting cartons out of a bag, his glasses sliding down the bridge of his nose as he did so. He appeared about as average and everyday as I felt.

He was the most stunning thing I'd ever seen.

It hadn't quite hit me in the hospital, the full reality of my new life. Yeah, I could touch things, eat things. I'd been ready to feel weak; I'd been prepared to have to deal with the loss of my invulnerability. What I *hadn't* been prepared for was the way being here, in my new apartment with the person I was in love with, would make me feel. I felt right. I felt *strong*, like I'd just been given a power I had no idea existed before.

"I was going to cook for you," he said when he saw me, pausing to push his glasses up his nose. "But then this arrived, a gift from our mutual friends, and I thought it would be better fresh. Besides, you've never gotten to try this soup, and it actually is delicious." He smiled at me. "Welcome home, by the way. I hope you like your new—"

That was as far as he got before I was on him, pulling him in close to my body and winding my hands around his head as I kissed him so hard it hurt. I should slow down, I needed to slow down, but it was too much of what I wanted all at once, and I couldn't—but I would. I lightened my grip, tried to take a step back, and then it was Ari's turn to reel me in, his fingers tight in my hair before traveling down, bunching the fabric of my shirt as he slid his hands under the hem. They were warm, but I still got goose bumps where he touched me.

We leaned against the edge of the counter, and I spread my thighs so Ari's leg could fit between them. I rocked against him hard and shuddered, recalling the last time I'd ground against someone until I came. I'd been sixteen, I think. If I wasn't careful, I'd be reliving my youth in another minute. "Can we—" I gasped between kisses. "Can we please—"

"Anything," Ari said, low and breathless as he pressed his lips to the side of my neck and bared his teeth, scraping them across my skin.

"Can we go to bed?" I managed. "'Cause otherwise I'm gonna come all over you right now, and I don't think I'll be worth much after that."

Ari leaned back, a familiar line appearing between his eyebrows. "Are you too tired for this? Should we eat instead? I can—"

"Shut the fuck up," I snapped, because there was no way we were waiting until *after* dinner to have sex. "Are you kidding me? I just don't want to get off in my pants and then have to go take a freaking nap when I'd rather have you fuck me until I come."

Ari's big blue eyes darkened. "That's what you want, then? For me to spread you out across your bed, open you up, and fuck you so hard that you come on my cock?"

Son of a bitch. "If that's what you want, you better stop talking and get me there fast."

This apartment was smaller than my old one, which was nice because we were able to make it to the bedroom in about ten floundering footsteps, culminating with us falling back onto the bed together in a graceless, desperate tangle of groping hands and desperate attempts to get out of our clothes.

I was faster at that than him, thanks to skipping the whole button-down thing. I let go of Ari long enough to drag my T-shirt over my head and kick my pants and underwear down my legs, and then lay on the bed, reaching for him. He'd settled back on his knees, though, hands paused on his own shirt as he gazed at me. The scrutiny made me blush.

"Not as pretty as I was before, I know." Not that I'd ever been very pretty, but I had fresh scars all over my body now.

Ari frowned, but it seemed more contemplative than disturbed. "The first time we did this," he said slowly as he unbuttoned his shirt with one hand and touched my knee with the other, "I couldn't really feel you. I held the weight of you, I could imagine touching you, but the glove kept me from knowing what this would actually be like. I could imagine the texture of your hair," his fingertips swirled down the inside of my thigh, "and the grain of your skin," he lingered on the goose bumps that every touch engendered in me, "but I could not verify. I am a scientist; I like to verify my hypotheses. We were too rushed in the hospital. I want to take my time with you, taste every part of you, catalogue every reaction I can elicit." His long fingers touched the tip of my cock, already starting to leak, and I had to pull his hand away.

"I want you in me first. Please." I hadn't been fucked very often before I became a Hero, but I was so ready to change that. I wanted it with Ari, and I wanted him to get why. "I swear to God, I'll let you do anything you want to me next time. You can tie me up and make me beg, you can fuck my mouth, you can ask me to rim you all day and I'll do it, but I've been thinking about this for way too long and I just— Ari—"

"Your turn to stop talking before *I* come," he said. He finished undressing, letting his clothes fall to the floor while I searched my battered bed stand for the lube I was positive I still had in there.

"I brought new," Ari held up a small bottle. "And condoms."

"Oh, good," I said with a grin. "'Cause my condoms have probably been expired since two presidents ago."

Ari smiled. He slicked his middle finger with lube, spread my thighs wide with his own as he moved in close to me again, and then reached down to brush his fingertip across my hole. "Are you sure?"

"So sure," I said, and then I couldn't say anything because he was pressing inside me, his long, thin finger moving slowly and steadily until he was as far as he could go. I didn't need slow. I didn't *want* slow. I'd had too many medical procedures over the years to be surprised by the feel of something inside my ass, but I'd never *wanted* anything like I wanted this.

I couldn't move a muscle without feeling Ari move too, and everything he did resonated through me like sound, carried on the current in my blood. I bit my lip and pushed down to deepen the sensation, and Ari rewarded me by adding another finger. They twisted together and slid into me, stretching my clenching hole, sliding straight and deep until his hand felt rooted between my legs. It was exactly what I wanted, what I *needed.*

"Mmm, fuck," I groaned. "Just like that. Oh, fuck."

"I could curl my fingers," Ari told me, and the darkness in his voice was addictive, throaty, wicked, and wonderful. "Touch them to your prostate and you would come for me, wouldn't you? I wouldn't even have to lay a hand on your cock; you would come untouched."

"Yes, I would." It was all I could do not to come just from him talking about it, honestly. Cock ring: definitely going on my "To Buy" list.

"I wonder how long you'll be this sensitive." He slipped his fingers out, and I made a noise I wasn't exactly proud of but couldn't stop, somewhere between a whine and a moan. "I wonder how many times I could make you come after you've recovered your strength."

"You can find out," I promised him. "Keep a spreadsheet, make a graph, whatever you want. Just, now, please." I couldn't wait through any more preparation and foreplay.

Ari opened a condom and rolled it slowly down his length, and oh my god I had to stop looking. I grabbed the base of my cock hard and shut my eyes as Ari leaned over me and gently kissed my open mouth. He felt like a weighted blanket, part comforting and part smothering, pressing me down deeper into my sweat-drenched sheets. I panted against his lips, twitching and itching and unable to stop, caught between wanting to beg him to slow down and demand that he speed up.

I could ask him to stop and he would, but I didn't know if I could bear the build-up again, and more than anything else right now, I wanted Ari in me.

"It'll be easier if you roll over; you might pull your stitches this way."

"This isn't going to be easy any way. It's just going to be *fast*, fuck," I gasped. "I'm sorry, I can't— Don't stop, okay? Don't stop, even when I come, I want to feel you in me."

"You don't have to be sorry," Ari said roughly as he lifted my hips and positioned himself. "You never have to be sorry with me. You're exactly what I want." He started to press inside of me, slow and careful but so much *more* than anything I remembered, almost more than I could take. As my body stretched to accommodate him, I rode the edge of pain and bliss, unwilling to let go of my cock for even a split second, because the instant I did I would come, I knew it. My thigh ached from where I had it hooked high against Ari's waist, and the cuts along my shoulders burned, and every grinding, persistent pain that had stuck with me since I first woke up somehow transmuted into desperate pleasure.

When Ari was as deep as he could go, he stopped moving for a moment. I didn't want stillness, though; I wanted to feel even more, for it to be as overwhelming for him as it was for me. I reached up with my free hand and shakily removed his glasses, then hauled him down by his neck into a kiss. It bent me in half; it *hurt*, and I loved it.

"Move," I muttered against his lips, and Ari took me at my word.

He pulled away and thrust in, bending to scrape his teeth across my chest, light, sharp nips that made my skin sing. I scraped my nails down his back, and he moaned and thrust in harder. I couldn't move; I couldn't breathe; I was shaking and breaking; I felt like I was drowning again, every cell in my body straining for something to keep it alive; and I couldn't hold off anymore. I stroked myself once, just once, a short, stuttering movement that was apparently the last signal my body needed before it decided that, yeah, too much was just enough. Every muscle clenched as I came, drawing Ari even tighter to me, holding him brutally close for the eternity it took to orgasm. He didn't stop moving, though there was barely an inch of give in his hips, just ground deeper and deeper until he gave a guttural cry of release.

I could have let him go then, but I didn't, just loosened up a little so we could both breathe. Aftershocks tingled up and down my spine, perky reminders that this was the first time I'd been fucked in what felt like forever and sex was fun, wasn't it fun? Holy shit, was it ever. And I wanted to tell Ari that; I wanted to explain how amazing he was, but I was also exhausted and could feel every bump and bruise I wore, and my shoulders were *really* aching. I turned my head to kiss his temple, finding his bare skin damp with sweat. "Ari?"

"Mmm." He looked as fucked out as I felt, which was something. He leaned up to kiss me again, one last butterfly touch of our lips together, before he slowly backed out of my embrace. It almost hurt to feel him leave, my hungry skin immediately aching for him to return, but I was too tired to chase him.

Ari helped me straighten my tingling limbs out, and checked my stitches for any sign of tears. He left for long enough to get rid of the condom and grab a washcloth, and then he nestled in beside me again, wiping my cum away before he tugged the comforter up over the top of us.

I smiled loopily. "Neat freak."

"You'll thank me when you're starving for dinner and don't have to take the time to go shower," he countered.

"I don't know, a shower could be fun."

"Maybe when you're steady on your feet," Ari said dryly.

"I think I'd be okay if you were there to hold me up."

"I will be." He looked me straight in the eyes as he said it, a tacit declaration that settled into my soul. "I always will be, if you want me there." He held my gaze to the last word, finally tucking his head underneath my chin and wrapping his arms around my waist. "You should rest. The food can wait."

And I actually could have gone for a nap right then, but there was something I had to do first. It might have been too soon for hearts and flowers, but fuck that. I was tired of living my life according to someone else's schedule. I could give him words he was comfortable with, that he would understand, and that still let him know how I felt. "I do want you there. I always will." *I love you.*

His lips curved into a smile against my shoulder. "Good." *I love you too.*

The food from Flower Pepper reheated fine an hour later. We ate it on the bed because I didn't have a new couch but I didn't want to be an entire chair's-distance away from Ari yet. The soup really was good; almost too spicy for me, but I'd get used to it eventually.

"How long before you're officially signed on over at Abbott's?" I asked after retreating to a bowl of plain white rice to cool my mouth down.

"It should be next week sometime. There's a petition going around to rename the prison that's already collected a hundred thousand signatures, apparently."

Sudden dread gripped my guts. "Please tell me they don't want to rename it anything embarrassing." *Like after me.*

"You don't like Haney's Penitentiary? I think it has a nice ring to it." Ari laughed as I whapped his hand with my plastic spoon. "No, your name isn't on the petition. They want to name it after the city. It's a motion that's likely to pass, too; Mayor Wright is in a frenzy to reshape himself in a more positive light after all that's happened lately."

"He's such a jackass."

"He's the jackass currently in power, though. Unless he's recalled, he has another three years on his term, so we must be patient with him." Ari snipped a dumpling in two with his chopsticks, and dipped it in the soy-vinegar sauce.

"He can't be innocent in this, can he? He had to know what was going on at the Abattoir."

Ari shrugged. "He says it was put into place by previous administrators and that he had no clue who Dr. Steuben really was. Heads are rolling, and the people in power are doing everything they can to excise themselves from the dead weight. It will be interesting to see who's still standing at the end of this purge."

Speaking of still standing . . . "Any idea what happened to Ray? My manager? I haven't heard from him at all."

"Nobody has. He's disappeared. He probably took what he could and ran. I know he was facing an inquiry by GenCorp over his handling of both you and Mr. Fabulous."

Ray was Panopolis born and bred; I couldn't imagine him being comfortable anywhere else, especially given how he liked to run people's lives. Frankly though, he'd been great at getting us exposure but shit at understanding what we needed. Who would hire Ray to manage any Hero after what had happened to me and Zane? I put my spoon down, my throat suddenly too tight. "Did Zane's younger brother take on his persona?"

"GenCorp has officially asked, but he hasn't decided. The boy is only eighteen. We're lucky there's such a lull in Villain activity right now, honestly. Our current roster of Heroes is more than sufficient for the time being."

And Edward and Raul were working hard to keep it that way, to make Z Street a better place for the people who had been shunted there over the years. I wasn't sure how long they'd be able to maintain that, though. For the moment, the public loved them for helping to break me out of the Abattoir, but how long before something happened to turn the tide the other way? It wasn't like I could help them anymore; I suspected I'd have my hands full just keeping myself alive, after this.

"All we can do is wait and see." I kept my eyes on my bowl, swirling vegetables and broth in a slow circle. That was going to be hard. I was used to being an active participant; now I would be nothing more than support staff, if that.

Ari set his hand on mine, stilling my circles. "You don't have to be on the front lines to make a difference. It will take time, but I promise: we'll do good work together. We can change people's lives for the better, Craig."

I smiled crookedly at him. "You might have to remind me of that every now and then."

"As often as you need, for as long as you need it. But you'll see." Ari's quiet confidence infused the air between us, and his gaze was as potent as any touch. "You'll see. Things are going to be different in Panopolis from here on out."

Explore more of the *Panopolis* series:
www.riptidepublishing.com/titles/series/panopolis

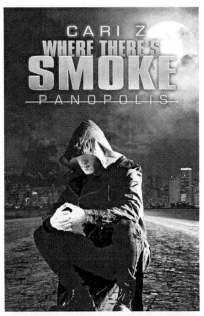

Dear Reader,

Thank you for reading Cari Z's *Where There's a Will*!

We know your time is precious and you have many, many entertainment options, so it means a lot that you've chosen to spend your time reading. We really hope you enjoyed it.

We'd be honored if you'd consider posting a review—good or bad—on sites like **Amazon, Barnes & Noble, Kobo, Goodreads, Twitter, Facebook, Tumblr,** and your blog or website. We'd also be honored if you told your friends and family about this book. Word of mouth is a book's lifeblood!

For more information on upcoming releases, author interviews, blog tours, contests, giveaways, and more, please sign up for our weekly, spam-free newsletter and visit us around the web:

Newsletter: tinyurl.com/RiptideSignup
Twitter: twitter.com/RiptideBooks
Facebook: facebook.com/RiptidePublishing
Goodreads: tinyurl.com/RiptideOnGoodreads
Tumblr: riptidepublishing.tumblr.com

Thank you so much for Reading the Rainbow!

RiptidePublishing.com

ACKNOWLEDGMENTS

Huge thanks to my betas Tiffany, Caitlin, and Charlie, without whom I would still be going "What now?!"

ALSO BY
CARI Z

Panopolis
Where There's Smoke
Where There's Fire

House Rules (in the *Rules to Live By* anthology)
Tempest
Shadows & Light
Changing Worlds
Cambion: Dark Around the Edges
A Blinded Mind
Surviving The Change
Camellia and Camellia: Spring Blossom, with Caitlin Ricci

ABOUT THE AUTHOR

Cari Z is a Colorado girl who loves snow and sunshine. She likes edged weapons, prefers books to television shows, and goes weak at the knees for interesting men and exciting explosions (but not at exactly the same time—that would be so messy).

You can find her at carizerotica.blogspot.com, follow her on Facebook at facebook.com/people/Cari-Zee, or on Twitter as @author_cariz.

Enjoy more stories like
Where There's a Will
at RiptidePublishing.com!

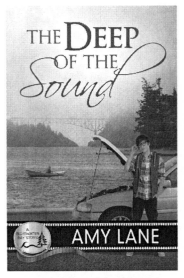

The Deep of the Sound
ISBN: 978-1-62649-276-9

Too Stupid to Live
ISBN: 978-1-937551-85-8

Earn Bonus Bucks!

Earn 1 Bonus Buck for each dollar you spend. Find out how at
RiptidePublishing.com/news/bonus-bucks.

Win Free Ebooks for a Year!

Pre-order coming soon titles directly through our site and you'll
receive one entry into a drawing for a chance to win free books for
a year! Get the details at RiptidePublishing.com/contests.

CPSIA information can be obtained
at www.ICGtesting.com
Printed in the USA
LVOW12s1244161116
513212LV00001B/233/P